TELEPHONE ROAD

ANN SWANN

5 PRINCE PUBLISHING

Published by 5 PRINCE PUBLISHING & BOOKS, LLC

PO Box 865, Arvada, CO 80001

www.5PrinceBooks.com

ISBN digital: 978-1-63112-248-4

ISBN print: 978-1-63112-249-1

Cover Credit: Marianne Nowicki

TELEPHONE ROAD

Ann Swann

Dedicated to my sweet hubby for
always supporting me.
And to all the kind readers who are so patient when asking when the
next book is coming. For them I say, "I'll write faster one of these days.
I promise!"

ACKNOWLEDGMENTS

Special thanks to Bernadette for always giving me the leeway to write what I want without boundaries.

Many thanks as well to Cate Byers, super ed! She pushes and pulls and tells it like it is. For that, I am grateful.

Thanks also goes out to my critique buddies at Brew Street Cafe. It's been a while since we looked at this one, but I always take your comments to heart.

Muchas gracias!

TELEPHONE ROAD

Ann Swann

1

TWENTY-THREE STEPS

When I walked into the long narrow art gallery behind my roommate, Joanna, it felt as if I were being funneled toward him. Preston Stevensen. Perfect hair and a smirk for a smile, he appeared to be the man of the hour. Even gazing at me over the head of a ponytailed patron in a slick, yellow shirt, he somehow made *me* feel like the center of attention.

Twenty-three steps.

His eyes were on me the whole way.

My name is Marlena Matthews. Joanna calls me Marlena "Miss Priss" Matthews. She thinks I've led a sheltered small-town life and she's right. That's why I felt so fortunate to be accidentally paired with her my freshman year. We were both serious students.

Joanna's friend, Antonio, is the one who invited us to the Visual Arts Gallery. He had several pieces of his beautiful high-glaze pottery on display.

But nothing compared to Preston's art. It took up the entire back wall. Every piece featured some sort of wide-slashed mouth or other wide-open gash. Some of the mouths were created from melted red lipstick and some were splash-painted on canvas; a couple were fashioned of metal, then shellacked onto blank mannequin faces made of charred or broken plastic. I overheard a girl walking ahead of us refer to the mouths as Freudian. "Yeah," her companion snickered. "All about sex. Weird sex." They both laughed behind their hands.

Twenty-three steps. Each one carried me closer and closer to the guy who would change my entire life. In hindsight it seems obvious that Preston's art should have been a big red flag. But Joanna didn't call me Miss Priss, The Sheltered One, for nothing.

By the time we reached them, the patron in the yellow shirt had decided to make Preston an offer he couldn't refuse. "I am *so* in love with your work," we heard the man gush. "I want to purchase several for my condo in Corpus Christi."

Joanna gave me a tiny shove and we moved on to Antonio's exhibit. "I wonder if Preston's art would be the feature if his father didn't contribute so much money to the school?"

Antonio whispered, "He told me he only does art to anger his father. He doesn't want to follow in Daddy's footsteps, but he has to if he doesn't want to be cut off from the bank account."

We all three laughed at the trials and tribulations of a poor little rich boy.

Red flag #2.

I should have taken those joking comments about anger more seriously. But I didn't. Once he turned that charismatic, upperclassman charm on me, I lost my common sense like a rabbit in the middle of the highway, too stunned by the bright lights to even see the car.

The three of us stood in front of Antonio's work. He'd glazed the pottery in shades of muted blue. Several sold, but the gallery talk centered around Preston's garish work. It seemed to reach out and grab everyone who walked by. "What does he want to do if not the family business?" I asked.

Antonio flashed me a bright smile. "I think I heard him mention travelling around Europe."

"That's not a career."

He pointed at me and clicked his trigger finger. "Bingo!"

Joanna rolled her eyes and I couldn't tell if he'd been joking or not. He smoothed his dark shoulder length hair off his face and grinned again. Antonio was one of my favorite people. So easygoing. Just like Joanna.

My first few months of college had turned out to be even better than I had hoped.

When Preston joined us, smiling apologetically, Antonio made the introductions. He nodded his perfect profile toward his classmate, then toward Joanna, and then he reached for my hand. "I've seen you," he said. "You worked at the Copper Kettle over the summer. I noticed you when I got back to school in August." He kept my hand in his. "Now you work at The Twisted Pasta Bar."

I looked at Joanna and Antonio to see if they'd heard what I just heard. Preston Stevensen had noticed me. *Me*, a lowly freshman, a nobody.

Of course I recalled seeing *him* at both places. With his GQ looks and flash-the-cash personality, it would have been impossible not to notice him.

Within moments, he had his other hand beneath my elbow, escorting me around the gallery, introducing me to everyone he knew as if we were long-lost lovers. I felt overwhelmed, dumbfounded, and completely flattered.

By the time we landed back in Antonio's display corner, I had begun to feel like a specimen. I figured the way he acted had to be some sort of joke, some kind of prank. Visions of *Carrie* at the prom flitted through my head.

I looked to Joanna for guidance. She just shrugged.

As the night wore on, Preston won me over. Attending the University of Texas on partial-scholarships and grants, having a rich boy like Preston Stevensen squire me around made me feel as if I'd stepped into one of those sweet romance stories I'd enjoyed as a kid.

Remembered premises ran through my head: rich guy woos poor girl, she wins over his jaded family and friends with her charm and innocence. Who knows, maybe the trope had some basis in fact.

Before the night ended, Preston asked if I'd like to do a pub-crawl down Sixth Street with him and a couple of friends that weekend. "The zombies will be out," he said.

Of course I said yes, although my suspicious nature still gave me pause, waiting for the other *Carrie* shoe to fall. Why would he want me? He could have any girl on campus. And what the heck did he mean about the zombies being out?

Before we could discuss it further, another patron came to inquire about buying the two mannequin heads. I don't think my mouth fell open but only because I consciously prevented it at the last second. I couldn't imagine anyone wanting those creepy twin creations in their home. Country-bumpkin, through and through, I just couldn't see them hanging on someone's wall. Takes all kinds, I suppose.

I gave Preston my phone number when he asked, and then he hurried off to complete the transaction. I stared after him, still feeling as if I'd stepped into a movie.

~

"WHAT SHOULD I WEAR FOR A PUB-CRAWL?" I asked Joanna after we left the gallery that night.

She laughed. "Comfortable shoes, that's the main thing."

I had been down Sixth Street a few times since moving to Austin the previous summer, but since I had not yet turned twenty-one, I couldn't drink alcohol. Of course that didn't prevent me from enjoying a ton of live music up and down the famous street. I didn't care for drinking that much anyway.

"What did he mean about the zombies being out?"

"It's October," Joanna said. "There's a Zombie Walk every weekend. Anyone can dress up and join. It's a lot of fun."

"Oooh, let's do it sometime, you and me."

She nodded and made the turn onto our street. We shared an off campus university apartment nearby. We both knew I shouldn't have been chosen to be her roommate. Freshmen were not allowed to live off campus. Someone had made a mistake down at the housing office. I wasn't going to look a gift horse in the mouth by speaking up, though. Living in a noisy freshman dorm? No thanks, not if I had another choice. Besides, Joanna and I had clicked right away.

The gallery showing took place on Wednesday. When Preston didn't call or contact me by the time Friday rolled around, I tried not to feel rejected. It must have been a joke, after all.

"I'm sort of relieved," I told Joanna. "I'm sure I would've been in over my head with him—"

As soon as the words left my mouth, a knock came at the door.

Joanna smirked. "Well that's either Preston or destiny. Whichever, I guess you'd better answer it."

I felt like an idiot as I opened the door. There he stood, expensive jeans, designer shirt, and leather jacket with the sleeves casually pushed up. I glanced down at my ripped jeans and t-shirt. "Come on in." I held the door open. "Just let me grab a sweater."

He stepped inside and I'd swear he was so tall he had to duck through the doorway. "Hey, Joanna."

She looked up from her book. "Hey, Preston."

He perched on the arm of the loveseat. "You and 'Tonio got plans?"

She shook her head. "He's doing the guy thing tonight. Poker, I think." She yawned, covered her mouth. "Gonna do the Zombie Walk tomorrow night, though."

I came back from my bedroom, pulling on my favorite sweater. "That's going to be fun."

Preston stood. His gaze took in my casual outfit. "You look great," he said. He opened the door and stood aside for me to exit first.

"Don't wait up," I told Joanna.

She raised one eyebrow. It was a joke between us. In the two months we'd been roomies, I'd had one other "date." She always told me I should live a little—just not too much.

He opened the door to his Mustang and I slid into the cozy leather seat. *Such manners. I could get used to this.*

"How about a bite to eat before we crawl?"

"Sure," I said.

We started at The Burger Bar a couple blocks off Sixth. "Let's just leave the car here," he said after we finished eating. "A few friends are going to catch up to us along the way."

That first date checked all the boxes. We strolled and laughed and acted silly. I did see him take a few sips from a silver flask as we went from bar to bar up one side of Sixth and down the other. But he didn't seem too inebriated and he didn't try to force me to drink, either.

Halfway through the night, we morphed into a large group. He wasn't kidding about some of his friends joining us. We seemed to pick up one or two more at each place we stopped. They were all high or drunk. I didn't see anyone sober other than us—well, me. Preston may have been sober, but each bar was so loud and jam-packed, conversation became more and more impossible. All I had to go on was how well he could walk.

Some of our group couldn't even do that.

Lines of people snaked away down the packed sidewalks and away from the entrances to every place that featured music. The whole street throbbed with sound and the entire downtown area felt wrapped in laughter and drenched in lights.

My favorite places were those where the musicians either sat outside on the patio or set up their instruments on small stages right inside the front windows. KEEP AUSTIN WEIRD signs decorated many of the buildings.

Around midnight, members of the group began to leave. "Everyone's going to the lake. You in?"

I shook my head. "I've got work tomorrow. I should go on home this time."

He didn't argue.

Outside my apartment complex, we sat in his car looking at the stars. Preston turned to me for a goodnight kiss.

"I had so much fun," I said. "Thanks for taking me."

He didn't reply, just kissed me again. Then his fingers began to travel. "The night doesn't have to end."

His lips were full and softly curved. As always, one corner of his mouth rose higher than the other. His brown hair was thick and well cut, streaked either by the sun or by a skilled beautician. I knew it didn't matter, but the perfect highlights kind of threw me.

None of the boys from my tiny high school did the hair salon thing. They were either oilfield offspring or kids of ranch families. They went to barber shops, not salons. If anyone had accused them of paying to have their hair streaked, they likely would have been roped and hogtied.

The swirl of thoughts cut off any desire I had for a longer

night with more kisses. "Sorry. I really do need to get inside." I kissed him lightly, one hand on the door handle. "Thanks again for a great evening."

He let me out and waited in the car until I got inside the apartment. I wondered if we would ever go out again.

The next week he invited me to dinner and a movie. But he wasn't very talkative. I did most of the sharing. Afterward, I felt like I'd been on social media the whole evening because now he knew everything about me and I knew zip about him.

We saw the *Joker* movie and it really depressed me. Later, Preston admitted he'd already seen it a couple of times. That was the one piece of information he shared without prompting. "I think it may be one of my favorite movies of all time," he said.

That surprised me. But after that, he didn't say much more. In fact, he began to seem downright bored.

"That will probably be the last time I go out with him," I told Joanna.

"What happened?" Her voice sounded sleepy. She'd dozed off on the loveseat, reading.

"What's that old movie? *He's Just Not That Into Me*?"

"Something like that." She yawned and gave her blonde ponytail a little shake. "His loss, sweetie. You are way too good for him anyway."

I searched her face for sarcasm, but she seemed serious.

Turns out I was wrong. Way wrong.

He *was* into me.

Big time.

2

PRUDE

The next day I found a handmade card from Preston on my car. It said how much he enjoyed our date and how he hoped we could do it again. A tiny set of melted wax lips sealed the envelope closed.

My phone trilled as I stood there reading the card.

"How's it going, gorgeous?"

I grinned. "Everything's great, Preston. I love the card. I can't believe you made it."

"No biggie," he said. "Just a bit of art. I don't sleep a lot."

An awkward pause.

"Well, I enjoyed the movie and dinner, too." I plunged ahead. "I'd love to do it again sometime."

"Kegger at the river this weekend," he said. "Sound good?"

"Sure." I don't *have* to drink.

"Bathing suits are optional," he said. "But it's totally up to you. Just be sure to bring your appetite. Nothing is off the table."

What does that mean?

After thinking it over, I decided I'm a prude. No doubt about it. I don't want to go skinny-dipping with a bunch of people I don't know—or even a bunch I do know—and that last line about nothing being off the table? I took that to mean anything goes. Nope. Not me. Not even. Buh-bye, rich boy.

I told Joanna and showed her the note before I tossed it.

"You've hit the big time, kiddo. Those parties are legendary."

I shook my head. "Not what I'm here for." I leaned over the trashcan as if to retrieve the paper. "I'll give it to you so maybe you and 'Tonio can go in my place."

She laughed. "No, that's all right. I'm with you on this one. Can you imagine the dope floating around a party like that?"

"And the diseases," I added. "Can we say *herpes*?"

Joanna grimaced. "Just talking about it makes me feel ill."

I agreed. There was no way I would jeopardize my college career over a night of getting high and getting laid. Even if I did like the idea of being part of the "legendary" crowd, I couldn't afford that. If I flunked out, my scholarships and grants would be null and void. I would not pass go. I would not collect my degree.

I had no rich-family pocketbook to fall back on in case of a too-much-fun emergency. My father had been partially disabled in a car accident. He only worked part-time. Any extra money went toward his catastrophic medical bills.

To tell the truth, I wouldn't have participated anyway. You can take the girl out of the small town, but... well, you know the rest.

Imagine my surprise when Preston arrived even after I had told him I'd have to take a rain check.

"We'll just go for a bit," he said, "let you see how it is. I promise. It isn't what you think. The guys are just blowing off steam. Tons of hotdogs on the grill. Lots of cold beer and hard lemonade. That's it." He planted himself in front of me, one hand on each of my shoulders, and stared into my eyes. "Would I lie to you?"

That smile. That smirky one-corner-higher-than-the-other

smile. It took me by surprise. I'd assumed he would wash his hands of me when he learned I wasn't into stuff like the skinny-dipping invitation.

"I'm sorry," I said. "I'm just not a party girl. But you go on and have fun, okay?"

His gaze slid away, his fingers tightened on my shoulders, he seemed about to speak, and then he sighed. "We don't have to go to the kegger." He leaned in and kissed me lightly. "I just want to be with you, it doesn't matter what we do."

"Seriously?" The word popped out of my mouth on its own.

"Of course."

I weighed my options. Go out with this rich, handsome, BMOC, or stay home and study and probably wind up watching YouTube videos until I fell asleep. "I have to work until ten," I said.

"No problem. I'll pick you up at ten—"

I laughed. "Maybe eleven? I'll want to change clothes. I always smell like garlic bread when I get off—"

He dropped his voice into a cartoon growl. "All the better to eat you, my dear." He cocked an eyebrow and leered at me.

"Oh, you." I pushed his shoulder playfully.

So, that's how we wound up at the river that Friday night for the weekly kegger.

"I thought you said we were just going for a drive," I murmured after he turned off the highway onto the single-lane road. I could see the campfire up ahead. Behind it was a well-lit lakehouse with a huge deck and immense windows facing the water.

Preston shrugged. "I decided if you saw the place for yourself, you'd realize you were just being silly to think you wouldn't fit in."

I clamped my lips shut and tried to think of the best way to tell him he was an ass. "It's not that I'm afraid I won't fit in," I said. "It's that I don't want to go to a party with a bunch of drunk skinny-dippers."

He had the good grace to look shocked. I believe he really thought I was worried about my popularity.

"We won't stay long," he said. Then something came over his face. Even in the moonlit confines of the Mustang, I could see the hardening. "The only thing is, you'll have to at least strip and take one dip in the water if you don't want to walk home."

My hand found the door handle before I knew I even planned to get out. "I don't think so." Ultimatums were not my thing. "Just let me out here."

He slowed and stopped, calling my bluff.

I took a deep breath, stepped out, and started walking back the way we had come. Though my outside appearance was calm, my insides were like waves white-capping near the shore. It was a long way back to the main road. I hoped and prayed someone I knew would come along and give me a ride. It wouldn't be Joanna, though. She and Antonio were doing the Zombie Walk again. This time there would be a prize for the best look. How I wished I'd gone with them.

When Preston realized I wasn't bluffing, he turned the car around and drove alongside me as I strode down the shoulder of the road, arms crossed over my chest.

I could hear him attempting to apologize, but this time his words fell into the gap between us like pebbles dropped into a dry well. "I was only joking," he said. "You know I would never make you do anything you didn't want."

I didn't buy it. I was done trying to keep up with Gatsby. He'd lied when he said we were just going for a drive. And I'd seen the change come over his face when he said I'd have to prove myself by taking at least one nude dip.

Skinny-dipping might have been okay if it were only the two of us and we'd been seeing each other exclusively, but skinny-dipping as a group, and as a requirement? Not happening. Besides, it had become apparent that the real reason he'd latched on to me, an unknown frosh, was because he'd already burned through most of the girls in his own class and all that was left were the drunks. Fresh fish. That was me.

I only wish I'd come to my senses a little sooner. When I pulled out my phone and called an Uber, he glared at me and sped away. He seemed determined to cover me with dirt from those wide back tires. But before my driver arrived, Preston reappeared. He actually parked his car and got out to walk beside me until my ride came. To keep me safe, he said.

That almost made me rethink my low opinion of him. Almost.

He called a couple times after that night, to ask me out, and he came to Twisted Pasta to eat a few times, but I didn't let my guard down. Relationships should be fun, not stressful. That's what Joanna and I decided in our late night chitchats anyway.

Unfortunately, he seemed to take my rejection as a challenge. The more I retreated, the more he charged ahead. Soon, I had a stalker.

Sometimes he would be sitting in his Mustang at the edge of the apartment complex parking lot. I would go out for my early morning run and he would be there, stepping out of his car, hair sleep-smushed, clothes wrinkled and soiled. He seemed to want me to know he'd slept in his car outside my apartment. I think he wanted me to see him as some kind of martyr, sacrificing comfort just to catch a glimpse of me.

To avoid him, I stopped running.

I thought it would be only temporary. I was nothing special. I figured after a while he would give up and go away. But I didn't know Preston.

He did not take rejection well at all.

He began to follow me to work, never bothering me, just

being there, in the parking lot. He even attended some of my classes, sitting in the back, watching. His demeanor was never violent or angry, just persistent. And really, I told myself, how could a well-known rich kid be a stalker? That would be ridiculous. Besides, he didn't accost me or try to make me interact with him, he just always showed up.

Joanna told me to call the cops anyway. She said he seemed to be trying to intimidate me even if he didn't talk to me.

But I didn't call them. Every time I made up my mind to do it, that would be the day he *wouldn't* show. I guess he had to attend at least some of his classes.

It became almost a joke. He would be there, like a puppy, waiting for a pat on the head. I never gave it to him. Never acknowledged him at all. Some days I forgot all about him. He became part of the landscape, part of the background.

"If this is stalking," I told Joanna one day, "it must be the slow-motion variety." But in the end, it was all a ruse so he could play out his line, set the hook, reel me in.

That's how I wound up running from him that night on Telephone Road. Running for my life through the trees, the brush, through the cold, dark night.

I didn't want to go with him that evening. Of course I didn't. He tricked me. He tricked me and he almost killed me, but I got lucky, and then I ran.

I ran for my life.

3

BREAK

We were starting our last week before Thanksgiving break. No classes for four days. I looked forward to spending time with my family. I loved my university, but the small-town girl in me often felt overwhelmed. Meeting Preston hadn't helped.

It seemed to be getting worse. After I'd said no to him a few times, I accidentally wound up at a party at his frat house. A girl from my psychology class asked me to drop her off because her boyfriend planned to meet her there.

I didn't even go inside because I didn't want to take a chance on running into Preston. No way would I actually attend the party. Especially when I thought he'd finally got the message that I didn't want to go out with him again.

Driving away, I thanked my lucky stars I hadn't seen him.

When he called from an unknown number the next day, the anger in his voice perplexed me. He said he'd watched me leaving and knew I'd been there with one of his friends. Then he said he'd get to the bottom of things and find out why I lied to him. He acted as if we were engaged or something.

Later that week, the next to the last day before we broke for

Thanksgiving, I found him sleeping in his car outside our apartment again. I'd thought those days were over. It had been the first time in a while that I'd gone out early for a run.

This time I got angry. "What are you doing here?"

I expected him to say it was a simple coincidence that he'd pulled into the nearest lot and passed out on the way home from a party or whatever.

But he'd just smirked that little smirk I'd once found appealing. "I'm here to take you out for breakfast."

I clenched my fists. "The last time we spoke you were ticked off and certain I was seeing one of your friends—not that it would matter if I did—"

He shook his head, ran his hand through his hair. "All is forgiven. I questioned everyone and no one saw you actually at the party. They all said you just dropped off Kenisha and left. Sorry I didn't believe you."

I had to force myself to keep my mouth shut. On the one hand, it made me furious that he seemed convinced we were a couple. On the other hand, I felt nauseated and a little disgusted that he'd questioned everyone about me as if we were not only a couple, but as if I belonged to him. Like property. Did he really assume I would drop everything and go with him to breakfast now?

Looking down at my leggings and running shoes, I made a small gesture of sarcastic regret. "Sorry, I'm just out for my morning run." I wanted to tell him off. To inform him that if I'd wanted to go to that stupid party I would have. I didn't need either his permission, or his "forgiveness." What a piece of work he'd turned out to be. And yet, something kept me from speaking my mind. I jokingly told myself it was just too early in the morning to antagonize the beast.

He frowned. "But you stopped running."

Not a question. A statement.

I stood there, wordless, for several seconds. I knew he'd been watching me. Hearing him admit it made it even creepier.

He must have taken my silence for agreement because he walked over, opened his passenger door, and motioned for me to get in the car.

"No," I huffed. "I really need to run this morning. Got a lot on my mind."

His blue eyes went dark. "I came all the way over here, spent the night in my car, and now you act like this?"

"You could have called." I held up my cell phone. "Saved yourself the trip." I don't know where I got the guts to say that, but I as I backed away, I saw his hands ball up into fists.

He started toward me and the look on his face made me think of an animal in a zoo. One that would eat you if the glass wall should break.

Just as his fingers unclenched enough to grasp my wrist, Joanna walked out. She also wore running gear. For a moment, his fingers tightened and I felt my bones grind against each other. Then Joanna called out, "Good morning," and he let his hand fall to his side.

Pretty certain he would've dragged me to the car if she hadn't appeared.

I took a couple more steps back.

Jo had become a good friend in the few months we'd shared the apartment. Since she majored in kinesiology, we didn't have many of the same classes, but I knew I could depend on her. Sometimes—before Preston—we would hit the running trail together, but not always. She often took a different route. I think she just didn't want to hurt my feelings because I couldn't keep up with her.

I gave her a little wave and a nod. She glanced at Preston and nodded almost imperceptibly. Then she took out her phone and looked from it to Preston and back to the phone again.

Preston glanced at her, then at me, and then he took one giant step back to the car and slammed the passenger door. Without another word, he strode around to the driver's side, folded his six-foot-plus frame behind the wheel, and fired up the engine.

Jamming the transmission into reverse, he flipped the Mustang's stereo all the way up to shake-the-frame level before executing a tire-screeching donut and fishtailing out of the parking lot and onto the street. It reminded me of the night I got out and called an Uber.

"What's his problem?" Joanna asked.

I didn't realize she'd jogged up beside me. "For some reason he thought I'd simply forget all the water under the bridge and join him for breakfast." I wiped a trembling hand across the back of my neck, underneath my ponytail. Adrenalin lit up my veins. I could feel it urging me to go, just run.

Joanna shook her head. "What a jerk." She tapped the volume on her iPhone, tucked it into her hydration belt, and nodded toward the trail that started behind the complex. "I guess he thought I was calling security or something." There was a jolly tone to her voice. "At least now we can run in peace. Ready?"

"So glad you came out when you did. I'm not sure what would have happened if you hadn't." I said it jokingly, and I don't know how much she actually heard since she had put her earbuds in, but at that moment, I meant it. Preston's temper tantrum had scared me.

Joanna jogged on slowly and I caught up to her. We parted ways after a mile. She took the fork to the long run, all the way around, while I opted for the shorter one, across the middle of campus. The joy had gone out of it for me, thanks to Preston.

As I jogged through the wooded areas of the trail, I began to feel a little nervous, as if someone might be watching me. But I didn't really think it could be Preston. I'd seen him speed away. If he were anywhere near, I would know it. The muffler on that Mustang would tell me.

After another couple of miles, I jogged back around to the parking lot of our apartment complex. I felt my already pounding heart quicken even more. A man stood outside our door. It appeared he'd already rung the bell and was simply waiting on someone to answer.

For a moment I thought about running right on by, as if I didn't live there. But I couldn't do that. What if he had a

message about my dad? The man certainly looked official. No one wearing a suit ever visited us.

At least it wasn't Preston. I scanned the parking lot as I slowed to a walk and sure enough, a nondescript car waited under a tree. I'd never seen the car before. It looked like one of those unmarked police cars on TV. Then it hit me. Joanna. Something might have happened to Joanna.

I approached the man from the side. "Hello?"

He turned, all business. Steely-eyed, square-jawed, he looked like a detective created just to match the TV-detective-car.

Looking down at his phone, he said, "Marlena Matthews?"

I peered at his screen and saw my school ID photo. "Yes, I'm Marlena. Is everything okay?"

He slid his phone into the inside pocket of his sport coat. When his hand reemerged, it held a business card, which he offered to me. "Detective Lapuli," he said. "I need to talk to you and your roommate if you have a moment."

I glanced at the card in my hand.

Detective Elko Lapuli
Campus Liaison
Austin PD/UTPD

It had an official-looking insignia that made it appear legit. If he wanted to talk to both of us, then Joanna must be all right.

"My roommate isn't back from her run yet. She took the long trail. Has something happened to one of our cars?" Since Joanna was alright, it was all I could think of that would warrant a visit to both of us. But I could see my little car from where we stood. It appeared to be just fine. Maybe Joanna's car had been broken into. I couldn't see it from here.

"No," Detective Lapuli said. "Nothing like that. I came by to ask about the girl who was supposed to be Joanna's roommate. Mariah Leathers? She's from Chicago. Never showed up to claim her spot."

"Oh." My mind went blank. "I don't know anything about her." I scratched at a bead of sweat trickling down between my shoulder blades. "When I first moved to Austin at the start of the summer, I shared a little trailer with a couple of girls from the Copper Kettle where we all worked. But when classes began I had to move into the freshman dorm. Regulations, you know." I scratched again, and then smoothed a hand over my hair. "When the housing clerk called and said I could move in here, right off campus, I jumped at the chance. I liked it much better than the noisy dorm or the trailer. It wasn't university-approved anyway." I shifted my weight. Nerves wouldn't let me stand still. "I figured getting to move in here was just some kind of clerical error."

The detective nodded. "I understand. Now that classes are underway, you should really be in the dorm, right? Seeing as how it's your first year and all."

"Right. That's what I meant about regulations. The university usually requires freshmen to live on campus. I was just sharing rent on the little trailer because I was so excited to go to UT I couldn't wait to get here. Thought I'd make a little extra money before school started. When the housing office called and said I had a place off campus, I couldn't believe it." I couldn't seem to stop babbling. Something about the man made me feel like a criminal. Like I had to prove my innocence.

He stood there letting me ramble. He seemed to have all day just to watch me talk. I didn't know why he made me so nervous, but I had a feeling if we stood there long enough, I would confess to something just to get a reaction from him.

Finally he said, "Did you know Mariah hasn't been seen since she left home?"

"What?" My brain was so focused on how I only had half an hour to get cleaned up and head off to class, that I couldn't really comprehend what he had just said. "Who?"

"Mariah Leathers," he said. "The girl who should be standing where you are standing."

"Standing here?" I looked down at the sidewalk. I still didn't understand what he meant.

He waited like a stone. Letting me draw my own conclusions.

"Oh," I thumped my forehead with the heel of my hand. "She should be standing here because she was going to be Joanna's roomie..." I shook my head. "I'm sorry, I didn't even know there was supposed to be a different roommate until just now."

"I see." His words sounded cryptic.

See what? I hadn't said anything for him to 'see'. Had I? "Really, Detective—" I looked at his card again. "Lapuli. I didn't even know the girl's name until just now when you said it." I shifted my weight, scratched the back of my right calf with the top of my left foot. "Is she like, missing? Maybe she just decided not to return to school."

"Her folks waved at her as she drove away in August—on her way back to school after being at home for the summer—that's the last time anyone has seen her."

It finally hit me. "That's awful. You mean they saw her off and yet she never got here? Maybe she ran away, you know, with a boy or something." I chewed the edge of my lip as possible scenarios flooded my brain. "Still, I can't believe that's why I got her spot."

His expression didn't change. His heavy-lidded eyes didn't blink. He watched my face like a lizard watching a fly.

"But it's almost Thanksgiving," I said. "Where could she be?"

He shrugged. "You sure you've never heard of her?"

The sun beat down on the top of my head as if it were high summer. "Me?" My voice squeaked. "Of course not. I was just glad I didn't have to stay in the freshman dorm. But if I had known she was missing, or whatever, I never would've taken the spot." I shivered. "It's creepy."

"How well do you know your roommate, Joanna Muirwood? Were you acquainted before this year?" He flipped open a small notebook and took out a pen, prepared to write down my answer.

"How well do I know her?" I thought for a moment. "Well, she's sweet, and kind, very smart. I just met her when we became roomies."

The detective wrote something down. "Will she be back soon? I'd like to speak with her, find out if she knew Miss Leathers."

I wished Joanna *would* come. I had no idea if she knew Mariah Leathers or not.

Detective Lapuli looked at his watch. Then he looked at the door to the apartment.

"I don't know when she'll be back. Like I said, she took the long route."

His eyes scanned the area. "And you say you didn't know Miss Muirwood before August?"

"No, we'd never met. I had already moved into the dorm when the housing clerk called and said a student apartment had opened up if I wanted it." I knew I'd said that already, but I couldn't seem to get it through his head.

He let his gaze come to rest on me. "Why do you suppose they chose you, Miss Matthews? Out of the thousands of students at UT, both new and returning, why do you suppose they chose you, a lowly freshman, to fill the gap left by Miss Leathers?" His gaze drilled into mine.

I took half a step back. Was he accusing me of somehow making the other girl disappear so I could have her spot? So I could move in with Joanna? It sounded like the ridiculous plot of an old movie. I couldn't wrap my head around it. "Sir," I began. "I have no idea why they chose me."

"Ahhh," the detective tilted his head back slightly. "So it's just a coincidence that the part-time clerk 'forgot' to put in a call to Mariah's parents when she didn't show up to claim her spot, but then turned right around and called you to tell you it was all yours. Just a little coincidence…"

I shivered. Moments before I'd been warm, perspiring, the sun beating down, sweat trickling. Now, my whole body felt cold, as if a cloud had crossed the sun. "I thought it was a little strange, too, getting that call out of the blue. But I wasn't about to look a gift horse in the mouth, you know?" I rubbed my hands up and down my arms to warm them. "The dorm was so crowded. So crazy. Besides, now that I know what happened, it doesn't really sound like coincidence at all. It sounds more like that clerk in the housing office was in a hurry to go to lunch or something."

"Which brings me to my next question," he said. "How well do you know Kyla Becker, the part-time clerk?"

I couldn't help it. I rolled my eyes. "I've never heard of her, either!" The whole conversation felt like a nightmare. I wished Joanna would hurry and get here so she could clear it all up.

He wrote in his little notebook again. "How far did you say she intended to run?"

"Ten miles. The distance around the perimeter—"

"Right," he interrupted. "I know that path well."

I didn't know what to say to that, so for once I didn't say anything, just rubbed my cold arms, retied both shoes, then unfastened my phone from the band on my arm and checked my texts and email. Being the campus liaison between the University PD and the Austin PD, the detective probably knew everything about *everything*.

At last he got a message on his phone. He slid the notebook back into his coat pocket. "I have to go," he said. "Please give this to Miss Muirwood." He handed me another business card. "Tell her to call me as soon as she comes in. Detective Andrews from Chicago may want to speak with her as well."

That got my attention. "May I ask you a question?"

He stopped, waited.

I flicked the edge of the card back and forth with my fingernail, unsure how to proceed.

Detective Lapuli drew in a breath, let it out, made a show of checking his phone again.

Finally, I said, "I just wondered why it took so long for anyone to start looking for her."

The cloud moved and the sun beat down on the top of my head again. It also touched my shoulders and the back of my neck.

I waited.

He peered down at his phone.

I began to think he wouldn't answer but then he said, "Good question. Apparently her folks assumed she was here all along. They had been receiving texts from her phone the entire time."

"Wait, if she's been texting them, that's not the same as missing, right? Maybe she just wanted to get away for a while."

He simply looked at me. "Well, that's one possibility, of course. Except for the fact that we now know there has been no activity on her credit or debit cards. Not even for gasoline. She had her own bank account so her folks didn't notice." He clamped his lips together.

I worried he might not tell me anything else, so I rushed ahead. "That doesn't sound good. It would be hard to run away without money, unless someone kidnapped her." What a horrible idea. My mind went into overdrive. "Could that be it? Has she been kidnapped? Oh, man. Can't you guys trace the phone or something?"

Detective Lapuli held up one hand like a stop sign. "We've been asking exactly those kinds of questions. The thing is this, after her mom texted her that they were going to call the university, the messages stopped. Completely. The phone has probably been turned off or destroyed. The call log showed that each message appeared to come from some place on campus. A different public spot each time."

"Oh, wow. That's spooky. Did they have a lot of, you know, family problems?"

He shook his head. "Not to our knowledge. Very well respected family. They said she loved UT, couldn't wait to get back. Sort of like you. Coming down early because you couldn't wait to start school."

I let that statement pass. "So that's how they learned she never came back... when her mom called the university?"

"Yes, that started the ball rolling. Chicago PD is investigating from their end—to make sure she actually left town—while we investigate here, to make sure she arrived."

His phone dinged again. It must've been important because he immediately turned to walk back to his car. "Thank you for your time," he called. "Please don't forget to tell Miss Muirwood to contact me."

I heard the distinct sound of the remote button unlocking his car door just as Joanna came jogging up from behind the complex.

"Hey, Detective," I yelled. "Hold up!"

He had already opened the door and climbed into the driver's seat.

I waved to direct his attention to Joanna, and then I loped over to intercept her.

Once I relayed the information, she immediately headed toward the detective's car. I saw him lean over and open the passenger door. Oh, no, I thought. He's taking her downtown. But instead, she just climbed inside and sat there with one long leg sticking out the open passenger door.

They visited for so long that I finally went inside the apartment, but I didn't shut the door. I wanted to hear if the car started up.

A few minutes later, Joanna came inside. Her interview had gone about the same as mine. She didn't know Mariah Leathers and she didn't know why my name had been drawn to be her roommate.

By the time the Thanksgiving break began, I couldn't wait to go home for a visit. I hadn't heard from Preston directly, but I'd seen him near the apartment once or twice.

I also began to get odd calls from various private numbers on my cell. But I didn't answer them. I no longer answered any call I didn't recognize. After Detective Lapuli's visit, my nerves kept me on high alert. I mentioned the calls to Joanna but she said she hadn't received any. That made me even more certain it was Preston trying to trick me into talking to him.

Although Joanna and I didn't discuss Preston much after

that, we did talk about Mariah Leathers. We both thought it extremely weird that the girl from Chicago, a place neither of us had ever been, had continued to pretend she was here on campus.

"Can't they trace her phone?" Joanna wondered.

I told her I had asked the detective that very thing and he told me how her phone had gone silent after her mom said she planned to call the school.

"That's really scary," Joanna said. "Do you think someone else could have had her phone? Like maybe they were pretending to be her?"

The skin on the back of my neck crimped up into gooseflesh as I thought about all the strange calls I'd been receiving. Especially since I had pretty much decided Preston was behind them, pretending to be someone else so I would answer.

I DROVE the four hours back to my tiny hometown of Window with my stereo blaring. I couldn't wait to see my mom and dad. My sister, Carrie, and her husband, Dixon, were also on their way from their home in Colorado. I felt certain it would be a perfect holiday.

Of course I longed to tell my best friend, Lana, about Preston so I could get her opinion. I'd also tell her about the missing girl. Lana would appreciate the eerie circumstances that allowed me to get such a great apartment. She loved a good mystery. No way would I tell my mom, though. She'd want me to report Preston to the campus police for harassment, and if I mentioned the missing roommate, she'd yank me out of school so fast I'd get whiplash.

I rolled down my window to clear my head. The further I got from school, the lighter I felt. The sky was melted-crayon blue, the clouds were fluffy cotton balls, and the sun shone as if it were spring instead of fall. I guess the events of the last few days had been weighing on me more than I realized. Maybe the trip home would reset my mood, reboot my happy.

Seasons in Texas could be almost nonexistent. They would often fade one into the other with little to no demarcation. There weren't that many trees where I grew up, and the ones that dotted the fields and rest areas west of Austin were likely to be mesquites and junipers rather than deciduous trees. In other words, there wasn't a lot of fall color on the trip home. But I loved it just the same. The further west I drove, the emptier the land became.

As I passed the city limits sign, I marveled at my tiny West Texas hometown. It felt like a step back in time. Red brick streets surrounded the courthouse square, shops with real window displays lined the sidewalks, and an old fashioned drugstore still stood right there on the corner of the square. I could almost taste their yummy root beer floats.

I sighed, amazed at how good it felt to be back.

Pulling into the driveway of my childhood home, I did my best to put my worries aside. I'd called first Mom, and then Lana, on the way home. Lana and I were already looking forward to attending the Settlers' Fair later that night. Mom is the one who encouraged us to go. "You need a little down time," she'd said. "I know how difficult the first year away from home can be."

Suddenly anxious to see my parents, I flung myself from the car, dashed up the walk, and burst through the door. Mom greeted me inside the entryway. She looked the same, small, plump, and slightly out of breath. Her fluffy brown hair sprang away from her temples in unruly tendrils.

We hugged for eons. "You look wonderful!" She patted me and pressed her palms to the sides of my face, forcing me to stand still while she examined me. "A little thinner maybe. No freshman fifteen for you, huh?"

I shook my head. "No way. My roommate is a runner and a kinesiology major. She doesn't eat much sugar either." I realized how I sounded, as if Joanna made all the rules. "She's a good example, I think."

Mom smiled, her eyes crinkling at the corners. "You don't know how good it is to hear that. I just knew you'd wind up with a party-girl for a roommate."

"Me, too," I said. "I probably would have if I'd stayed in the dorm." Her worry furthered my resolve not to mention party-boy-Preston.

I hurried back to the car to grab my luggage and laundry. I hadn't meant for it to pile up, but knowing I could do it all at home had made it easy to put off going down to the shared laundry room at our complex.

"Where's Dad?" I looked back toward the driveway, my eye searching for his truck. Only Mom's Fiat sat in its customary place outside the garage.

"We sold the truck, honey. Dad isn't feeling well." She pulled the door closed behind me. "He sits in his recliner drinking iced tea and watching westerns most of the day now."

My dad had suffered a traumatic brain injury when a drunk-driver hit him head-on two years earlier. Insurance had paid for a new truck, and with the help of rehab he'd recovered most of his cognitive function, but he still had problems with balance and short-term memory. "But doesn't he need his truck for work?"

Mom shook her head slightly. "He's not allowed to drive anymore. Couldn't pass the exam to have his license renewed." She took one of my bags of laundry from me. "Seeing it sitting in the drive depressed him, so I sold it and took some of the money to purchase an automatic-lift recliner. He has a little trouble getting to his feet without assistance."

My overnight bag and second duffle full of dirty clothes hit the floor. Sure, Dad had been moving slowly and taking a boatload of medicine, but this news hit me like a ton of bricks. My dad could no longer drive? That meant Mom must be driving him back and forth every day.

Dad had only recently gone back to work full-time. Since the accident he'd been on part-time duty in the refinery office. He'd been looking forward to going back to work in the plant itself.

"Are you able to take him and pick him up every day?"

Mom bent to retrieve one of the bags I'd dropped. "They let him go, sweetie. Even with the medicine, his balance kept getting worse. He stumbled a lot. They were afraid he would fall and hurt himself. Maybe even cause an accident in the plant somehow." She shouldered both bags and headed toward the utility room. "I think they were right."

I grabbed my overnight bag and followed her. "Mo-o-m. Why didn't you tell me?"

She shook her head, setting her brown curls bouncing. Following behind her, I couldn't see her face.

"It wasn't totally unexpected." She opened the lid of the washing machine and started the water. "The neurologist said some areas of his brain just haven't recovered, and likely never will." She began to sort clothes into piles of colors and lights. "It's what they call atrophy." She stopped and turned to face me. "I'm sorry. I know that's a horrible word, but we have to face the truth, kiddo."

The news devastated me. I had never thought of my dad as an invalid until now. "So he can't work anymore?"

Mom dumped my other duffle onto the floor and continued sorting. "Maybe the Step-Up people can help us find a job he can do that doesn't require walking or standing. They're part of the state-funded disability program he's involved with. They've been very helpful, you know."

I turned on my heel and headed to the living room.

Dad sat in his recliner, oblivious to the fact that I'd arrived.

"Hey, Dad." I leaned down and gave him a hug. "How's it going?"

He looked into my face and for a moment, it seemed as if he didn't recognize me at all. Then the fog lifted and he smiled. "Hey, baby girl, when did you get home?"

I pulled the footstool over and sat beside him. His hair appeared longer than usual, thinner, too. His eyes seemed a little unfocussed. "I just came in," I said. "It was a nice drive down from Austin."

"Good weather?"

I glanced out the picture window. "Beautiful weather." My gaze fell on the wheelchair tucked out of the way in the corner of the room. He'd used it the first few months after the accident, but then he'd worked hard in physical therapy and graduated to a walker. The wheelchair had been moved to the storehouse. Did he need it again? Was he a complete invalid?

Giving Dad another hug, I promised to be back after I unpacked. He nodded absently and went back to his western.

After putting the things from my overnight bag into the bathroom, and helping Mom with my laundry, I poured a glass of iced tea and went back to the living room to visit with Dad. But he'd fallen asleep.

It broke my heart to see him sitting there with his head bent over on one shoulder. He looked incredibly old. Ancient. Not like my dad at all.

Mom had moved on to the kitchen. She must've seen something in my face when I sat down at the breakfast bar. "He's had some problems," she said. "The doctor said he may have had a TIA at some point in the past few weeks."

"What's that?"

She explained that a TIA is a transient ischemic attack, which is like a mini-stroke. It means blood flow to the brain had been interrupted for some reason. "It can be a precursor to a major stroke," she said.

"What do we need to do?"

"They've put him on some medicine to help prevent that—"

"Is he back in the wheelchair?"

Mom nodded. "Hopefully it's temporary. His balance just got worse and worse."

The stress I'd been feeling at school suddenly reappeared in a new form. "I need to be here to help you. How does he get around while you're at work?"

Mom came and stood across from where I sat. "I've hired an aide from a program called Home Help. She comes in for a couple hours each day to help him bathe and make certain he takes his medicine." She wiped her hands on a dishtowel. "There's also an occupational therapist who is teaching him how to transfer himself from the recliner to the wheelchair. He's actually doing pretty well, all things considered."

I wanted to ask what she meant by "all things considered," but just then Lana arrived. She came in the back door like she always had when we were growing up.

Her cheeks were pink and her enviably straight blonde hair still gleamed from a long summer spent outdoors at the community pool where she worked as a lifeguard. Instead of a big university, she'd opted to attend the junior college one town over. It seemed to agree with her.

Maybe that's what I should do, I thought, transfer to the good old JuCo just a few miles away. I could be a lot of help to Mom and Dad if I were closer.

Lana grabbed me and hugged me tightly. "Ready for the carnival?"

I hesitated. With all this new information about Dad and his problems, I didn't know if I wanted to go to the carnival at all. It seemed I would be leaving almost before we'd even said hello.

Mom sensed my reluctance. "Go on," she said. "Have fun. Tomorrow we'll cook our turkey and dressing—"

"And sweet potatoes?"

Mom nodded. "And green beans and corn on the cob and broccoli-rice-casserole—"

"And caramel pie?"

She grinned. "Of course. But now that you're all grown up, some of that will be your job."

I hurried over to kiss her on the cheek. "I can't wait to get cooking."

She laughed and kissed me back. "It's so good to have you home."

Picking up my phone, I accompanied Lana out the door with a little wave. "I'll be back early," I called.

Mom just waved and went on with her cooking.

Lana and I jumped in her car and away we went into the early fall evening.

4

JIM

Lana insisted on driving. On the way, I showed her a picture of Preston on my phone. She commented on his blue eyes and thick, wavy hair. When I told her about his little fit in the parking lot, she agreed it was a definite red flag.

She popped a piece of gum into her mouth. "Sounds like a control freak. Who needs some guy calling the shots? Isn't that what parents are for?"

I nodded. "That's why we went to college, to get away from our parents."

Lana laughed. She liked living in a residence hall at the junior college. And she'd also enjoyed driving to Austin to visit me and check out the live music scene. We didn't get crazy though. It's true what they say, you can take the girl out of the small town, but you can't always take the small town out of the girl.

Driving down the streets of our hometown felt like going back in time. Not just back in time to a historical small town, but back in time to my childhood. I'd sat at every booth in the corner drug store, ridden my bike down nearly every sidewalk, and learned to drive right there in the high school parking lot. It seemed idyllic and slightly unreal. As if all my memories were simply figments of my imagination.

Nearing the agriculture center, where they held the fair each year, we began to encounter traffic. In a town the size of Window, the annual fair is a big, big deal. It suddenly occurred to me that I didn't know if Mom had entered any of her canned goods in the homemade contest the way she always did. I hadn't even thought to ask.

"We'll have to go through Barn G and look at the homemade stuff," I told Lana as we searched for a parking spot. "I want to see if Mom entered her Christmas pickles."

"Surely she did," Lana said. "They always win."

"I know," I shrugged. "It's just with Dad's health problems..." Then I gave her a brief update on everything Mom had said.

"He can't work at all?"

I shook my head and stepped out of the car into the dusty parking lot. "It was a shock to me. Mom never said a thing about it on the phone. Said she didn't want to distract me from studying." I rolled my eyes and frowned. "I didn't tell her I'd already been distracted by Preston and his weirdness."

Lana clicked the lock on her Ford Focus. "Yeah. I guess it's not a good idea. As long as you're not going to keep seeing him that is."

I thought about that. "No way. No matter who he is, or how perfect he looks, I don't need that nonsense. I don't think anyone does."

"He sounds kinda psycho," Lana said.

"I can't argue with that."

We linked arms and strolled through the multitude of cars. The night was warm for November. Dust from the unpaved parking lot permeated the air. Clanky carnival music wafted across the lot to greet us accompanied by the smell of frying dough and melting sugar—funnel cakes and cotton candy—two of my favorite fair foods.

"Ahhh," I inhaled deeply. "It's going to be a great night."

Lana laughed and began to jog, dragging me along into the gathering twilight. We skirted the carnival rides and hurried toward the large metal buildings at the rear of the property. By the time we rushed through the baked goods and arts and crafts, watching for Mom's pickles amongst the home-canned vegetables, beans, peppers, and salsa, darkness had fallen and the colorful rides whirled against the night sky in all their neon splendor.

The small-town atmosphere was as thick as the powdered sugar dusting the tops of the funnel cakes.

"Are you okay?" Lana asked.

I nodded. "I'm just sort of dumbfounded about my folks having all these problems I didn't even know about."

Lana knew what I meant. "Yeah, your mom's pickles always win. I can't believe she didn't enter them at all."

I thought of the multiple blue ribbons she'd won over the years. The bakery where she worked displayed them proudly. "Yeah. She really has her hands full with Dad's problems. And she never once told me how much trouble he was having. She didn't say a word. Not one."

LANA NODDED IN SYMPATHY. "Maybe after a few rides and games, we'll feel better."

I made myself smile. "It's certainly worth a try." We linked arms and strolled toward the carnival games, promising each other we wouldn't get suckered in by the fast talking barkers.

We'd been there about an hour when I spied Jimmy Allan with his buddy, Dash. We had all attended the same high school, but Jim hung out at the agriculture building and I worked half a day in the vocational ed program. I don't think we shared a single class. Same way with Dash. I knew his name, but I didn't really *know* either of them.

Jimmy came from a ranching family, and Dash had been our high school track star. We'd shared the same hallways, but even in a town as small as Window, we still seemed to stay within our own little circles of friends.

They made a handsome pair in their western shirts and jeans. Jim even wore his old Ag-Club jacket.

Lana and I had just given up on the carnival games. We were standing between the roller coaster and The Scrambler when Dash and Jimmy ambled over. I elbowed my bestie in the ribs. She'd had a crush on Dash all through our senior year.

He stopped beside her and smiled that dazzling yearbook smile. "How y'all doing?" Somehow, that line reminded me of Joey Tribbiani on the sitcom *Friends*.

I murmured hello and looked from him to his buddy.

Jimmy nodded a greeting and then glanced away, hands jammed into the tops of his front pockets.

Dash said he recognized us from school, and then he asked if we were home from college. He said he'd torn a ligament in his knee and had to delay his own college career until it healed. "Scholarship says I've got to be able to run track, you know?"

We both nodded in understanding. The rumor mill said his torn ligament had been the result of a drunken motorcycle accident, but it was none of my business.

He turned his attention to Lana. His teeth were white and perfect in the sodium arc lights. Glancing upward, he indicated the towering Ferris wheel with a tilt of his dimpled chin. "You ever been kissed at the top?"

Lana shook her head. A slight giggle escaped her lips.

"Well," he held out his hand, "Let's give it a whirl, shall we?"

Lana nodded and slipped her hand into his. She shot me an apologetic smile as they strolled away.

That left me standing on the midway with Jimmy Allan.

Uncertainty filled the warm night air between us. I would glance at him just as he looked away, then in a few seconds he would look back at me with a sweet smile. It felt sort of like that first boy-girl dance way back in junior high.

Just as I opened my mouth to ask him about his college, Lana sent me a text asking if I wanted to meet her and Dash at the gate later, or did I think Jimmy would drive me home?

I replied with a happy face and told her not to worry about me, that I would find my own ride. Then I urged her to be careful. It didn't really bother me to be ditched before we'd even reconnected—okay, it did bother me a little—but what really worried me was Dash's love 'em and leave 'em reputation. Definitely the kind of guy every girl's mama warns her about. Plus, we'd all heard that disturbing DUI rumor. At least Lana would be the one doing the driving; after all, we had come to the fair in her car.

Jimmy smiled again as I looked up from my phone, and I smiled back. I'd heard he went off to Tarleton State or Sul Ross, one of those Texas agriculture colleges. I remembered seeing him at school in that very same dark blue jacket, climbing out of his red pickup truck with The Double L Ranch sign on the door. I'd always admired how the bright gold embroidery stood out against the navy corduroy fabric of that jacket. Now I noticed how the deep blue color made his gray eyes look as mysterious as rain clouds.

"Which bear do you want?" He nodded toward the nearby Pitch-Till-U-Win game booth.

"The blue one," I said, "if you think you can win it." I don't know what made me so bold. He just seemed so shy. Or maybe the night simply required it. The air was thick with the scent of popcorn and possibility.

Jimmy grinned, paid the barker a five, picked up his three balls, threw them in quick succession, wham, wham, wham, and all three weighted milk bottles toppled one after the other. The dark blue bear belonged to me. It almost matched the shade of his jacket.

I hugged it to my chest as we ambled away.

"I'm sorry you got stuck with me," he murmured. "Do you like roller coasters?" His voice was soft, but deep.

"I love roller coasters. And I'm sorry *you* got stuck with *me*." I tried to sound lighthearted. "The coaster here is pretty rough. Lana and I rode it first thing. Have you ridden it yet?"

He shook his head. "We just got here. You wanna ride it again?"

"Sure, but I warn you, it really slings you around, even buckled in."

He stopped short. "Look at that line."

I looked. The line for The Whip had grown all the way around the corner and out of sight. "Wow. I'm glad I rode it already."

Jimmy laughed. "How about the Tunnel of Death instead?"

"Sure. I wanted to go earlier, but Lana is terrified of things like that."

He grabbed my hand. "C'mon."

All at once the clanky music sounded clearer, and the sparkling neon lights shone even brighter.

We dashed across the midway, kicking up sawdust as we ran. I clutched my blue bear in one hand and Jimmy's work-hardened fingers in the other. The feel of his skin conjured up pictures of roping and riding and branding, things I associated with a real ranch. Overhead, the stars had begun to pop out, but they were no match for the lights of the rides and booths.

The line for the spook house curved around the front of the building. Not as long as the one for the roller coaster, but it still gave us time to chat.

While we stood, he told me a little bit about life on the ranch where his father raised cattle. "My great-grandpa actually helped settle the area." He looked around at the flashing lights and whirling rides. "I wonder what he would think of this celebration." A chuckle rose from his throat. "He would probably cuss and spit and call it a waste of time."

I agreed with everything he said. My own folks were transplants from Oklahoma, so our roots didn't run that deep, but I could easily recall how my own Gramps felt about frivolous things. "Mine would probably do the same," I said.

"What are you majoring in at school?" He asked.

I told him I had lots of ideas about a major but none set in stone. "What about you?"

He ducked his head. "I'm going to Sul Ross to learn the business side of ranching. And to learn as much as I can about genetics and other aspects of animal husbandry."

"Oh, I guess I didn't know there was so much more to it than just rounding them up and shipping them to the feedlots up in the panhandle."

A slight frown from Jimmy made me stop talking. "That's what most people think, but there's so much more to it than that. My dad is great at what he does, but technology always seems one step ahead of us in the breeding department." He shifted his feet. "What about you, what does your family do? Your dad, I mean."

I wasn't sure how much to tell him, but he seemed genuinely interested so I wound up just blurting it all out. "My dad had an accident a while back. He can't work anymore." I didn't go into detail. I didn't want to see the expected look of pity cross his face. "A car accident," I explained. "Traumatic brain injury."

Jimmy didn't recoil, nor did he seem to want to grill me the way some people did. "I'm sorry to hear that. It must be pretty challenging."

"Yeah," I said. "Getting laid off is a recent thing. Up until the last couple of months, he worked part-time."

I tried not to feel embarrassed or ashamed, or even worse, panicked. All I knew was that in blue-collar Window, Texas, people worked and made a living, and no one went on welfare or disability unless they'd come to their last straw. But Mom said Dad still received a small disability check so I had to ask myself, was this my family's last straw? The one that broke the camel's back?

Once again, the idea crossed my mind that I could do more at home than at college. How long could I continue to go anyway? I had a partial scholarship and a work-study program. That left a lot of things unpaid. Things that my parents would no longer be able to afford.

"That is really tough." The concern in Jim's voice sounded real.

For a second, I'd forgotten all about him. Now, I forced myself to relax.

His gaze never left my face. I began to feel a little uncomfortable. Finally he said, "I can't imagine how hard it would be not to go to work everyday. To be stuck in the house..."

I nodded. "Yeah. It's completely new to me. Mom didn't want to worry me, so I wasn't aware that he'd lost his job until today, when I got home." I glanced at the other people in line to make sure they weren't listening. "I'm thinking I may need to come home and help out. I don't see how my mom can keep working and taking care of Dad all by herself."

"Aren't you at UT Austin?"

I nodded. "Hook'em Horns." I made the requisite Longhorn symbol with my fingers, wondering how he had known. "I also work at The Twisted Pasta Bar after school and on weekends. Sometimes I fill in at the Copper Kettle where I worked over the summer." I took a shallow breath and pressed on. In for a penny, in for a pound my Gramps used to say. "I actually pull in pretty good money in tips. If I came home and went to work, Mom and I could share Dad's care and I could contribute financially as well."

Jimmy shook his head. "It's nice that you want to help out, but I seriously doubt you'd find any place in Window that could guarantee you the same tips you make in Austin. I've been down Sixth Street a time or two." He swiped one hand across his lips as if subconsciously wiping away a foam of beer. "I think there are more people walking up and down that one street than there are in our whole little town."

I had to smile at the imagery. "You know, you're probably right. I didn't think of it like that. Most of the time Window rolls up the sidewalks at dusk. How could I make any money here?" I let my mind wander to all the possible jobs for a high school graduate with only a few college classes under her belt. The pickings were pretty slim.

"Right," he said. "But think how much more you will be able to contribute after you get your degree."

I smiled a little. He made very good points. This would definitely require more thought. Maybe I will take fewer classes and work more shifts, that way I can at least pay for more of my own education. I turned to tell him this idea, but the line had started moving and we were almost to the front.

"Maybe we can talk more about it after the carnival?" he said. "If you'll let me drive you home, that is..."

"That would be great." I was relieved I didn't have to ask for a ride. Maybe the two boys had made a plan before they walked over to us in line. I didn't have time to ponder because we were up for our turn in the Tunnel of Death.

We climbed in the sleigh-shaped car and clipped on our lap belts. In moments, the six-car train started up with a jerk. Once we went through the black fabric opening to the "tunnel," the terror began. Spiders fell into our laps from a multitude of webs —only to be jerked back up again almost immediately—ghouls popped out of walls, shrieking witches flew past on glowing brooms, and when the train ground to a halt halfway through the tunnel, a chainsaw-wielding Michael Myers-lookalike burst out of the pitch black shadows and stood spotlighted in a shaft of white light.

The sound of the chainsaw made me grab my ears and hide my face on Jimmy's shoulder. He wrapped his arms around me and I closed my eyes and didn't open them until I felt the train begin to move once more.

The chainsaw man backed up into the shadows and we drew shaky breaths as the sound of his weapon faded to a soft growl. We were almost to the exit—I could see the glow of the outside lights around the edge of the heavy fabric curtain—when a bloody zombie shambled directly in front of us. Then the chainsaw guy revved up his weapon again and came at us from behind. Over the loud speaker a deep voice said "Do Not Get Out of The Car, No Matter What Happens, Remain Inside the Car!" Then the voice yelled, "Sir! Madam! What are you doing? Get back in the— No! Don't do that—"

We all turned around to see who was getting off, and that's when the little train's metal wheels began to shriek as if we were being pulled along the track against our will.

The voice on the speaker continued to urge the phantom couple to get back inside the car so the train could finish the circuit. In the confusion, the zombie reached us and stumbled past just as the chainsaw guy caught up from behind. The two figures met and began to scuffle.

As the battle raged, our little train chugged forward and we all finished the ride craning our necks to see who would win. Just before the black curtains closed behind us, the zombie appeared to lose an arm that flew off into the darkness. It was the best carnival spook house I'd ever experienced.

We left the ride screaming with laughter. Jimmy kept his arm around my shoulders as we climbed down the few steps to the ground. My knees trembled and I could only imagine the color in my cheeks.

"That was amazing," I said.

"Wanna go again?"

"No way!" I laughed self-consciously. "I really thought someone was getting off the train. I wonder what would happen if they did?"

Jimmy leaned his face into my hair and whispered into my ear. "Let's do it again and find out."

"Noooo," I squealed. "I'm not going and you can't make me." I took off toward the Funnel Cake booth with my brown hair streaming out behind me like a flag.

"You can run, but you can't hide," Jimmy called, shambling after me like a zombie.

I felt like a twelve-year-old kid again. Like I could be my silliest self and it would be all right. I couldn't remember ever enjoying the fair this much.

We ate our funnel cake—dusted with plenty of powdered sugar—standing at a wooden rail surrounding a pair of faux cowboys about to throw-down in a mock shootout at the O.K. Corral.

Jimmy looked at me. "Which one's Doc and which one's Wyatt?"

I shrugged. "Neither?"

He laughed and the sound was so reassuring I found myself pulling it out of my memory time and time again over the next few months. Every time I needed a dose of courage or comfort.

After our treat, we strolled around the fairgrounds stopping from time to time to try our hand at Balloon Darts and Washer Throws. I almost won a goldfish in a clear plastic bag, but apparently it wasn't meant to be.

When the carnies began to shut down the rides, Jimmy led me toward the parking lot. "It's still early... how about a ride out to the caprock?"

The caprock is a sharp bluff out on the edge of town perfect for viewing the desert night skies. Of course most of the kids used it as a place to go and drink beer and make out. "Let me text Lana and tell her, okay?"

"You bet." He stood there patiently. At that moment, I didn't care what Lana said, Jimmy Allan could've taken me anywhere. He'd easily won me the blue teddy bear at the Pitch-Till-U-Win booth. He'd won my heart that easily, too.

We left the carnival moments before it closed. The parking lot had thinned a little, but not much. The weeklong Settlers' Fair would culminate in an outdoor Fall Dance after Thanksgiving. A town-wide celebration.

The November night grew cool, nowhere near cold, but it definitely had an autumn feel to it. I took a deep breath. "My favorite time of year."

"Me, too," he said. "The season of turkey and dressing, pumpkin pie, and homemade rolls." He glanced at me from the corner of his eye. "Do you bake, Miss Marlena?"

I flung my hair back nonchalantly. "Why yes, sir, I do. Why do you ask?"

He saved himself from having to answer by clicking the remote in his hand.

I expected to hear his old red pickup truck roar to life, instead, the lights on a navy-blue Camaro flashed on and off. "Pretty car," I said. "It matches your jacket and my bear." I held up my stuffed prize.

He laughed. "She's my girl. My high school graduation gift. Dad made the down payment, I make the rest." I heard a touch of pride in his voice.

"You don't drive her around the ranch, do you?"

He shook his head as he opened the door. "Not on your life. Too low slung. When I'm home from school, Betsy lives in the garage."

I smiled and buckled my safety belt. The interior of the sports car felt warm and cozy. When he climbed in and pushed the starter button, I said, "Around the ranch you drive a red Ford pickup, right?"

He glanced at me before backing out. "How'd you know?"

I shrugged. "I may have noticed you arriving at school a time or two."

Jimmy grinned, then maneuvered us out of the dirt parking lot.

We didn't speak again as we drove toward the outskirts of town, but just past the city limits sign, my phone chirped and a text came in from my mom. "Dad fell again," it read. "Can you come home?"

I immediately hit reply. "I'll be there in ten minutes."

Jimmy looked at me questioningly. I held up my phone and showed him the text. Without a word he slowed the car and executed a perfect U-turn. "Just tell me where to go."

I gave him my address and also sent Lana a text telling her what happened. I'm not sure why I did that. We just told each other everything. We always had.

"I'm so sorry," I told Jim after I'd texted Lana. "As soon as you drop me off, you can go. I hate dragging you into my family's problems."

He took my hand, the one holding my phone, and held it in his. "Don't hurt my feelings like that," he said. "I would never drop you off and leave you to help your folks all by yourself." He squeezed my fingers gently. "If it's all right with you and your mom, I'll come on inside and see what I can do."

I exhaled. "That would be great." I squeezed his fingers back and then turned my palm up to access my phone.

When I called Mom, she sounded even more breathless than usual. "Don't rush," she said. "He isn't hurt, just slipped trying to get into the wheelchair. We are sitting here on the living room floor, leaned up against the chair. I just can't get him up this time. His legs don't seem to have any strength, and my back isn't what it used to be."

"Thank God he's alright. I was about to call 911."

"No, no, no," she said. "It's okay. I just need a bit of assistance with the lifting."

Jimmy raised his hand and then pointed to his chest with his thumb.

"I'm bringing some muscle," I said. "His name is Jimmy Allan and we went to school together."

Mom started to say something, but I continued, "We met up at the carnival and he was going to drive me home anyway, so it's okay."

When we arrived at my house a couple minutes later, he hopped out, saw that I was already out, and headed up the drive to the front door. We arrived on the porch at the same instant.

I opened the door, and we stepped inside together. "In here," Mom called.

Jimmy followed her voice to the living room.

Mom sat on the floor, smashed up between Dad on one side and the recliner on the other side. "It was the only way I could keep him from falling over," she explained. "I called the doctor just in case, and he said if there is no slurred speech or obvious weakness in his arms,"—she held up both of Dad's arms and they stayed put at the same level—"then it's just the balance thing again."

I had questions about that, like why his legs were so weak if it was a balance problem, but I held my tongue. Now was not the time.

Jim walked over to her and tipped the brim of an imaginary hat. Then he grasped one of Dad's hands and shook it in greeting. "Mr. Matthews, my name is Jim Allan and I'm a friend of Marlena's. I hope you don't mind if I help you up." And without another word he pulled Dad forward and up using the lift belt looped around Dad's middle. I quickly pushed the wheelchair forward and Jimmy lowered him in.

Dad's face was red. I don't know if it was from embarrassment or effort, but later Mom told me it was a sign of high blood pressure. She said the doctor adjusted the dosage on his meds so that it wouldn't spike that way again. We learned later that high blood pressure can cause further damage to a brain already injured by TBI. It could even explain the sudden weakness in his legs.

Once we had him settled, I hurried to help Mom up off the floor as well.

"Thank God for cell phones." She held hers up. "I've got to the point where I carry it with me at all times." She laughed and smoothed her blouse down with one hand and her hair back with the other. "In fact," she slipped her phone into her pants pocket, "nowadays, my sense of fashion depends on whether a garment has pockets. If it doesn't, back into the closet it goes."

I'd never heard my mom ramble that way. I glanced at Jimmy, but he didn't seem to notice. He simply stood beside me with a slight smile on his face.

"Thank you," I said.

He nodded. "Glad to help."

Mom added her thanks. I could tell she was a little unraveled. She patted my dad's shoulder. "Are you about ready for bed, Wallace?"

Dad nodded. "I think we both need some sleep." Then he grinned and for a moment I saw my old strong dad. The one who would lift me over his head and twirl me like a strand of spaghetti before plopping me back on the floor with a laugh.

Mom grasped the handles of his wheelchair and started down the hall. "Thank you again, young man. You've been very helpful."

I walked to the front door and Jim followed. "I really appreciate this. I guess I'd better go and make sure Mom can get him into bed."

He stepped out onto the porch then stopped and pulled out his phone. "I could stay," he said. "Make sure he's tucked in all right."

"Oh, I couldn't ask you to do that. But thank you for offering."

Before I could say goodnight, he reached for my hand. "Okay if I call you sometime?"

"Sure."

He placed his phone in my palm.

I entered my number into his contacts and handed it back. "I had a lot of fun. Thanks for the teddy." I held up the stuffed bear, surprised to find I was still holding it under my arm. "And for helping with Dad, of course."

"You're welcome." He hesitated. "But I wish I hadn't."

"Hadn't won me the bear, or hadn't helped with Dad?"

He grinned. "Wish I hadn't been forced to bring you *straight* home." He touched my hair as if it were a gem in a pirate's treasure chest. "Such a gorgeous night. Too bad we couldn't make that drive."

I started to reply that I was sorry, but Jimmy tugged a lock of my hair and said, "Maybe another night?"

I nodded, my fingers straying to the lock of hair he'd tugged. "That sounds like a good plan."

"Great. I'll call you, soon." He turned and sauntered back to his car. I admired his blue-jeaned silhouette. It was easy to see he'd spent his life on the back of a horse.

As soon as the Camaro turned the corner out of sight—yes, I was still watching—he sent me a text. "Just wanted to test your number, and to give you mine in case you and your mom need me."

I sent him a smiley face with the message, "Who is this?"

Then I went inside and immediately sent another text. "Just kidding. I had a great time at the carnival. Blue Bear looks very comfy on my bed."

He replied with a comical emoji followed by a string of bears. "You almost had me, there," he wrote. "I've heard of mean girls giving guys the wrong number on purpose."

I sent a big-eyed smiley face. "I can't imagine any girl ever doing that to you."

For a minute, nothing came through. Then he sent a large, shiny heart. "Sleep well," the message read. "I'll call you tomorrow."

I texted back a thumbs-up symbol. "TTYS," I wrote. Then I hurried to the bedroom to make sure Mom and Dad were okay. She already had him in his pajamas and sitting on the side of the bed.

"We're fine," she said. "Sorry to spoil your evening."

I waved her hand away. "Don't be ridiculous. We were already leaving the fair. I'm just glad Jimmy was here to help. But what if he hadn't been? I'm not sure I could've picked Dad up."

Mom helped him lift his legs and tuck them under the covers. As soon as his head hit the pillow, his eyes closed. I couldn't believe he could go to sleep that quickly.

"It's the medicine," Mom murmured, putting her finger to her lips. Once we were in the hallway, she said, "Mr. Nolan next door would have been my next choice, he helped out once before, but I knew it was about time for the fair to close down so I felt certain you would be on your way home anyway. Together, we would have got him up." She patted my back. "I never meant to ruin your date."

"Mo-o-o-m," I swatted her shoulder playfully. "It wasn't a date; we really did meet up while we were standing in line at the carnival. Lana went with his buddy, Dash, and Jim was going to bring me home anyway."

"Well," she said as we reached the kitchen. "I'm glad he did. That boy seems very nice. And not hard to look at either."

"I can't argue with that." I rummaged through the fridge. "In fact, he asked me out again."

Mom's eyes were bright. "I hope you said yes."

"I sure did." I pulled a soft drink from the fridge. "But Mom?"

She finished filling the tank of the ancient Mr. Coffee. "Yes?"

"Can we talk? About everything that's going on with you and Dad, I mean."

She slid the coffee maker back into its usual spot on the counter and yawned behind her hand. "Oh, honey. Can it wait until tomorrow? I'm sort of beat right now."

I nodded and popped the ring tab off the can of Diet Coke. "Of course. I just want to run a couple of ideas by you."

She hugged me and kissed the air near my cheek. "Sleep well, sweetie. We'll talk tomorrow while we cook."

I kissed her temple and she squeezed my upper arm and then disappeared down the hall toward their bedroom. I'll tell her tomorrow, I thought. I'll tell her I've decided I have to do something to help out.

Lana messaged to see how my dad was doing. We talked for a few minutes and made plans to have coffee soon. I still wanted her input regarding Preston, and what she thought I should do to get him to back off, but since I'd met up with Jim, Preston didn't seem quite as important or as intimidating as he had before.

I climbed in bed and snuggled Blue Bear into my arms. I'd never met anyone like Jimmy. Although I'd seen him around school for as long as I could remember, once we started talking

—and he came to my house to help with Dad—it seemed as if we'd known each other forever.

I drifted off with the image of him smiling back at me as we dashed from the spook house, laughing.

The next day—Thanksgiving—Mom let me sleep late. By the time I got up, she already had Dad dressed, in his chair, and had the turkey in the oven. I never heard a thing.

"Wow," I sat at the kitchen table. "I must've been exhausted."

Mom nodded. "I figured you were. That's quite a drive home from school. Not to mention school itself." She glanced at me as she took a two-quart casserole dish from the cabinet. I recognized it as the one that always held the sweet potatoes. "And then I had to call you home early from your first night out."

I shrugged. "That was no big deal. How's Dad this morning?"

Mom waved her hand toward the living room. "He's fine. Barely remembers the incident."

I didn't really understand how that could be, but Mom didn't seem to be worried. She handed me a large can of yams and instructed me to drain the juice off while she buttered the casserole dish.

When she was done, I poured in the yams and Mom handed me the potato masher and brown sugar.

I mashed, mixed, added vanilla, a quick squeeze of lemon juice, and a handful of pecan pieces before spreading the mixture and topping it with more pecans. After it baked in the oven for twenty or thirty minutes, I would add a layer of tiny marshmallows on top. When they melted, the casserole would taste more like dessert than a side dish.

I licked my fingers. "Good thing we only have this on holidays."

Mom gave me a little hug. "It is so good to have you home."

I hugged her back. "It's so good to be here."

As we were cooking, Lana called to catch-up. We'd barely

started discussing everything that had gone on after last night's carnival when Jim beeped in to ask me to the celebration-wrap-up dance on the courthouse square Saturday night.

When I told Lana I'd said yes, she squealed and said that she and Dash would be there, too. That's when I decided that if Preston kept bugging me when I returned to school, I was going to quit simply trying to avoid him. If he wouldn't leave me alone, I would get up my nerve to tell him, in no uncertain terms, that I couldn't see him anymore because I had met someone else.

6

FALL DANCE

Thanksgiving came and went and what a wonderful holiday it had been. We had a small turkey with cornbread dressing, along with the yummy brown sugar and pecan sweet potatoes, the requisite green bean casserole, and a big fruit salad. For dessert I'd made the simple but delicious caramel pie—just a can of sweetened condensed milk boiled in a pot of water for three hours, and then spooned directly from the can into a graham cracker crust before being cooled in the fridge and topped with whipped cream. Mom also taught me how to make Dad's favorite, pecan pie, and of course we had our basic drink, iced tea.

Mom and I briefly discussed how things were with her and Dad, her job, and his care. She insisted she had everything under control and that if Dad fell again, which was always possible, she would definitely call the neighbor next door. She said if nothing else she would just dial 911 and have the paramedics come. She told me not to worry; his doctor was doing everything he could to get Dad back on the path to recovery.

I allowed her to placate me. Deep in my heart, I wasn't completely convinced, but with my new relationship burgeoning, I didn't put up much of an argument. I wanted to go back to school. Once I got rid of Preston, I felt like things would be back to normal there, just as Mom insisted they would be here at home.

My sister, Carrie, and her husband, Dix, had arrived on Thursday just before the big meal. They were staying until Saturday, and I was going to wait and drive back to Austin on Sunday.

"So tell me about this new boy," Carrie said as soon as we'd finished our meal.

I shot Mom a look. "Someone's been gossiping."

Mom looked at the ceiling and whistled a tuneless song like a character in an old cartoon. Then she said, "I had to tell her how he came to our rescue when Dad slid out of his chair."

I rolled my eyes, but grinned. "I'm sure thankful he was there. And that Dad was okay." I reached over and squeezed my father's hand, which lay beside his dinner plate. He'd suffered no ill effects from the fall. But he still had no strength in his legs. Getting him in and out of bed and on and off the toilet was becoming extremely difficult.

It amazed me how he could be so lucid and Dad-like one day and so out-of-touch and stranger-like the next. His strength seemed to wax and wane as well.

"Jimmy really is a nice guy—"

"Jim Allan, right?" Carrie interrupted.

"Yes," I nodded. "Do you know him?"

"Sure. I remember him from school. A little younger than me, of course. Was he in your grade?"

"Yes," I said. "He wasn't in my circle of friends, though. And then in my senior year I started working half days, so I didn't socialize much."

"That's right." Carrie put down her fork down and sipped

her tea. "Jimmy was one of those agriculture guys, wasn't he? Dad owns a ranch or something?"

"Right. Now he goes to school at Sul Ross, down in Alpine. He said he's learning the business side of ranching."

"Ambitious, handsome, *and* polite," Mom said. "Not to mention he's a local boy. Sounds like a win-win to me."

"Mo-o-m, please! We haven't even been on a real date yet."

To prevent me scolding her further, Mom jumped up and began to clear the table. "Who's ready for dessert?"

Dad raised his hand. "I am!"

Up until then, he hadn't said a word.

We all laughed. Life was good.

I SPENT Friday visiting and catching up with my sister and her sweet husband. Saturday, Lana came over and we marveled over everything that had happened since I had come home. She and Dash had seemed to really hit it off. They were also planning a date later in the evening. For dinner we shredded the leftover turkey for sandwiches and wiped out the rest of the trimmings. We even heated up the remains of the pecan pie so we could melt scoops of vanilla ice cream on the last skinny wedges.

By the time evening arrived, Lana had gone and I was on pins and needles listening for Jimmy's car.

When I heard it pull up, I glanced out my bedroom window and watched as he stepped up on the porch in his blue plaid shirt and neatly pressed jeans. His hair appeared still damp from the shower. The glossy dark waves shone in the slanting rays of the setting sun.

Mom answered the door and brought him into the house. I could hear him making small talk with her in the entryway. "It smells delicious in here," he murmured. "Just like home."

"Did y'all have a nice Thanksgiving?" Mom asked.

"Wonderful," I heard him reply. "We have a lot to be thankful for."

Mom introduced him to Carrie and Dix and Jim said he remembered my sister from school.

I opened my door and walked down the hallway and into the living room just as Mom presented Jimmy to my Dad. It felt memorable, seeing him standing there just inside the front door, like looking at a postcard in the making. I saw them shake hands as if Wednesday night had never happened. After they released, Dad's hand hung in the air a beat longer than necessary.

Jimmy didn't flinch, didn't look away. "It's a pleasure to see you, again, sir." He smiled and turned his head toward me.

My breath caught in my chest. Even from across the room those gray, storm-cloud eyes pulled at my heartstrings.

"Hi," I said.

"Hey. You look beautiful." He stepped forward and handed me a small, clear box. Inside was a bracelet of fall flowers. Mom sprang into action and helped me put it on. Dad sat in his recliner watching John Wayne knock someone to the ground with one punch.

"It's lovely," I said. "And look," I held my wrist against my russet colored dress. "It matches."

Jimmy smiled and ducked his head. "My mom picked it out." Then he seemed to realize how that sounded. "But I asked her to."

I laughed. His innocent declaration was endearing.

From behind me, I heard Carrie say, "Well, whoever got it, it's perfect." She glanced at the two of us, then at Dix. "How come you never brought me a flower bracelet when we were dating?"

Dix grinned. "I brought you a jumbo frozen yogurt. Doesn't that count?"

Carrie leaned over and smooched his cheek. "Best fro-yo I ever tasted!"

I picked up my cell phone and tucked it into my gold cross-body bag.

It felt like we were back in high school. Like we'd gone back to last year in a time warp or something. I almost wished I *could* go back in time. Back before my Dad got hurt, back before I'd met Preston, back before adulthood happened.

I shook off thoughts of Preston and adulthood and walked through the door Jimmy held open. I called goodbye to the family pressed around the front door—you'd think I had never had a date before—and stepped off the porch to see "Betsy" waiting at the curb. The gorgeous little car made me smile. Jimmy opened the passenger door and I slid inside. "I must've been a teenage boy in another life."

Jim settled into the driver's seat. "What makes you say that? Is there something under that dress you aren't telling me about?"

I covered my mouth with my hand so I wouldn't snort-laugh and embarrass myself.

"No, everything under there is as it should be. I just meant I'm in love with your car."

Jimmy nodded and reached for the start button, and then he hesitated and cocked an eyebrow at me. "Wanna drive?"

I nodded. "I do. But not right this second. I'm too nervous. After the dance maybe."

He pushed start and revved the engine. "That's a deal. As long as you don't step on my toes, that is."

I groaned. "You've obviously seen me dance."

He smiled and touched the flowers at my wrist. "Actually, I have. Senior prom, you went with Caleb Mortensen. I took Amber Garza."

My eyes went to his face. "That's right. It was the one and

only time I went out with Caleb. I'm not even sure why he asked me. We never went out again."

Jimmy clicked on the turn signal. "Same here, Amber and I were just pals. But you... I couldn't take my eyes off you in that frilly blue dress you were wearing." He seemed to reminisce for a moment. "It kind of matched old Betsy, didn't it?"

"Come to think of it, yes. It did." I let my mind travel back to that momentous night that had turned out to be something of a flop. "I loved that dress. I can't believe you even noticed."

He didn't say anything.

I fiddled with the seat belt and visor mirror. "Why is it when you look forward to something so long it almost always turns out to be a letdown? I mean, it was senior prom, right? Supposed to be one of those leaving-childhood-behind milestones. And yet it turned out to be just another dance. Not even a very memorable one at that."

"You should have gone with *me*. We would have made some memories."

I felt my eyes widen. "You didn't ask—"

"But I wanted to," he said. Then he grinned. "I was just chicken."

I slugged him on the shoulder. "You should have asked." I felt like a tomboy again. Like the little girl who rode her bike with no hands and shinnied up every tree within a block of the house. I felt like I could be myself with this guy. And apparently my feelings weren't one sided. "It's a beautiful night, isn't it?"

Jimmy grasped my fingers and laid our clasped hands on his thigh. "It certainly is." Then he looked me in the eye. "Very."

We drove toward the downtown area. Most of the same shops still occupied the town square. In the here-and-now of Walmart and Amazon, that was almost a miracle.

The streets were crowded. We had to park a couple of blocks away from the square. "I could let you off nearer the bandstand,"

Jim said before killing the engine. "That way you won't have to walk so far."

I shook my head and held up one foot. "I wore my boots, not my heels. Walking won't bother me at all; also, when I step on your toes, you're gonna know it."

He laughed and turned off the engine.

We walked to the square hand-in-hand. A country band played a decent cover of a Jason Aldean song, and what promised to be a nearly full moon had just started its nightly ascent behind the picturesque bandstand. Crimson, orange, and gold leaves from the giant red oak trees littered the gutters and dotted the courthouse lawn. The colors made the autumn night complete.

The old wooden bandstand had been given a new coat of white paint, and lush pots of fall 'mums had been placed on each of the three wide steps leading to the platform where the band played. Bales of hay bordered a sawdust-covered dance floor pieced together on the lawn. Tiny orange pumpkins graced the white tablecloths on the foldout tables lining the sidewalks.

A few couples were two-stepping in the twilight.

"This is amazing," I said. "It feels like I'm seeing it all for the first time. Has our little town always been so awesome?"

Jimmy grinned. "I think everything looks better tonight."

We arrived at a wide table holding huge urns of coffee and cider. A banner advertising Oliver Orchards was pinned to the front of the table. Jinx Oliver, the owner of the apple orchard, was sitting behind the table. A couple of teens were doling out the drinks. "Mr. Oliver," Jimmy said. "How are you?"

The white-haired man nodded and held out his hand. "I'm fine, just fine, Jimmy Boy. It's good to see you. Say hello to your dad for me." He and Jimmy shook and then the older man tipped an imaginary hat in my direction before turning to answer a question from one of his workers.

I pulled my sweater close. The air grew crisp as the sun went down. The giant moon rose even higher.

"How about a cup of hot cider?" Jimmy asked.

I nodded. "I'll lay claim to a table before they're all gone." I couldn't believe how quickly they were filling up. It appeared the entire town had turned out. I'd heard about these dances, seen them mentioned in the weekly newspaper and on Facebook, but I'd never attended one. My high school friends had called them lame. Said they were for the old folks. The old "settlers." Guess something had changed my tune. Perhaps it was just being away from home for the past few months, or maybe it was Jimmy. Nothing seemed lame with him.

He proved to be an excellent dancer, too.

"Do you have to know how to waltz and two-step when you own a ranch?" I asked as he steered me around the floor.

"Oh, sure." He swung me in a tight circle. "I practiced on the steers every night growing up." When the song ended, he said, "And what about you, Miss I've-never-been-to-a-Settlers'-Day-dance? You're holding your own pretty well for a newbie."

I felt a little heat rise to my cheeks. "If I tell you, will you promise not to laugh?"

He crossed his heart and held up his fingers like a boy scout. "I would never laugh. Dancing is serious stuff."

I elbowed him in the ribs as we made our way back to our little table. There had been a Sharpie marker tucked in amongst the tiny pumpkins and we'd immediately decorated the round gourds with mustaches and triangular eyes, then Jimmy signed his with a flourish so of course I did the same. I think that's why no one sat there while we were dancing. The little pumpkins turned out to be excellent placeholders.

"So? Are you going to fess up or do I have to tickle it out of you?" He made crawly fingers in the air.

"No, no. You don't have to bring out the tickle-spiders. I'll tell you." I looked over my shoulder to make sure no one was listening, and then I leaned toward him and whispered, "Lana and I took dance lessons one summer. We learned all the basics plus a few line dances, too."

Jimmy threw his head back and laughed out loud.

"Hey!" I slapped his knee. "You promised not to laugh."

He couldn't seem to stop. "Sorry. It's too good not to laugh." Grinning, he leaned back in his folding chair and tried to get control of himself. "At least now I know why you had the cowgirl footwear."

I looked down at my beautiful turquoise-inlaid boots. "You didn't think I bought them just for tonight, did you?"

That shut him up. "Well, maybe I did. I mean—"

I let him off the hook. "Oh, it's all right." I patted him on the arm. "You can't help it if you're a guy."

He leaned back even further, and I swear if he'd been wearing a cowboy hat, he would have pushed it back on his head. "Just what does that mean?"

"Oh, you know, thinking I would buy a special pair of boots just to go on a first date with you. It's the male ego thing, that's all." I tried not to smirk when I said it, but I was enjoying this little sparring match.

"Egotistical? Me? Is that what you're saying?"

"Well," I twirled a hank of hair around my finger. "If the big word fits..."

"Oh, you are really asking for it, Marlena Matthews." He tilted my chair backward and caught it with his other hand.

I squealed and plopped my boots on the ground. "I can see I had you all wrong."

He raised his eyebrows.

"I figured you for a nice guy, and it's obvious you aren't trustworthy at all!"

Tipping me back again, he said, "Sugar, you ain't seen nothin' yet."

I couldn't believe this was the same shy boy who had won me the blue bear at the carnival.

"C'mon." He grabbed my hand and pulled me out of my chair as the band struck up a waltz. Holding me close, we danced the rest of the night with only a couple of breaks for refreshments. After a while it seemed I'd found a part of me that loved small town life after all. And Jim. We fit together like connecting links of a chain.

I was glad when Dash showed up with Lana in tow. She'd told me they would be here, but they were running extremely late. And she didn't seem nearly as exhilarated as I thought she'd be.

"Here," I patted the chair Jimmy offered her. "Sit by me. Where have y'all been?"

Lana rolled her eyes. "Party at Hart Monihan's house. Remember Hart?"

"Of course. It's only been a couple years since he graduated. Isn't he at some big university?"

Lana nodded. "LSU. Football scholarship. Big man on campus. Or so he says." She leaned into me. "Drugs everywhere," she whispered. "Dash is so high right now it's not even funny."

"Oh, Lan. I'm sorry. I didn't know he was like that. I mean, I heard stories back in school, but I didn't believe them. That sucks."

My best friend blinked. "Yeah. I had no idea." She squeezed her lips together tightly.

I could see she was on the verge of a meltdown. "Let us take you home. Don't get back in the car with him, okay?"

She nodded. Exhaled. "Thanks, Mar. I appreciate that." She

glanced at the two guys who appeared to be deep in conversation. "You don't think Jimmy will mind?"

"I don't think so. He is the sweetest guy I've ever met. He does love to tease, though." I showed her the pumpkins we'd decorated. Every time we came back to the table Jimmy had added to them. Now they read *Jimmy & Marlena, Dancing with The Stars.* Or *Marlena LOVES Jim: She just doesn't know it yet.* That one went around the whole pumpkin.

Lana read the silly words out loud and her face began to crumple.

"Oh, honey, what is it? They were supposed to make you laugh, not cry."

She shook her head and arranged the tiny gourds back in the center of the table. On the last one he'd written *Jim and Mar 4 Ever.* It was like something a junior high girl would write. Silliness to the max. And we weren't drinking anything but hot cider.

"Sorry." She wiped her eye with her knuckle. "I just—I mean." She glanced over at Dash and the look on her face said it all. He wasn't what she'd thought. It reminded me of my three dates with Preston, how each one had been worse than the one before.

"Not your Romeo after all?"

Lana looked at the ground. "He's awful. He drinks *a lot*. And then tonight, at the party, they had booze and coke and a huge bowl of pills. Oh, girl. It was surreal."

I put my arm around her shoulders. "We've just never been one of the cool kids, have we?"

She collapsed against me. Lana dreamed of being a preschool teacher. She adored little children. This wasn't her cup of tea at all. "It's okay," I said. "You're going home with me, no matter what."

"Thanks, Mar. It was a nightmare. I can't believe he is like this. I never want to see him again."

I hugged her tightly and then sent her off to the portable bathrooms while I tried to figure out a way to tell Dash he could go on home without her.

He and Jimmy had moved off away from the edge of the dance floor. They appeared to be deep in conversation. It took all my willpower to approach them, but I'd promised Lana she wouldn't have to leave with Dash. I intended to keep my promise.

"Hey, guys," I walked up beside Jimmy. "Lana feels kind of sick." I half-turned and indicated the direction she'd gone. "When she comes back, I think I'll let her ride home with us." I hesitated and looked at Jim. Even though I was certain our new connection was true, it occurred to me that I could be putting him in a very uncomfortable position with his buddy. "If you guys don't mind, that is."

Jimmy shook his head. "Of course not. I'll be glad to take her home. Dash isn't feeling that well himself. Maybe I should drive him home and let you drive Lana home." He dug into his pocket and produced the remote key. "You still want to drive Betsy, right? I'll take Dash home in his truck."

My heart melted. Even though we'd joked about it earlier, I couldn't believe he trusted me with his most treasured possession. "I'll follow you," I said. "After you drop Dash off, you can get back behind the wheel—"

"Bullshit!" Dash exploded. "I'm not sick." He took an unsteady step toward me. "And I'm not drunk. No matter what Little Miss Perfect says."

I cringed and retreated toward the table. My foot caught the leg of a folding chair and I stumbled. One of the mini pumpkins rolled toward the edge of the table. Somehow, I caught it and held it as I continued to back away.

Jimmy put one hand on Dash's chest. "You need to calm down."

"Get your hands off me," Dash yelled. "I know Goody-Two-Shoes thinks I'm drunk. She didn't want me to drive. It's my fuckin' truck, I'll drive it anywhere I want." He tried to push past Jimmy, coming toward me, or toward the area where Lana had gone, but Jim gave him a little shove toward the street.

"I'll take you home." He kept shoving Dash, gently but firmly. "Give me your keys."

I could feel people looking our way. A hush fell over the tables. The band played on, but tension permeated the previously jolly gathering.

Jimmy kept carefully manhandling Dash toward his truck, which was parked in one of the slanted spaces at the curb. "You don't want to make a scene, buddy. Let's all end the night on a good note. Just hand me your keys. You'll feel so much better at home, in your own bed."

That seemed to placate Dash a bit. I got the sudden impression this wasn't Jimmy's first go-round with a drunken Dash. He was way too good at it. But as he handed over the keys, Dash seemed to feel the need to get in one last bit of ugliness.

He turned back toward me, toward the tables, and raised his fist. "Tell that little Goody-Two-Shoes bitch she ain't no better than me. And I'm not drunk!" Then he turned and fell over the curb.

Jimmy caught him by the arm and opened the door, allowing him to fall heavily into the passenger seat.

"You just tell her," Dash roared before Jim could get the door closed.

He turned toward me and shook his head. "Sorry about that. I'll drive slowly so you two can catch up."

I glanced back and saw Lana walking toward me. It was clear she'd been watching. Her eyes were red and glassy. "I'm so embarrassed," she said. But it wasn't Lana's words that were ringing in my head. It was Dash's.

The tone of his voice alarmed me. How could anyone go from sweetly sarcastic to brute ugly like that? Did the two guys exist in the same body all the time? He'd seemed not only rude and crude; tonight, Dash had seemed downright dangerous.

7

DASH

Lana thanked me profusely. In her state of emotion she never noticed how my hands shook as I clicked the remote to unlock the Camaro. She didn't notice my silence or the fact that I couldn't seem to formulate a single coherent sentence. The tone of Dash's voice reminded me of Preston and how he'd protested when I wouldn't go to breakfast that day.

I shivered and realized I was still holding the tiny pumpkin decorated with *Marlena Loves Jim* written on it. I let it roll from my palm into the cup holder where it would stay put.

We followed Jimmy to the small house Dash shared with his Mom. He'd told Lana he had been working in the oilfield ever since his ankle injury. Unfortunately, lots of people used drugs to fuel those long, dirty, hours out at the rig. He seemed to find drugs and alcohol wherever he went. I suspected he sought them out the way some people seek out religion.

When Jim pulled into the driveway, Dash opened the door and fell out onto the concrete. He was still raving about everyone who had—in his opinion—ever wronged him. I parked halfway down the block so he wouldn't notice us and come over to the car.

Lana slumped deeper into the passenger seat the closer we got to the house.

"Don't worry," I said. "He won't bother us." I looked at her shivering beside me. "He must have scared you."

She nodded. I'd never seen my bubbly friend so subdued. But before I could say anything more, Jimmy was out of the car, lifting Dash to his feet, ushering him toward the house.

The porch light came on and a woman I assumed was Dash's mother opened the door. "That you, Dash?"

I looked at Lana. "His mom even calls him Dash?"

She nodded. "It's his real name. His granddad named him after some old friend of his or something." She gnawed at her pinkie-nail. "At first I thought it was sort of romantic. Like maybe that's what prodded him to be a track star." Her voice broke off and she didn't say anymore.

We watched Jimmy help him up the steps and say something to his mom. I had to remind myself that he and Dash had been friends for a long time. Jim had probably been to his home many times.

Sure enough, the mom stepped aside, still holding the door open, and allowed Jimmy to half-carry and half-drag Dash into the house. I imagined him laying his friend on the bed, taking off his shoes, making certain he had a trash can nearby in case he got sick in the night. I imagined his mom helping, tucking the quilt up under her son's chin, tsking over him, thanking Jimmy, maybe giving him a quick hug. In a way, it was almost an echo of how he'd picked up my dad and put him in his chair.

In moments, the door opened again and we saw Jimmy emerge and then turn back to hand a set of keys to Dash's mom. Even from where we waited, we could see her shake her head as she took the keys he offered.

"What must it be like to have a grown child like that?" I asked. It was strictly a rhetorical question, but Lana answered anyway.

"It must be torture. He'll never change as long as he's drinking and doing every drug that comes along. He's so self-centered. So controlling." With that, she actually closed her eyes and shuddered.

"Hey," I said. "Anything you want to tell me?"

She sat still, motionless, silent.

Jimmy rapped on the window, but I was already lowering it. "Hey, beautiful." His smile was kind. "I'll be glad to ride in back if you want to continue driving." His smile widened into a grin. "Betsy can be quite addictive, can't she?"

I laughed and opened the door. "As much as I love driving her—I'd feel better if you went ahead—"

Lana jumped out and flipped the passenger seat up, climbing into the back without a word. "I'll ride in back," she said. "I'm the third wheel here."

I turned and swatted her on the knee between the bucket seats as I prepared to exit the driver's door. "You are not a third wheel. Don't ever say that. It isn't your fault Dash got wasted."

She didn't reply so I got out and went around to the passenger side.

Jimmy met me there just to make sure I was able to get in okay. That cracked me up and made me feel special all at the same time. But I wished he'd taken a moment longer in the house. I wanted Lana to tell me what was really bothering her. Now, that moment might be lost forever.

Jimmy got back in behind the wheel. "Sorry about Dash." He put the car in drive and pulled away from the curb. "He can be a real ass sometimes. I swear, if we hadn't been friends since third grade I wouldn't put up with his crap at all." He glanced over his shoulder at Lana. "And you shouldn't either. No offense, but you can do a whole lot better."

Lana thanked him weakly. "I had a crush on him forever. Now, I can't remember why."

We all laughed a little and I glanced out the side window just in time to see a woman's shadow move past the curtains in Dash's house. What a lonely existence that must be, caring for someone who refuses to care for himself. I involuntarily shuddered the way Lana had done.

"Cold?" Jimmy reached over and turned on the heater.

I imagined myself back in his arms at the dance, waltzing and slow dancing with my cheekbone pressed to his shoulder, our hands clasped together loosely as we drifted around the makeshift floor. I could almost feel the sawdust grit beneath my boots again. I didn't realize I'd closed my eyes with the memories, but when I opened them we were stopped at the red light at Fourth and Bryan, and Jim was staring at my face.

He touched my wrist softly. "You all right?"

I nodded. "I'm okay. How about you?"

He nodded and touched the little pumpkin as if he'd just noticed it. Then he asked if we wanted to stop by the A&W drive-in for a milkshake.

From the back seat Lana piped up, "I'd like nothing more than a milkshake right now. Unless it was chocolate milk in my old yellow kitchen with my big dog, Rex, sitting by my knee."

"Didn't Rex die when you were about eleven?" I asked.

"Exactly." Lana's voice sounded hollow in the darkness. "What I wouldn't give to go back in time and start everything over again."

I turned around and peered between the seats to see her. In the intermittent streetlights, I could see the tracks of new tears streaking her face. "Oh, Lanny." Even to my ears my voice sounded motherly. "What happened?"

She shook her head sadly. "Let's just say I never want to be within fifty feet of that guy again."

"Here we are." Jim pulled into the parking lot. "Should I just go to the drive-in window?" he asked.

I looked at Lana.

"No. I'm all right." She forced a little steel into her voice. "I'll go into the restroom and wash my face. Y'all order for me, okay?"

After we parked, I got out and moved the seat forward for her. Then Jimmy was there, wedging himself between us, offering us both an elbow. I got the impression he kind of enjoyed playing the hero.

We went on into the restaurant, and when Lana came back from the bathroom she seemed almost back to normal. We drank our shakes and joked around and did our best to put a rose on the tail end of the night. It could've gone a lot worse if Jimmy hadn't stepped in and taken control of Dash. I wondered if we'd see him again, and if so, how he would act.

After a half hour of small talk and joking around, Lana seemed to feel better. We made our way back to the car and she thanked us both profusely.

"No need for thanks," Jimmy said. "I'm just sorry he acted like that. Being away at school, I guess I'd forgotten how bad he can be." He clicked the remote. "Or maybe he's gotten worse in the last few months."

"Maybe so," Lana agreed. "That night at the fair, he wasn't like this. Now, well, he scared me. I never want to see him again."

Later, after we dropped Lana off at her home, I asked Jim if it would be awkward the next time we saw Dash.

Jimmy looked at me like I'd gone crazy. "Awkward? Hell, he won't even remember it. He's got a real problem, that's become pretty obvious. He drinks until he blacks out or gets arrested or gets in a fight with someone. Afterward, he never remembers the details."

I chewed my thumbnail. "I can't imagine what happened between him and Lana. She seemed kind of terrified."

Jimmy and I were sitting in the turnaround that led to his father's ranch. He said it marked the beginning of the southern boundary. "I'd like to show you my favorite place," he said. "If you want to go."

He took my hand in his, and brought it to his lips. "Don't worry too much about Dash. With him, it could've been anything. He probably embarrassed Lana somehow. He was so out of it. Did you ask her?"

I nodded, but with his lips beginning to make their way from my hand to my wrist to the inside of my forearm, it was becoming more and more difficult to remember exactly why Lana's problems were so important.

Over the course of a few days Jimmy, the shy cowboy, had gone from a cute guy I'd seen around high school to a real man who went out of his way to take care of other people.

"Okay," he said, a little breathlessly. "It's just up this road. The remains of my granddad's first ranch house." He glanced at me in the dimness of the car. "Don't expect much, it's just a rock foundation and a few old trees, but for me, it's magical."

We drove a few more miles then turned on to a hard-rutted dirt road. "Gotta be careful here," he said. "I'm usually in the truck. Betsy's a little more delicate."

It was only about a mile and then the road ended where a stand of trees fanned out on either side of a small ruin consisting of a few tumbledown rock walls that might have once been a ranch house. "Oh, Jimmy. It's beautiful." Old growth elms and oaks towered over the little clearing. Fall wildflowers and tall, unchecked, prairie grasses caught the reflected light of the moon as they waved in the scant midnight breeze.

He stopped the car. "You really think so?"

I looked at him. The moonlight and shadows played across the planes of his face and I could see the question meant something to him. "Yes," I said. "I really think so. It's like a little nugget of history just waiting to be discovered."

He exhaled. "That's exactly what it is. My family's history, just disappearing in front of my eyes." He stared out at the ruins. "Someday I want to build my own ranch house, right in this clearing. Save as many of these stones as I can, use them for a fireplace chimney or as part of the façade, replant the gardens, put up new fencing, a metal roof so when it storms I can lie in bed and know how lucky I am listening to the rhythm of the rain —" He stopped talking and glanced at me as if just remembering I was there. "Sorry," he said. "I get a little carried awa—"

I placed my index finger over his lips. "Don't apologize." I looked out the window. The huge moon had reached its apex and started down the other side of the world. It laid a streak of smoky-white light across the road like a ghostly pathway. "I can almost feel your ancestors here." I laughed a little self-consciously. "I don't mean in a spooky way, just, like, I don't know, in a good way. Like a connection to the past. To something bigger."

He took my finger off his lips and kissed it. "I knew you'd understand." He kissed my palm. "I wanted you to see it." He pulled me close enough to kiss the tender place below my ear. "Couldn't wait to show it to you. From the moment we came out of that spook house, I've wanted to bring you here."

Before I could reply, or ask why, his lips found my mouth and all conversation stopped until we broke apart a few minutes later, shaky and somewhat delirious.

"What are we doing?" The question fell into the space between us before I even realized I was going to speak.

Jimmy pulled my hand back to his mouth and began to

explore my skin again. "I was going to ask you the same thing," he said. "But I think I know the answer. I think I know what we're doing, I'm just afraid it's too soon to say it out loud."

"Go ahead," I told him. "Say it." I couldn't believe how bold I sounded. He could've said anything. But I trusted him. After the things I'd seen, how he had acted to protect Lana and me, how considerate he'd been with my dad, I trusted him. Maybe I was stupid.

He leaned across the narrow console between the bucket seats and cupped my face with his hand. "I won't say it until I can be certain you feel the same way."

I might've said it, myself, right then and there, but his lips touched mine again and like a little girl, I remembered that silly line from *The Princess Bride*. The one about the most perfect kiss in the history of all kisses, because yes. That's what this was. The gentlest, sweetest, most perfect kiss I'd ever experienced. It left me breathless. It left me dizzy, it left me unable to think coherently. It left me wanting more. And more. And more.

"Jimmy—"

"Marlena—"

"Can we—"

He kissed me again, cutting off the rest of my question. When we broke apart this time, I had no idea what I'd been about to ask.

"What?" he asked. "Can we what?"

I shook my head. "Can we just keep doing this?"

He fell back into the driver's seat and laughed deeply. I'd never heard a man laugh that way. It was joyous, like a spring rain after a long winter drought. I sat still and listened and watched, and fell more deeply in love than I'd ever dreamed possible.

8

PASSION

W hen he stopped laughing, Jimmy tilted the driver's seat back and reached for me. I went willingly. With him, I was someone else. A girl who was sure of herself, not self-conscious, not timid at all.

He pulled me onto his lap and there was no more talk as we explored each other's lips and necks and faces. With my fingers buried in his thick, dark hair, his hands explored my body in ways that had always made me uncomfortable with other guys.

With Jimmy, it was different.

His passion mirrored my own.

In a husky voice, he said, "I have some blankets in the trunk."

Still not thinking clearly, I replied, "Why?"

He laughed again, but this time, I felt it in his chest. "For emergencies on the ranch. I bought them at the feed store, I just haven't put them in the truck yet."

My mouth on his skin, I murmured, "Is this an emergency?"

Pressing me tighter, he spoke into my neck. "This is definitely an emergency."

He opened the driver's door and we tumbled out in a heap,

laughing like two kids scuffling on the playground. When he helped me to my feet, he pulled me up against his body and there was no going back. "The trunk." He leaned past me into the car to press the release button.

While the lid opened soundlessly, Jimmy reached over and turned the radio volume up a bit louder. A disembodied voice crooned, "Sirius XM love songs—all night long. Feel it. Live it. Love it."

I giggled as he turned back to me.

He smiled and touched my face, my hair, the top of my shoulder. "Would you believe me if I told you I'd never done this before?"

My response was immediate. "No, I don't believe you. Why would—"

He silenced my speech with the pad of his thumb in an imitation of what I'd done to him only moments earlier. "I've never," he said. "Almost, many times, but something always held me back." He looked up at the starry sky. "I wanted to wait for the perfect time. The perfect night. The perfect girl." His thumb pulled my bottom lip down slightly. "Now, I've got all three."

I bit the tip of his thumb gently. He groaned and slid his other palm under the edge of my dress. The midnight air felt like cool silk as it found my bare skin.

"Jimmy, I—"

He stared into my eyes as his hand caressed my thigh. "What?" he asked. "Tell me anything, Mar." He leaned in and kissed me again. "Tell me anything. Tell me everything. I want to know it all."

I stepped out of his embrace and shrugged off my sweater and then the straps of my dress. It fell to the ground and I shook out my long, wavy hair and stood in a patch of moonlight in my peach colored bra and panties, a smattering of chill bumps coating my thighs, trembling in my cowgirl boots, and the fall flower bracelet he'd given me for the dance. I didn't have any more words. I didn't need them.

Dragging me to him, Jimmy whispered things in my ear that I almost couldn't hear. Things like "you're the one," and "I'm never going to let you go."

He half-walked, half-carried me to the trunk where he fished around blindly, pulling out a couple of rough horse blankets.

"C'mon." He grabbed my hand, pulling me half-naked and laughing across the short distance to the ruins. There, behind the remains of the tumbledown wall, he tossed the blankets on the ground in a heap and stood, breathless, seemingly uncertain how to proceed.

Taking the reins, I knelt and smoothed out the two thick blankets and then stood in the middle of them so I could reach him. I tugged the top of his western shirt and the pearl snap opened with a click. Delighted, I took both sides of the shirt and pulled it apart—click, click, click, click, click—until he stood bare-chested and beautiful in the silvery light of the moon.

I pushed the shirt completely off his shoulders and realized he was trembling, too. We both laughed when the sleeves of his shirt caught at his wrists. He unsnapped the cuffs with his teeth so that the garment fell to the ground, then he pulled me to his chest and the feel of my skin against his was so electrifying I immediately reached behind me and unsnapped the filmy barrier of my bra.

When I pressed myself to him this time, his chest was warm and smooth and solid. He pushed me away just far enough to get his hands beneath my breasts and then he devoured my mouth with abandon before slowly going to his knees, trailing kisses from my lips all the way to my belly button where he looked up at me with a sexy grin. "Pick up your foot."

I felt like a balky horse about to be shod, but I did as he said, one hand on the top of his head for balance.

With a little tug, he pulled off first one boot and then the other. I felt silly standing there in my long socks and panties. I quickly bent and pulled the socks off and flung them aside. For some reason, being nearly naked in front of Jim didn't feel strange. It felt natural. I liked the way his eyes fastened on mine as he kicked off his own boots and unbuckled his belt and jeans.

I stood still and watched.

If he felt self-conscious, it didn't show.

When the belt was loose and the buttons on his jeans hanging open, I could see a triangle of turquoise stretched almost to its limit.

With a smile, I reached forward and shoved the jeans off his hips. The turquoise knit boxers delighted me. I hadn't even thought about what he might be wearing underneath his jeans.

As soon as his pants were down, he had me in his arms. Together we stepped on the hems of his jeans so he could maneuver his legs free.

In tandem, we went all the way to the ground tugging at the last remaining articles of clothing separating us from total nudity.

The scratchy horse blankets softened our landing. "I knew it would be like this," he whispered. "With you."

"I'm just glad we're on private property."

He laughed, rolled over onto his back, and pulled me on top of him. "From now on, this will be our spot."

I nodded, but couldn't speak. He had rolled me back over onto the blanket and his mouth was on mine and we were busy figuring out how to get from point A to point B in the quickest, most pleasurable way possible.

"Wait!" His voice sounded urgent.

I waited while he scrambled around and located his pants. In a moment, he held up a condom, tore open the package, and then struggled to put it on. I looked away, trying to pretend I didn't know how much trouble he was having. He'd said he wasn't experienced, but I hadn't really believed him. Now, I did. It made me love him even more.

I caressed his back. "Anything I can do to help?" I wasn't experienced either, but I felt a need to lighten the moment.

He laughed shakily. "Sorry, guess I'm a little nervous."

I followed my caresses with my lips. "It's only me." I kissed his taut skin again, sat up and pressed my breasts to his back. "Just us."

A moan started in his chest. He leaned his head back. In the moonlight, I could see his eyes were closed. "I love that," he murmured.

My hands seemed to know where to go. They found their way around his waist into his lap, found his hands, caressed the backs of them as he rolled the condom the rest of the way down.

"I can't wait." He took my hands, turned in my embrace, and gently pressed me back. His kisses were urgent but sweet. They began at my mouth, trailed down my throat, lingered on my breasts, trickled down my belly and even lower.

The fragrant night breeze followed his path, enhancing every place his lips touched, every damp spot. Years later I could still recall that feeling, the sweet-scented wind, the cool touch of the night. It felt as if nature played a role in our first time. A strange and wonderful ménage à trois.

In a few minutes, everything was over and he lay sprawled and spent beside me, head on my chest. I let my hand play through his thick hair. He raised his head and his gray eyes met mine. "You okay?"

I loved that his first thought was of my wellbeing. "Better than okay," I said. "How about you?"

He grinned and kissed me softly. "Better than okay," he echoed. "Wonderful, in fact." He pushed himself up on one elbow. "Did you, um, you know..."

I squinted at the moon peeking over his shoulder. "I think so. I mean, it was my first time so I don't really know."

That got his attention. "Seriously? You couldn't tell?" His happy grin faded, replaced by a worried expression.

I laughed. I couldn't help it.

His worried expression deepened.

"I'm sorry, it isn't like that."

He rolled over on his back and I lay across him, breasts once again pressed into his chest. "I love the way you feel against me," I said.

That seemed to placate his worries. "Did it hurt?"

"No, not really—"

"But a little? I mean it did hurt? I'm so—"

"No, no, don't say sorry." I didn't want him to apologize. "It's not like you think. It was just a second." I wanted to look, to feel myself, to check for blood, but I felt suddenly shy.

He closed his eyes and wrapped his arms around me.

That gave me the courage to say, "But when you were kissing me, and you know, all that stuff, it felt wonderful. Like I was in heaven."

He clasped me even closer, kissing the top of my head. "Heaven, huh?"

I laughed. "Don't get that ego thing again."

"No," he said, "heaven sounds about right to me, too."

I studied his face. His smile was as wide as the Grand Canyon. "I'll never forget this night."

Jimmy sat up. "This is our spot, from now on, remember?" He reached for his clothes, pulled on his pants, walked to the car, and retrieved our pumpkin.

I began to pull my clothes on, too. "What are you doing?"

He searched around in the tall grass near the base of the rock wall.

"What are you looking for?" I grabbed my phone, touched

my flashlight app, and shined it on the area where he was bending the grass. "Did you lose something?"

He laughed and I realized what we'd both "lost." And then he picked up an old soft drink can and held it aloft. "Voila!"

"Have you lost your mind?" I trained my light on his smiling face.

He seized me, spun me around, and kissed me. "You know I've fallen completely in love with you, right?"

That took me by surprise. "Well, I—"

"No, no," he shushed me. "You don't have to say it back. It's okay. I changed my mind. I don't have to wait for you to say it, too."

I took his hand and made him look at me. "But I do," I said. "I feel the same." I enclosed his hand in both of mine. "These last few days have been magical." I laughed, embarrassed at using a word he'd uttered only an hour ago.

He tilted my chin up with our clasped hands, made me look him in the eye. "Exactly what I was thinking. I've never felt like this with anyone else. Ever."

"Me either," I whispered.

He let go my hand and kissed me deeply, one finger still beneath my chin. "I never want to let you go."

"Me, either," I murmured again. "Never."

This time, our kiss lasted a long while. At last, we parted.

"Now," he said. "This will make our place even more special." He bent down, picked up the forgotten soft drink can, crushed it between his palms, shaped the flattened can into a sharp tool, and cleared the grass away from a small area at the base of the wall. Then he began to dig.

"What—"

"Hand me the pumpkin," he said.

Then I finally understood. Beneath the prairie grass, and the top layer of sandy soil, a few inches down, rich dark earth became visible. I gave him the tiny pumpkin.

He broke it open, just a bit to expose the seeds. "To let the process begin," he said. And then he planted it in the moonlight.

I knelt and helped him cover the hole with the good rich soil. When we were finished, he folded the crushed Coke can into a stick-like shape and stuck it down into the soil as a marker. "We'll check it every now and then," he said. "See what happens. See what grows."

I ran back to the car, returned with the remains of a bottle of water I'd noticed earlier, poured it around the base of the small mound of earth. "There," I said. "How long before it sprouts."

Jimmy laughed. "Next year, I think. Pumpkins are gourds. Plant 'em in the fall, harvest 'em the next fall." He scratched his jaw. "At least I think that's how it works. My gran always grew 'em." He laughed and picked up rocks to pile around the base of our little planting. "It could be all different this year, though. I don't recall November ever being this warm. But what do I know? I'm a rancher, not a farmer. Guess we'll find out this time next year."

I smiled inwardly. *Next year.* I liked the sound of that. It sounded like a future.

Our future.

9

BACK AT SCHOOL

"Next year?" Lana couldn't believe it when I told her about planting the little pumpkin. "Wow. He's really planning ahead, isn't he?"

I was on the way back to school and we were talking on the phone. Again. I'd spent Sunday morning with the family, and I wanted to get a somewhat early start on the trip back to school.

When he brought me home Saturday night, Jim had warned me we wouldn't be able to talk much today since he and his dad were going up in the northern part of the ranch in search of strays. "You'd love it, Marlena." His voice had taken on a wistful note. "It's wild, unspoiled—only accessible by horseback—most of the ranch is really good grazing land, but up there it's like a different world. Like a little bit of the old west. Sort of like what you said about the ranch house." His lips had grazed my hair as he spoke.

I leaned in even closer. We were sitting in his car outside my house. "Sounds amazing," I said.

"Wish you could go up with me. You like horses?"

I nodded. "I've only ridden a few times, but I can't wait to see it. One of these days."

He'd squeezed me even tighter. I didn't want to let him leave. We wouldn't see each other again until Christmas. But at last we had to part. What a night we'd had. I went on inside, and he went back to the ranch to prepare for a Sunday in the wild.

Now I was driving back to Austin with Lana on the phone, happy for the chance to finally find out what had gone wrong with Dash.

We talked for over an hour before she finally got up the nerve to tell me. "I wanted to tell you right away," she said. "But it's so surreal I'm not even sure how it all happened."

"What was it, exactly?"

I heard her take a deep breath. "He stopped his truck on the I-20 overpass and pretended he was going to climb over the side and leap to his death."

"Oh, my God. Was he drunk already?"

"Yes," she said. "And when I got out of the truck to beg him to stop, he laughed and grabbed *me*. Pretended he was going to take me over with him." She hesitated. "At least I think he was pretending. He had me bent over the concrete barrier, telling me he wanted one last *forever* kiss."

Her voice cracked as if the memory terrified her. "I looked over my shoulder and the ground was so far away the highway looked like death."

"Oh, Lana..."

"I really thought he was going to push me over, he was so drunk and so heavy I couldn't get him off me. He had me in a bear hug, stumbling around like an idiot, trying to kiss me, pushing me up against the barrier over and over." She inhaled again and this time it turned into a ragged sob. "I just couldn't get *loose*."

"What made him finally stop?" I asked gently.

She sniffled and I could imagine her wiping her eyes with a

tissue. "I could see a car coming toward the bridge. I told him it was the cops and that made him hesitate long enough for me to break away."

I pictured the scene in my mind.

"Of course he grabbed me again and dragged me back to the truck. Then he started apologizing." She cleared her throat and I knew she was reliving the moment. "I really thought he was going to kill me. Or himself. Or both of us."

"I have to tell Jim all that. I don't think he realizes how dangerous Dash has become. Maybe there's something he can do. Some way he can get the guy some help before he hurts himself—"

"—or someone else," Lana said.

I must have gone silent for a moment because she called me back down to earth. "Hey, Mar?"

I glanced in my rearview mirror to change lanes. "Yeah?" I put on my turn signal and waited for a semi to pass.

Lana cleared her throat again. "It's really none of my business—"

"It's okay, go ahead."

She dove in. "Are you going to tell Preston to get lost once and for all when you get back? I mean you and Jimmy seem so perfect together."

I laughed and set my cruise control. "I sure am. I'll tell him right away, because you're right, Lan. Jim is perfect." I sighed and then giggled when I realized what I'd said. "I think he's the one. I don't want to be with anyone else." I glanced at my starry-eyed reflection as I checked my rearview again. "He says the same thing." I dug about in my memory. "He says I'm the only girl he's ever felt this way about."

Lana sighed, too. "I knew it. I could see by the way you two treated each other. It's love. No doubt about it."

I wanted to tell her everything, but she'd had such a horrible date with Dash I'd made a concerted effort not to talk too much about Jimmy and our incredible time together. "I can't wait for semester break. Spending Christmas at home, with you, and Jimmy, and my folks. It's going to be great. What should I get him? It has to be something important, but not too important. You know what I mean?"

"Marlena! Hey," she interrupted. "You didn't answer me."

I stopped talking and thought back over our conversation. What had I missed? I'd been so caught up in telling her about Jim I might have said something I didn't intend.

Lana blew out an exasperated breath. "I said when are you going to tell Preston? I'm afraid he's not going to take kindly to being rejected."

I tapped the speaker icon so I could take the phone away from my ear. "Oh, I thought I told you. I got a text from him yesterday. Seems he felt bad about how he acted outside my apartment the other morning. Says he wants to make it up to me." I recalled the message he'd sent. "You know, I think he stayed at school for the holiday. I don't really understand about his home life... all that money, and yet he didn't even have a family Thanksgiving dinner?"

"How sad," Lana said. "Poor little rich boy, huh?"

I pictured his face in my mind. He never seemed sad. But I had seen him mad, that's for sure. "I'm just going to be honest with him. Tell him I met someone. I'm not even going to suggest being friends. In a way, he reminds me of Dash, only without the drugs." I waited for her response.

"Yes. Make a clean break," Lana said. "Don't trust him at all. If he's anywhere near as unpredictable as Dash, you need to stay far away. He might be even worse if he acts that way stone cold sober. Dash didn't scare me until he got stinking drunk."

I hadn't thought of it like that. "You're right. We only went out a few times. He got possessive almost immediately." I shuddered just remembering the look on his face when I turned down breakfast that morning. "He is kind of a psycho. The sooner I get rid of him, the better."

My phone dinged with a new text message. "Hang on." I clicked over, expecting to see a heart or a smiley face from Jim.

"Oh, hell," I said, when I clicked back into my conversation with Lana. "Speak of the devil and he rings a bell."

"Preston?"

"Yes. He just messaged me to meet him at a restaurant downtown, so he can *truly* apologize for his 'assiness', his word, not mine."

Lana sucked in a breath. "Don't go," she said. "Tell him now, in a text. Or better yet, just call him, tell him you've met the love of your life and you won't be seeing other guys, ever."

I appreciated her concern. "Yeah. Maybe you're right. I don't *want* to see him. I'll call him right now. Talk to you later."

"Call me back," she said. "I want to know how he takes it."

"Okay," I said. But when I pressed his number in recent calls, my phone beeped with a NO SERVICE message. Ugh. How can it be good one second and not the next? That's Texas, though. Cell towers can be few and far between on the plains.

I summoned Siri and sent him a voice text instead. "Hey, Preston, I got your message. Sorry. I can't make it to the restaurant tonight." I hesitated, unsure how to proceed. Then I plunged ahead. "I met someone over the holidays. We really hit it off. I won't be dating anyone else now that I'm with Jim. We're, you know, exclusive."

There. That ought to do it. I sent it and hoped for the best.

A little red memo popped up. MESSAGE NOT DELIVERED.

"Oh, no." I immediately tried calling Lana back to tell her, but of course I couldn't get her either. Not for a few more miles.

I looked at the red words on my phone. Maybe I should just delete it and go on to the restaurant, meet him and get it over with. That way I wouldn't have to worry about him showing up at the apartment later, claiming he never got the message.

That's what I'll do. It would be better, more final. I'll be on my toes the whole time. Besides, we'll be in a restaurant, in the midst of all those people. Nothing can happen there.

I called Lana as soon as I had service again. She didn't seem convinced. "I don't like it. Just cut him off, now. Resend the message."

I laughed a little. Her suspicious nature was one of the things I loved about her. "Don't worry, Mama Bear. I need to do this my way. I'll just make a clean break. Besides, we'll be in a restaurant with a million people—"

Lana huffed. I'd seen her do it a thousand times. Her voice came out gruff. "Okay. But what restaurant is it? Just for my peace of mind."

"It's a new one downtown. Double Dog Dare Ya. Some name, huh?"

"Sounds like a bar. Be careful, okay? Promise me."

"Okay, okay," I agreed. Then I recalled how terrified she'd been after the date with Dash. I felt terrible. We'd just decided Preston was every bit as scary. "Hey, you know what? You're right. Let me call him now that I have service again. I'll call you right back."

"Thank you," she said. "I've got a bad feeling about that guy. Maybe it's just because of my own recent scare, but still..."

I reassured her that I would call her back as soon as I told him. But of course it didn't work out that way.

To begin with, he didn't answer.

I called Lana back and told her it appeared I would have to

meet him after all. "If I don't," I said. "He'll show up at my place and that's where I definitely don't want to see him. I'll go on to the restaurant and let him down easy. I don't want to make an enemy of him. But trust me, I never intend to go out with him again." I hesitated a moment. "Even if I hadn't found Jimmy, I wouldn't go out with Preston again, he's just too—"

"Creepy? Psychotic? Ted Bundy-ish?"

I laughed. "Yeah. Or in light of this weekend, too Dash-ish."

She chuckled, but I could tell it wasn't a real laugh. "Just promise me you'll end it and go right home." She started to hang up, and then she said, "And if you need anything, call me. I'm not going anywhere tonight."

"You're several hours away, Mama Bear, but if I need you, I will definitely call." I hesitated. "But don't seriously expect to hear from me until I get home, okay? Dinner shouldn't last more than a couple of hours at most." I broke our connection, patted Blue Bear on the head—he was riding shotgun—and then clicked on my newest playlist to try and enjoy the rest of my trip. Before long, I was back at school and ready to get things over with.

The message from Preston, and knowing I had to meet him and possibly endure some sort of scene, dampened the weekend only a little bit. What had really put a damper on it was when I'd said goodbye to Jimmy. It didn't feel like my heart was breaking, it felt more like it was melting. A slow-motion dissolve deep inside my chest, right down into my gut. I'd never felt so thoroughly undone by anyone. Ever.

When I approached the university, I subconsciously caught myself watching for Preston's Mustang. I realized then just how much I dreaded this encounter. Maybe Lana was right, and I should try calling him again.

I pressed his name in my contacts list before I could back

out, but he still didn't answer. It cut off before the voicemail alert came on.

With a sigh, I clicked END. Maybe he was out of range like I'd been. Or maybe he had an accident or something. Maybe I'll show up and he won't be there, and I'll never even know why. That wouldn't hurt my feelings, not at all.

I pulled into the parking area, found a slot right in front of the apartment, grabbed Blue Bear by the arm, and retrieved my bags from the trunk. I had quite a load to take inside.

When I turned from the car, a bag over each shoulder and my wheeled overnight case—with Blue Bear sitting on top—by the handle, I got the distinct feeling I was being watched. The back of my neck felt naked, vulnerable.

That convinced me to listen to my intuition. I pulled my phone out of my pocket and sent the message again. Best not to face him at all.

But the same red alert popped up. MESSAGE NOT DELIVERED.

What the heck?

I glanced around the parking lot. It was nearly deserted. A lot of kids must be waiting until the last second to return. Not me, though. I didn't like being on the road alone when it got late. Especially on that one funky stretch where there was no cell service. That's why I'd left before noon even though I could tell Mom would've liked me to stay a little longer.

Hurrying across the sidewalk to our ground level apartment, I stuck my key in the door and went in, glad to be home, but sad to be leaving Jimmy behind. Of course, I hadn't really left him in our hometown. After helping his dad with the strays, he'd had to go back to school, too. Sul Ross was three hours from Window in the opposite direction.

I unpacked my clothes, put them away, and tried to call Preston again. Still no answer and no voice mail. I placed Blue

Bear in between my two bed pillows, and then went to the bathroom and ran a bath. I added a few lavender bath beads to soak away the drive. By the time ten o'clock rolled around, the date with Preston would be over and I could stop looking over my shoulder all the time.

10

DOUBLE DOG DARE YA

With dread pressing on my chest like a weight, I drove to the restaurant, parked down the street and walked for several blocks. I'd only decided to take my car at the last minute. I just couldn't imagine breaking it off with him and then going down to wait for a bus. At least with my car I could leave at a moment's notice.

When I saw the line waiting to get in, though, second thoughts crossed my mind. He'd better have reservations, or I'd tell him the truth right there on the packed and breathing sidewalk.

As soon as I approached the restaurant door, Preston stepped out of the shadows. "Hey, gorgeous. Looking great, as always."

His hand went toward my hair but I ducked away under the guise of studying the menu posted beside the door. "Hmm, thank you, Preston." I noticed his Mustang parked a few feet away at the curb. How long had he been here? I ran my finger down the menu. "Did you get any of my messages?"

He smoothed his hair off his brow. "Messages? Not a one."

He didn't ask what the messages said. He leaned forward and whispered, "I'm sorry."

I stopped studying the menu. "Sorry?" I thought he meant about the messages.

"They lost my reservation." He waved a hand toward the long line snaking the opposite direction down the sidewalk. "The hostess said the wait will be at least an hour, maybe more." He shook his head. "I'm so pissed at them."

But he didn't seem pissed. In fact, he had a smile playing at the corners of his mouth. It seemed very odd in light of the fact they'd lost his reservation.

I straightened and started back down the street the way I'd come.

Preston loped alongside me. "Where are you going?"

"Home," I said. "I'm not going to stand around on the sidewalk for hours. Thanks but no thanks." I realized I hadn't broken it off with him, so I came to a stop. "We do need to talk, though." My nerves zinged as I tried to gather the courage to tell him about Jim.

Preston stopped. He towered over me by at least six inches. "I said I was sorry for their ineptitude." He shot a withering glance toward the restaurant. "But I've got a bottle of merlot in the car. We can grab a pizza. Have a little picnic out on Telephone Road. Have you seen the new picnic area near the lake? There's a hidden stream nearby. It feeds right into—"

I shook my head and resumed walking, a bit more slowly this time. "No. I haven't been to the lake lately. Too much craziness out there for me."

"Exactly." He put his hand under my elbow. "That's why this place is so cool. It's brand new. Sort of undiscovered." His gaze traveled backward over his shoulder toward the milling crowds. "That probably won't last long, though."

I nodded. He was definitely right about that. Austin was so

crowded. Especially on weekends. "Sounds nice," I began. "But I'm not in the mood for a picnic. In fact," I gathered my courage and turned to face him. "I just came to tell you that I've started seeing someone. And it's serious." I stopped walking so that I could be certain he was hearing me. It took everything I had to look him in the eye.

To keep myself from glancing away—which I thought might be a sign of weakness—I pictured Jimmy, bare-chested, in the moonlight.

"Seeing someone? How? When?" His voice took on a strident note. "I mean, we just went out last week, when have you had time—"

"Preston..." I gently pulled my elbow out of his grasp. I didn't even bother to correct him on the circumstances of the last time he'd asked—or demanded—we go out. "I ran into an old friend at Thanksgiving. We really hit it off. We kind of decided to see each other, you know, exclusively." We'd never discussed anything of the sort, but he'd said he loved me. Wasn't that the same thing?

Preston started to take my arm again. His facial expression hinted that he no longer understood the language I was speaking. "No," he said. "That can't be."

I took a couple of quick steps forward, hoping he wouldn't come with me this time. It didn't work. He hurried to catch up, his hand cupping my elbow again.

"You can't just go off one day and decide you're going to see someone else exclusively. I made reservations."

"Look, I'm sorry. I didn't intend to get involved with someone so quickly, but I did. It just happened." *Besides, you and I weren't even dating. You were practically stalking me.*

"Seriously." His voice sounded like that of a petulant child. "Let's just go for a drive, get a pizza, talk it over."

I shook my head. Alarm bells were beginning to sound. He

was making it very difficult to let him down gently. "I don't think I want to do that." I tried to keep my voice level.

Preston stopped, smashed a hand through his stylish hair, and then resumed his speech. "All right, then. Have a great life. I would've given you the world, you understand? But go on back to your hick-town boyfriend. I hope you will be very happy."

Relief washed over me. I realized I'd been gearing myself up for a real battle. I recalled the times he would be waiting for me after my classes, having skipped out early on his own to be there. Or when I would head out to the student union building or to the library or for a run with Joanna and he would be sitting there, in his car, just waiting, watching.

"Can I call you?" he asked.

I'd started walking again. Uh-oh. Something in his tone almost stopped me, made me want to soften the blow after all. But I pictured Jim again. "I'm sorry," I said. "I don't think it's a good idea."

"But we can be friends, right?"

I felt like a heel. Wasn't that supposed to be my line? I started to say, *Sure, of course we can,* then I remembered the hick-town boyfriend remark. "I think we'd better just say goodbye now, so both of us can move on." I stumbled a bit when I came to the curb, looking back at him to gauge the effect of my words, but I set my jaw and forced myself to continue walking.

Later, I had to wonder if that hesitant little stumble might've given him the idea to follow me that night. To do the things he did. It was a victim's move, that hesitation, that stumble. Uncertainty spoke volumes, or so I learned later, in therapy, and in my self-defense classes in Denver.

"Okay, then," he muttered. "Guess I'll see you around."

My step quickened, I sensed freedom.

Then I heard him mutter, "You have a nice life, now, *bitch.*" The tone of his voice had changed yet again. That last word was so low I wasn't certain I'd really heard it. Had he called me bitch? I didn't doubt it. The civility he'd exhibited had shocked me, the word bitch? Not so much. It reminded me of Dash that night at the street dance.

Eager to get back to my car, I went with the flow of people, hurrying back to the place where I would feel safe. All around me vehicles crawled up and down the street, engines revving, and the sidewalks were so crowded, even the crosswalks were jammed with couples, trios, and groups, some linked arm in arm, intent on going nowhere, their main objective to have fun.

I noticed very few single revelers out and about. Soon I began to feel not like a salmon swimming upstream, but more like a human pinball, bouncing off first one partier and then another.

Outside a small café I stopped to catch my breath. This was a place I would have liked to visit. An acoustic guitarist was tuning up inside, his chair and mic stand on a tiny stage built into the bay window. I imagined he would play classic folk music like my parents liked.

Leaning against the rough brick wall, one hand on my chest, and one on my purse, I wondered, could it really be over with Preston? Could it have ended that quickly, that easily? I hoped so. I prayed it was so, but behind the hand covering my heart, my insides vibrated as if someone had strummed them the way the guy in the window strummed the strings of his guitar.

One good thing about being on Sixth Street, no one even noticed that I was on the verge of a full-blown panic attack. It was weird though, being alone in a crowd. I felt like an alien, invisible, there but not there.

I inhaled slowly and deeply to quell the internal vibrations, then looked back toward the restaurant to make sure he hadn't followed me. When I was certain he was nowhere in sight, I resumed my trek toward my car and my freedom. How had he disappeared so quickly? I hadn't seen him pass me. Hadn't even noticed him get in his car. I turned and stood on tiptoe to see over the crowd of revelers. To make certain he wasn't coming.

Eventually, I made it back to my Nissan. But even from half a block away I could see that something was off. My little car seemed to be listing to one side.

When I got closer, the problem became obvious. The front left tire was completely flat. That made no sense. The tires were fairly new. Dad had seen to that, a few months earlier when he was more himself.

Exasperated, I dug my keys out of my purse to unlock my hatch for the spare. That's when I saw that the rear tire was almost flat as well. Bending down, I could actually hear the air escaping. "Dammit." Had I run over something without realizing it?

"Hey, gorgeous."

I looked up. Preston's black Mustang idled beside me. He had the top down and the early evening sunset made his handsome face glow. I recalled how he'd bragged about the cost of the triple row of custom silver pinstripes that ran the length of his car. "Preston? What are you doing here?"

He jerked his thumb over his shoulder. "Saw you walking, made a U-turn. I feel terrible about the reservations." He indicated my flat tires with a nod of his head. "Looks like you could use a little help."

I pressed my lips together. How convenient that he was just passing by. On the other hand, two flats and one spare didn't add up to a great scenario. Still… I'd just made up my mind to be done with him. Wouldn't accepting his help set me back? "Nah, it's okay," I said. "I'll call my roomie—"

Preston laughed good-naturedly. "What's Joanna going to do? Bring you another spare?" He leaned over and popped his passenger door open. "C'mon, hop in. I'll find a place to park and then I'll get that tire off, take it to Discount." He made a show of looking at his watch. "We can get it fixed and put the spare on for the other one. I think we can make it before they close if we hurry."

I hesitated. Maybe he was right. I couldn't imagine Joanna bringing me a second spare and then the two of us putting them both on the car. Maybe I should at least let him help me get the tire off. I nodded and pointed up the street. "You go ahead and find a parking space and I'll dig out the lug wrench."

Preston's perfectly curved lips turned down in a frown, but only for a second, then he seemed to realize how it looked. He turned the frown into a grin. "Sure," he agreed. "I see a spot opening up. Be right back."

With a slight feeling of unease, I stuck my head back into the hatch to retrieve the lug wrench. I'd used it once before, when I had a blow out on the highway, but that had been over a year earlier. It was that incident that prompted my dad to spring for a new set of tires.

I opened the spare tire well in the hatchback's storage area. Everything was just as I remembered. I unscrewed the bolt holding the jack and lug wrench in place and just as I removed it from the well, Preston walked up and took it from my hand.

It took a good five or ten minutes to get the rear tire off the vehicle.

"They use those pneumatic lug wrenches when they put the tires on at the shop." He took off his jacket and handed it to me. Perspiration had darkened the area between his shoulder blades. With the heel of his good shoe, he began stomping down on the handle of the wrench to loosen the lug nuts. "I'll get it in a minute."

He was working so hard to help me out, I felt a little guilty for the way I'd left him on the street in front of the restaurant.

At last, the first lug nut loosened up and he moved on to the second and then the third, fourth, and finally, the fifth.

Wiping his brow with the back of his wrist, Preston smiled. "I've got it now." He slid the jack into place, fit the lug wrench onto the jack as a handle, and then began to pump. "Thankfully it's fairly level here," he said. And then just like that, he had the flat off. Without another word, he rolled the tire up the sidewalk to his Mustang, opened the hatch rehotely, and stowed my tire inside.

"C'mon," he called. He climbed into the driver's seat without waiting for a reply.

I looked at my little car, my lifeline between home and school, sitting up on the jack, and I knew it was wrong to leave it there unattended. I walked over to the Mustang. "Shouldn't we at least take it down off the jack? I mean, what if someone comes along and takes the other tires, or even the jack?"

Clenching his jaw, Preston stepped back out of the car. "Sure," he said. "Someone might do that." He waved his hand at the milling people a couple blocks away. "Of course there would be a lot of witnesses, wouldn't there?"

I thought that was an odd thing to say, but he was right. There were a lot of people around, but still. The little Nissan was my baby. I couldn't stand to go off and leave it jacked up that way.

To humor me, he walked back to my car, lowered the jack, removed it, and stowed it back in the hatch. Now my car really looked sad. But at least it was all locked up. Without another word, I accompanied him to his Mustang and got into the passenger seat.

He drove us straight to Discount Tire. They took pity on me and put my tire right on the machine even though they were just about to close.

In a moment, the technician came back to the waiting area.

"I'm sorry, ma'am. We can't fix your tire. It looks like someone slashed the sidewall on purpose." He looked at the ground as if he expected me to dispute his word. "You can see it if you want."

Preston sprang into action. "Of course we want to see it." The tone of his voice had changed. It sounded as if he didn't believe the guy. "You're just trying to sell her a new tire, that's all."

The technician sighed as if he'd expected just this sort of accusation. He dragged a rough red rag across his palm and led us back to the garage.

Sure enough, once they had it on the machine, the huge cut on the curve of the tire was easily visible.

"You say your other tire is flat, too?"

I nodded.

The technician looked at me. His black hair shone under the high fluorescents of the garage. "You got any enemies?"

That question surprised me but it immediately made sense. "No," I said. "Not that I know of." I looked at the obvious slash mark. "But I see what you mean."

The technician, the patch on his uniform said his name was Juan, pointed at a row of tires above our head. "I've got a couple used ones I can sell you, if you want."

I thought back to my dad handing me the paperwork on my brand new set. "Hey," I said. "I think these may be under warranty. They aren't even a year old yet."

"Did you get them here?" Juan's voice sounded hopeful. I liked this guy. I'd known him five minutes and I already liked and trusted him more than Preston.

I shook my head. "My dad bought them for me back in my hometown. Window? Do you know it?"

The guy shook his head. "Sorry. No. But if it was at Discount then it doesn't matter which town."

Preston made a noise in the back of his throat. It was obvious he was growing impatient. "Look, I'll spring for a new tire, then you can find out about your warranty and even check your insurance policy tomorrow." He stuck his fingers into the front of his rich-boy haircut and ruffled his bangs again. Then he smiled as if that would endear him to me, as if I hadn't seen that move a dozen times.

I pulled out my Visa card and handed it to Juan. "Please mount a new tire and I'll bring the other one in tomorrow as well." I wished I'd been able to bring them both, I knew it wasn't good to drive on the spare for long, but I hated to ask any more of Preston.

The technician nodded and led me back to the cashier. Preston tagged along. A woman stood behind the counter. She must have been somewhere else when we came in.

Juan gave her my card, wrote up a quick ticket, and said, "I'll have it mounted in a few minutes." He didn't speak to Preston again.

11

TELEPHONE ROAD

Preston took me back to my car, put on the new tire, removed the other flat—which also appeared to have been slashed or cut—and put on the spare. It was a lot of work. He never complained, and I didn't argue. I didn't want him to do all that, didn't want to feel indebted to him, but he insisted and I felt it would be rude to refuse. How can you tell someone you don't want their help when they're right there doing it?

"Whew!" He laughed while he wiped his hands on a clutch of fast food napkins from my car. "Hey," he held up the napkins. "This gives me an idea."

I didn't want to hear it. I knew what it was going to be; I just didn't know how to bow out gracefully. Not now.

"Our picnic," he said. "I'll call ahead, order a takeout pizza, I've got the wine in the car." He raised an eyebrow in my direction. "It'll be a nice way to unwind after all this." He glanced back at the ruined tire in my hatch. "You can follow me there, and after we eat and relax, you can head home." He peeled a napkin out of the wad and swiped at his forehead. "I don't know about you, but I've worked up quite an appetite."

I shrugged. It was the very last thing I wanted to do, but I did feel indebted, I couldn't help it. "Hey, I have a different idea. For all your help, why don't you let me buy *you* dinner." That piqued his interest.

"We could just go in to the Pizza Hut, have our pizza there. It'll be so much quicker, and I'll foot the bil—"

He started shaking his head before I even finished speaking. "I'm way too sweaty and grimy to go in anywhere. Unless we go by my apartment so I can clean up first—"

"No, no, that's all right." I made a show of glancing at the horizon. "It's getting sort of late, now." I definitely didn't want to go to his apartment. Whatever it took, I was ready to be done with this day, and with him. "Let's just have our picnic. I'm pretty tired—"

He barked a harsh laugh. "*You're* tired?"

"I'm sorry, you know what I mean. It's been a little unsettling finding out someone has it in for me." I watched a couple cross the street, arm in arm, laughing and talking, enjoying each other's company. It reminded me of the fall street dance with Jimmy.

I must have had a look of longing on my face. Preston smiled. The setting sun was at his back; the pastel colors illuminating the end of day. "Looks like they're in love, doesn't it?" He nodded toward the couple crossing the street.

I shrugged. "Who knows, maybe it's their first date." I hurried on to cover the tone that had crept into my voice. I don't know why I was having so much trouble simply being nice to the guy. Oh, yeah, that bitch comment. And the nonexistent reservations. I took a deep breath. "Really, thank you for all you've done." I had to keep reminding myself that he really had stepped in and saved the day, or at least a big towing bill.

"No problem," he muttered. "Glad to do it." He opened my car door and I slid into the driver's seat.

When I glanced up to pull the door closed, his silhouette loomed over my small car. For the first time, I noticed a smear of black across his forehead from the tires. He *had* put out a lot of effort for me.

Could Preston have a jealous girlfriend I didn't know about? Could she have slashed my tires?

He pulled out his cell phone and called a nearby pizza place and ordered a take out pizza half pepperoni and half veggie. I was surprised he remembered that I preferred all vegetables. We'd only shared pizza once, and that had been the first time we'd gone out with his friends. He closed my door and tapped the roof as if to say I was good to go.

Against my better judgment, I followed him as he stopped, picked up the pizza, and led me straight out Telephone Road toward the lake.

I'd been to a couple of parties down this road. If you went far enough, it ended right at Cameron Cove, a popular place to hang out. There were usually dozens of people at The Cove, laughing, drinking, swimming, even lounging about on inner tubes and inflatable rafts. There wasn't a place for boating, it was too shallow, but there were several grills and picnic tables.

I assumed we were headed for a newly built or cleared site near there.

When Preston followed a different road just before we got to The Cove, my heart fluttered in my chest. This road was more like a lane; narrow and unpaved. It appeared to be the future continuance of Telephone Road.

I didn't like this. Too secluded, too rough. I watched for a place wide enough to turn the car around. By the time I found one, I was already there.

Preston had a picnic blanket dangling from one hand, pizza box balanced on the other. Even though it was November, the day seemed mild. Little did I know a cold mist would follow the sunset.

"I thought I'd lost you," he called.

I glanced around. It was definitely hidden, but I didn't see a stream. "I thought you said there was a stream."

He laid the blanket on the hood of the Mustang and set the pizza box on top of it. Then he leaned back inside and emerged holding a bottle of wine and two glasses.

I was surprised. "Do you always carry wine glasses in your car, just in case?"

He stopped perfectly still. I saw his shoulders tense, saw his mouth form a thin, hard line. I hesitated getting out of the car, taking a moment to push the button to roll up the window. That seemed to send him a signal.

Laughing, he held up the glasses. "Plastic," he called. "I bought them at the liquor store."

As I sat there, debating whether to turn off the engine and join him for the picnic or turn around and gun it back for town, he strode over, opened my door, and held out a glass. "C'mon," he said. "I'll show you the hidden stream." He popped the cork out with a device on his key ring, and then glanced across the hood of my car toward the trees. "When you turn off the engine, you can hear it." He smiled and I pushed away the little voice inside my head that kept telling me to slam his hand in the door, jam the gear shift into reverse, and hightail it out of there.

I turned off the engine and took a sip of the wine. He was right. I could hear a stream burbling somewhere close by. I stepped out, stuck my keys down in my front pocket, and my phone in my back pocket. "Just a slice and a glass, and then I'll need to head home."

He smiled, and I thought I must have misjudged him all along. That's why I allowed him to lead me away from my car toward the hidden stream and into a new version of the future that didn't include any of the things I'd ever planned.

12

SURVIVAL

The red wine made a startling contrast to the savory pizza. I took a few more sips, glad I'd also brought along a bottle of water. Even though Preston urged me to have more, I shook my head and retrieved a bottle of water from my car. A brief shadow crossed his face, but he didn't try to convince me otherwise. He finished off the wine without me.

That gave me a moment's pause, thinking about a drunken Dash, but not nearly as much pause as when we first broke through the thick trees and arrived at the beautiful stream. Preston had obviously done some prep work ahead of time. He'd made a fire ring in a sandy spot on the bank. The beach was the size of a postage stamp, just wide enough for the circle of stones. There was a long campfire lighter balanced on one of the flat rocks. *When did he do all this?*

The remains of the sunset reflecting across the rippling water drew me to lean down and dip my fingers into the cold, bubbling flow. The sounds lent a storybook feel to the scene. The air was cool and still, fragrant with the loamy, nose-tickling scent of damp earth and fresh water. Multicolored leaves and drifts of pine needles carpeted the ground, softening our steps and turning the whole area into a painter's fall palette.

I sat cross-legged on the plaid blanket he'd spread. "This is kind of amazing," I admitted around a mouthful of pizza. "How'd you find it?"

Preston looked into the distance. "I spend a lot of time in the woods," he said. "It's my refuge. I just needed you to share it with me."

He looked at me and I knew, suddenly and without a shred of doubt, that I had made a huge mistake. His light blue eyes had gone as cold as the water in the creek.

I tried not to panic, tried to keep my suspicions in check, but alarm bells clanged inside my head. "It's really beautiful," I said. "Thank you for sharing it with me." I put one hand down to push myself to my feet. "Now I've really got to get bac—"

He grabbed my shoulder, forcing me to remain seated on the blanket. For a moment, I had a ridiculous hope that he was playing, roughhousing the way Jim and I had done. But when he held me there, when his other hand clamped down on my opposite shoulder, when he smashed me backward onto the remains of the pizza, I knew this was no game.

"Stop!" I cried. "What are you—?"

His face came closer and closer, his lips questing.

I jerked my head from side to side. "Preston, stop! What're you *doing*?"

His weight pinned me to the blanket, his hard chin dug into the side of my neck. He tried to hold my face still without using his hands.

"I love you." His voice had gone as hard and cold as his eyes. "I know you love me, too. I don't know why you won't show it."

His lips found mine and he let go of my right shoulder long enough to tangle his fingers into my hair.

My head was trapped. Anger crashed through my body. I

jerked my head aside to get his mouth off mine. Strands of my hair were ripped out of my scalp, but suddenly my hands were fighting, clawing, raking at his face, his clothing, his skin. Anything to get him off me.

He tightened his grip on my hair but his other hand came up holding the campfire lighter. Just as he depressed the trigger to ignite it, my right hand found the wine bottle lying on its side. I wrapped my fingers around the neck of the bottle and swung it through the air, smashing it into the side of his head with as much force as I could muster.

The sound was intense, a bone-cracking whack muted by a layer of flesh.

He fell away, holding his temple. "You bitch!" He appeared to be in shock, touching his head, assessing the damage.

I struggled to my feet and ran directly into the cold creek, wading up to my knees before I got across.

"Come back here," he screamed. "I'll kill you for that."

Part of me *still* wanted to insist that this was all a mistake, a game, a twisted version of hide and seek. But he continued to scream out my name. Telling me he'd get me. That he would kill me. That he would burn me. Burn me. Burn me.

The sound of his voice spurred me on. Branches clawed at my face the way I'd clawed at his. I didn't feel the pain. I pushed my way through, my breath harsh as fire in my throat. Damp night had crept in as the sun disappeared. The sweet loamy air turned acrid. Away from the clearing, the pretty fall landscape had gone dark, alien, and terrifying.

When I came out of the creek I fell over an invisible root, knocking all the breath from my lungs. Stunned, I lay perfectly still, hoping I'd gotten far enough away so I could simply stay put until he gave up, until I could take stock of my surroundings and figure out how to get back to my car without being found.

He's probably already regretting his impulsive actions, I

thought. Probably praying I don't say anything to anyone. Probably packing up his Mustang and heading home right this minute. He didn't really mean he would burn me, kill me, did he? That was just anger talking, right? Anger and alcohol?

Wrong.

His voice hissed out of the darkness beside me.

"Run, little rabbit." It was him, but a different him. This Preston sounded gleeful. As if he were having *fun*. As if this nightmare chase was the real reason we were here, the only reason we were here. As if my car and all that had happened today had occurred simply as a means to channel me into this moment. Sort of like the first time I'd seen him at the art gallery.

"*Run*," he hissed again.

So I did.

I dragged myself to my feet and took off like a wounded animal. Behind me I could hear him clicking the trigger on the long-barreled campfire lighter. *Click, whoooshhhh. Click, whooosh-hhh. Click, whooosshhhh.*

"Run, little rabbit," he snickered. "Run fast. I burn little rabbits. Burn off all their fur."

Sobs tore through me, making it nearly impossible to suck in enough air to keep going. I crashed through the brush, through the branches, looking behind me every chance I got, trying to hear over the sound of my own panicked flight. Was that him, was he coming? Was he right behind me? I couldn't tell. My ragged breathing clogged my ears; all I could hear was the pounding of my own heart.

I had to slow down. A soft rain had begun to fall, blurring my vision even more. The rain hit the earth and mist rose like fog. I bent over at the waist, gasping for air, pulling in one pained lungful at a time.

After a second, I went on again, more slowly. All at once my world had shrunk to rain, cold, towering trees, thick brush, darkness. Fear. Running, running, running.

Tree limbs sliced my cheeks and snatched my hair. The ground swelled with roots and caught my toe again. It threw me to the earth, face down in the rich, loamy soil and I tasted it, breathed it in, tried my best to panic in silence. Tried my best to survive without making a sound.

A twig snapped.

My body froze,

Was that him?

Was it?

Panic guided my feet, but I couldn't hear anything more.

I got to my feet as quietly as possible, I'd lost a shoe and my bare foot found every sharp stick and jagged rock. No matter what, I couldn't run quietly. Every time something pierced my heel or the ball of my foot, I cried out.

When I fell a third time, he was on me.

He'd been right behind me all along. There was nothing playful this time. He struck out with his fist and my vision doubled, then tripled, and then went away. I came to as he dragged me deeper into the bushes. Flinging me to the ground, he fell on top of me again.

All the breath went out of my lungs. I tried to scream. Tried to breathe. Impossible. Then I saw it. The silvery suggestion of a knife slicing through the air.

I jerked my head away.

The blade gashed the side of my neck.

Quick warmth ran down. My brain refused to accept that he had stabbed me—instead, it focused on the idea that this was probably the same knife that had slashed my tires.

All my instincts told me to play dead. Be still. Pretend to be somewhere else. It wasn't hard to do. He didn't seem to realize he had missed the mark. He was too busy doing other things.

I let my whole body go slack. I knew he would kill me if he realized the flow of blood had slowed.

When I stopped struggling, his body weight lessened. Only his shoulder held me down. That, and the tip of the knife.

As least I could breathe a little better.

It was clear now. He'd orchestrated the entire evening just to get me here. He was a rapist, pure and simple. A rapist and a wannabe murderer.

All those thoughts ran through my head as he did what he wanted. I didn't resist. I didn't try to fight. I lay there, forever, even when he prised open my mouth, even when he flipped me over, even then. I imagined myself as a ragdoll. A dead ragdoll.

I silently recited The Lord's Prayer and The Hail Mary over and over and over.

When he finally stopped thrusting and jumped up, I heard the click, whoooshhh of the lighter and I knew my days on earth were done. Now he would finish me off and set me on fire. Burn my body to cover his evil actions.

I lay completely still, praying, just praying.

Then I realized he was gone, the knife was gone, the sound of the firestarter was gone. I was still face down in the dirt. Was that him crashing through the brush, running away? Where was the fire he'd started, where was the flame?

I held my breath to listen.

In the distance, I could hear voices, but I couldn't make out the words.

I opened my mouth to scream for help, but then I realized he had stopped crashing. He must be standing still, nearby. What if he was he waiting for me to scream, to jump up and run again? Was this still a part of his twisted game?

A feminine laugh floated to me on the lilting fog. Probably a couple on an outing, maybe even a group of kids having a kegger, enjoying the lake. They could be nearby or clear across the water. It was impossible to tell. I wasn't even sure how close we were to the lake. The soggy air disguised sound. Warped it. I'd forded the stream, but I hadn't seen the lake.

I lay perfectly still as long as I could stand it. Earth and leaves clogged my nose, stuck to the stickiness on my neck.

Already I could feel my face swelling, throbbing, my entire body singing with pain. Eventually I rolled myself beneath the bushes. Something small and hard wiggled beneath me. I dug my hand under my body and swept out what felt like a beetle.

My heart banged inside my chest. If Preston was still nearby, I felt certain he could hear it. I forced myself to spit quietly and inhale slowly as I peered out between the thin- branched bushes.

Damp fall cooled my skin as stray shafts of moonlight reflected off the mist. It appeared to be growing denser by the moment. I couldn't hear the voices anymore. Either they'd moved farther away, or the sounds had been a fluke to begin with, carried *from* far away. I made up my mind not to think about it. Somehow, I had to get back to my car and hope that he was gone.

13
___

THE GAME?

Head pounding, I struggled to fasten my jeans. He'd only shoved them halfway down my thighs, and they were soaking wet around the bottoms from where I'd forded the stream. I'd been holding them up with one hand while I ran. I fastened them closed and tried not to think of how he'd ripped my panties off and flung them away. The mist clung like cold skin. Where had the mild evening gone? It felt as if I'd fumbled my way straight into a hellish parallel universe.

My fingers gingerly explored the swelling around my eye, my tongue tasted the blood on my lips. I tried to ignore the torn, burning pain between my legs and the other places my memory refused to acknowledge.

The horrid thought of sodomy battered my senses as surely as another blow from a fist. I didn't know what to do. I simply lay there in the bushes, numb, broken, unable to think, unable to plan, unable to even feel grateful to be alive. I knew action was my only hope. I would have to get back across the creek, that's where I would find my car. I'd begun to shiver. I longed for the sweater I'd left on the front seat.

I put one hand to my throat, remembering the knife, but I

felt only a smear of moisture that might have been blood. Wait, what's this flap of skin? No, don't touch it. Don't touch it. Just go. Survive. Live.

On my hands and knees, I began to crawl along beneath the bushes, going as slow as a snail to keep from making any noise. I wasn't sure how long he'd been gone. It felt like a long time, but in the back of my mind I figured it had only been a few minutes.

What if he was still watching? Again I thought, what if this was part of his game?

I continued to crawl, and then something occurred to me.

I felt in my pants pocket. No phone. It must have fallen out when he yanked at my pants. Losing my phone was like losing my eyesight. Finding it would save me. I had to go back to the place where he'd yanked down my pants. If I had my phone, I had a chance.

No, a voice said. Just keep going. Listen for water. Follow the stream to the lake. Don't think about what happened. Don't think. Don't think. Just go. Go. Keep going.

I turned and went back. It had only been a few yards.

But in the darkness, there was nothing. I'd thought I could see the messed up leaves, churned earth, but no. The night was too thick. The mist a damp veil.

Feeling around on the ground yielded nothing. Not even my keys. I'd thought I might at least find my keys. They had to be here. Had to be here somewhere.

A small voice nattered at my brain.

I heeded that small voice and started moving again, crawling along beneath the safety of the brush, trying to move quietly, listening for the sound of running water or people's voices.

My palms and knees were stabbed with twigs and stones, yet I felt little except the burning need to get home.

Every now and then I would put my hand in something mushy, but I never looked to see what it was. The night grew lighter as the moon rose higher, but the greedy mist hugged the ground as if attempting to swallow the earth.

My teeth chattered. I wanted to stand up and run, warm myself, hurry, but there were too many obstacles hidden in the mist. It would be like asking for another fall. Like sending up a come-and-get-me signal. I was afraid I would weaken if I used too much energy. I didn't want to think about how he had cut my neck, but how could I not? Surely I didn't imagine that liquid warmth running down.

Once or twice I thought I heard a bear. I knew bears didn't live in Central Texas, but I'd never spent the night alone in the forest. What I did know was a pair of glowing yellow eyes. Staring.

I stopped, tried to control my breathing, tried to be extra quiet in hopes it was only my imagination, but of course I snapped a stick beneath my knee and reality sprang to life. My mind went blank. Panic set in. My body said run so I ran.

And ran.

And the thing disappeared.

Not knowing where the animal had gone was even worse than seeing the yellow eyes. What if it had circled behind me? It might be a cougar or a bobcat, a coyote, or even a wolf. Did wolves live in Texas?

I searched my memory but came up blank. Then I recalled some newsperson saying noise would scare away most any wild animal—noise and light—if only I had my phone with its flashlight app—but all I had were my bloody knees, battered body, one bare foot, and my desperation.

I couldn't make myself yell, or make noise.

It could attract a worse animal than the one I was trying to scare away.

I collapsed on the ground and pulled my knees to my chest, wrapped my arms around my legs and closed my eyes. I give up.

I can't do this. He wins. He's won. I'll lie here until sunup, or until he comes back, until he finds me. Until I—

Everything seemed suddenly still, too quiet. Shouldn't there be crickets, or was the wispy fog masking every sound? When I opened my eyes would I be face to face with a snout full of teeth? Or the smiling rictus of a madman?

My eyes popped open.

Nothing.

Nothing but white, cold, mist.

I felt around for a sharp stick or a rock, anything to make me feel not quite so helpless. In moments I'd found one of each. Just holding them made me feel stronger. I am strong, I told myself. I am.

Muscles growing stiff, bruises aching in the sharp air, I began to crawl again. In my left hand I clutched a jagged stone, in my right, a short, sharp branch. The smell of the mist was the only thing good about this whole place. It was a deep, clean scent. I breathed it in and willed myself to keep going.

After a few minutes, sounds began to return. Was it only my terrified mind that had temporarily shut them out?

Now there were crickets and the stealthy rustlings of small animals. I stopped, but the noises didn't. I felt better. I knew that whatever was there wasn't stalking me or it would have stopped, too.

And then I became aware of another sound.

A sound that made my heart soar.

It was the sound of water bubbling along a rocky bed. I was nearing the stream.

I continued creeping, restraining myself from rushing toward the sound. Instead, I hung back, studying the area from beneath the foliage, from beneath the cover of the mist. Somehow, I had to get up the nerve to cross the stream again.

After a few minutes, I grew so cold my muscles began to cramp. I had to get moving. If I was close, he might be close, too.

An owl hooted softly and the hair on my neck rose in response.

I thought I could smell charred wood, but he had never even lit the campfire. He'd only used the fire starter to scare me.

Standing, I carefully worked a cramp out of my calf and made my way along the edge of the stream. It wasn't wide, I could see the other bank and smell the scent of someone's campfire. I didn't think it was still going, I couldn't hear the crackle of flames, but I was almost certain the odor was fresh.

It occurred to me that I could be going the wrong direction, away from the place where my car was parked. Could I be fooling myself? Kids had campfires everywhere near the lake. This could be an entirely different place.

I began to doubt myself completely. In Girl Scouts all those years ago, I'd learned the best thing to do if lost in the woods was to sit still and wait for rescue. But if I sat still out here, he might find me before any rescuer. No one even expected me back except for Lana. She would notice if I didn't call soon. Besides, my mind was growing as foggy as the night. My body wanted to lie down and rest. Go to sleep. I knew that wasn't good.

I trundled along, arguing with myself in my head. At least moving kept me warmer. That was the best reason to keep going—

And then I was there. Right across the stream from where I'd started. I could see the little spot where he'd laid the blanket. There was no sign of it now, though.

I hid behind a juniper bush. My car should be nearby. I imagined it sitting there, wrapped in fog. Anxiety gripped me and for a few seconds I could do nothing but shiver. Then I took a deep breath, stepped into the water, and bit back a scream. It was cold before, but now it was downright frigid.

I made it across the stream in half a dozen sliding steps. I needed to come up with a plan in case he was sitting there in his Mustang, waiting. I'd stowed my purse under the front seat of my Nissan and stuck the keys down into my pocket.

But of course my keys weren't there anymore. Either the key ring had fallen out when he yanked my pants down (my mind shied away from that image as if it were a snake), or he'd found them and taken them with him.

I fell to my knees and crawled out onto the muddy bank trying to keep my body sheltered behind the low bushes edging the little postage stamp "beach." I'd made it back, made it all the way back, but even if my Nissan sat there, beneath the mist, there was no way to get inside without that key. No way to start the engine—

A fragment of memory struck me like a hammer; there *was* another key; a second key in a magnetic box under the front fender. It had been a Christmas joke-gift from my big sister almost two years earlier when I was still in high school. She'd said she'd grown tired of rescuing me every time I locked my keys in my car.

Oddly enough, I'd never had to use it since then. As if just acknowledging my forgetfulness had helped me overcome it.

Would it still be under the fender after all this time? Could it possibly have clung there that long? Yes, my mind insisted. It will be there. Unless Preston saw the box when he changed the tire—*or when he was slashing it.*

Only one way to find out.

I rose to my feet using the rough trunk of a cottonwood to help me. I walked hunched over and apelike across the small clearing, still holding my stone and my stick.

My little Nissan appeared out of the mist like a miracle. Even if he's flattened the tires again, I will drive it out of here. My dad's face tried to creep into my mind—buying me those new tires had been one of the last independent things he had done.

I straightened my spine and prayed the monster wasn't nearby, watching.

The owl hooted again and I almost fainted, my rage fading along with my courage.

THE KEY

In the clearing, the mist reflected the moonlight so brightly it seemed like day instead of night. I had hoped it would afford me a bit of cover as I crossed the parking area; instead, I felt like an actor in the spotlight.

There was nothing else to do, though. If I went slowly enough, I thought I might be able to crawl up to the driver's side and feel around under the fender. If the key was still there, I might be able to get into the car without anyone seeing me.

I clenched my teeth and began to crawl again.

I needn't have worried.

There were no other vehicles in the small turnaround.

A puff of air escaped my lips as I dropped my stick and rock. Hearing those floating voices must have really frightened him. I knelt beside the Nissan and ran my hands under the driver's side fender. Nothing.

In desperation, I stuck my head under the car and shoved my arm into the wheel well as far as it would go.

Thick mud coated the curved area inside the fender.

Behind me, a twig snapped.

I froze.

Nothing moved.

I swiveled my head around, one hand pressing the center of my chest, ragged breaths burning the back of my throat. I didn't think he would leave me alive if he found me again. No way I'd be that lucky.

That thought broke my paralysis.

I jammed my hand under the fender once more. Hooking my fingers into claws, I scraped at the fresh mud and the hardened mud and just when I felt certain the little metal box must have been knocked off at some point, there it was, just a shape, buried deep beneath a layer of crusty muck.

I dug it out with my fingernails. I'd forgotten how tiny and flat it was. No wonder it had stayed on. The mud had probably anchored it in place.

By the time I got it out from under the fender I'd broken three fingernails, one down to the bloody quick, but I barely noticed. I had the distinct turtle-without-a-shell feeling of being watched.

The key box had become so encased in mud it might as well have been sealed shut at the factory. With a little cry, I dug at the seam with my strong thumbnail, attempting to pry it open, so afraid the treasure wouldn't be there after all.

When my thumbnail broke off, I felt around on the ground for my rock or the sharp stick I'd dropped.

The owl glided overhead. Was it the same one? I knew nothing about nocturnal birds of prey but this one seemed to have taken a special interest in me. Dear God, I began to pray, you've got me this far, please help me just a little more. I know I should have listened to that small voice that kept telling me not to come here with him, but I didn't heed it and now I'm in a bind. I really need your help. I need a mira—

My hand found a sharp stick and with a sob I began to stab the edge of the tiny box. The mud had turned to cement. No wonder some people built houses out of this stuff, my tortured mind whispered.

The point of the stick broke and the box fell from my hand and disappeared into the thick ground mist. In frustration I stomped my foot and felt it connect with the thin metal. I stomped it again and again, tears building in my throat, until I felt rather than heard, a minute crack. I reached down with both hands, scrabbling along the ground, until I found it again.

I snatched it up and sure enough, I'd crushed the edge a tiny bit. Just enough to see that there was indeed a spare car key, waiting, just like the old TV ad had promised.

I found another stick and forced the gap until it opened far enough to let the key fall into my open palm.

Salvation.

A miracle.

Thank you, God, thank you. I unlocked the car, pulled the door open, and crawled into the driver's seat. The key went into the ignition smoothly. I started the engine and began to sob. In a flash I reversed, jamming on the brakes at the last second to keep from backing off into the hidden stream.

My foot juddered on the accelerator. I seemed to have no control over my frozen extremities. Why didn't he disable my car? Stab the tires again on his way past? Were there people here, right here, watching him? Or had he lost the knife in the woods? What I wouldn't give to have that knife now, to take to the police.

Wait.

I have to go to the police?

What will they do, will they go and find him, arrest him? Will I have to identify him in a lineup or go to the hospital, have pictures taken? Oh my God, will my picture be taken? I don't want the whole campus talking about it, about how stupid I'd been to come out here. But yes. He raped me. He would have killed me if not for the voices floating over the water.

What happens when you report a rape? Is it his word against mine?

I turned the heater on high and felt around in the passenger seat until I located the sweater I'd left there. Once I pulled it around me, I felt more normal.

I drove back down the lane to the cut off. In a minute, I'd be out on the highway headed toward my apartment. I longed for my phone, I needed to call Lana and I needed to call the police. Regardless of what I had to do, I would turn him in. I had to. I was strong. No matter what—I could not let him get away with this.

Mind made up, my breathing slowed, and my foot stopped jumping up and down on the accelerator. I began to feel sleepy, tired. Only ten minutes to town. If I just followed the road I would come to the highway. Pretty sure I'd know which way to go from there.

And I did. When I turned off of Telephone Road, I barely even noticed. It would haunt me later, but just then, all I saw in my rearview mirror was the back of a sign for a red dirt road.

Once on the highway, the mist disappeared except for the low-lying areas, and then it was like driving through milk froth. But it didn't matter. I was okay. I'd made it out. I was alive. I'd made it back to my car alive.

I hated to think of the look on Mom's face, the one that would say why did you go with him? We thought you were grown up, we thought you were an adult, a college student, not a stupid kid.

When I called her, she would probably jump in the car and rush right up here, she might even beg me to leave school. Come home. I hated to do that to my mom. She had enough to worry about with Dad.

Maybe I'd better think about this.

At least I'm not lost in the woods anymore.

I let my foot remain on the accelerator while my mind dashed in a dozen different directions. Every car light terrified me. I knew he would show up in my mirror at any moment, that he'd been lying in wait, watching for me to leave the parking area and start back home. I couldn't let go of the idea it was still a part of the game.

The black highway stretched out before me like the humps of a sea monster, visible only when it rose between the mist-shrouded dips. My eyes wanted to close. It grew harder and harder to concentrate. I was alive but so very tired. I started my incantations again, my prayers, "Our Father who art in Heaven, hallowed be thy name..."

I don't know how many repetitions it took to get me back to town, but before long, I found myself on campus. I looked for signs directing me to the Police Department. Of course I'd seen it on our orientation tour, but in my agitation, I couldn't locate the correct street. All the curvy avenues seemed to lead in circles. *You can't get there from here*, my tired mind insisted. I giggled. It felt like hysteria.

In desperation, I went around one more curve and there it was.

Almost sobbing, I pulled into a slanted space as close to the front door as possible. It was marked blue for handicapped, but I didn't care. I felt handicapped. The night seemed pitch-black even though tall sodium arcs lit the parking lot. Shadows loomed across the building from all sides. The thick glass doors looked as if they might be locked. *Do police stations ever close?*

I'd driven out of the mist. Now the night was hazy but no longer wrapped in white. *Should I have gone to the city police station downtown?* I grasped the inside door with my bruised fingers and broken nails. It took a supreme act of courage to pull that handle. More than anything I wanted to put the car in reverse and drive back to the apartment, but how would I even get in? My apartment key hung on my missing key ring.

Maybe I could get a key from the Community Advisor, go in my safe little apartment, stand under a scalding shower, climb into my little bed and cover my head. But not like this. *Look at me. Look at my face.*

I thought of Blue Bear sitting on my bed where I'd left him. My heart sank. Blue Bear belonged to another lifetime, to another girl. What would Jimmy think if he knew the things Preston had done, the things he'd made me do? Would his kind face change? Would the look in his eyes be the same?

I yanked the key from the ignition. I wasn't stupid. I knew I had to report this and the sooner the better. I couldn't go to the apartment office looking like this, besides, what if Preston had a disease? God. What if I got pregnant? Oh, God. No. I prayed a silent monotonous prayer—please, no, God, please, no—as I stepped out and crossed the sidewalk to the entrance.

By the time I got within shouting distance of the doors, I no longer felt sleepy, now I was running—shuffling might be a better description—I no longer thought about having only one shoe. I didn't think about my swollen eye or the cut on my neck or the scrapes all over my arms and face. I didn't even think about the condition of my wet clothing. I just thought about safety. Get me out of the empty night. Lord, just get me inside where there are people with uniforms and badges.

My hands clutched the handles of the heavy glass doors and I pulled them open and rushed inside. "*Help.*" My voice came out ragged and low. "Help me, someone."

A dispatcher glanced up from her console. My appearance etched her face into a mask of shock.

"Oh, honey." She came around the counter and wrapped me in her arms. "What happened?"

My legs weakened and I knew they were about to buckle.

She led me to a row of chairs against the wall. "Chuck," she called. "Need a little help here."

I saw a second head pop up above a different console. Chuck pulled off his headset and came around the counter, too. They were both older than me, not middle aged but not young. The woman had fluffy blonde hair and a comfortable bosom. She pressed me back into the chair and looked around at Chuck.

He was short and stout like a bulldog on two legs. I felt safe with them. "Let me get you some water," he said. And all of a sudden I realized how parched and raw my throat felt. Water sounded like the best thing in the whole wide world.

I nodded.

But the woman—her nametag read D. Prine—shook her head and frowned at Chuck. "Not until she's been examined at the hospital. There could be evidence."

Oh, my God. Evidence. In my mouth? Did they know what he'd done? Could they tell that easily? I closed my eyes and slumped back in the chair. No water. My throat burned. I licked my lips, tasted blood. My bottom lip felt huge. Twice the size it should've been.

D. Prine instructed Chuck to sit beside me and not let me slide off the chair. Then she walked back around the counter, picked up a phone receiver, and spoke into it. In a matter of minutes a patrol officer arrived followed closely by paramedics.

Through the glass door I could see an ambulance.

There were no lights or sirens.

The officer who came in told me he would follow me to the hospital. Then he took my car key and purse and told me not to worry. I wondered if he would move my Nissan to a proper parking slot. But I didn't have time to ask. I was being loaded onto a gurney and whisked out to the ambulance where an IV was inserted into my arm. They covered me with a funny silver blanket. No one asked what happened. Maybe they'd seen it all before.

We arrived at the ER after what seemed like a lifetime. They wheeled me into an exam room and a nurse appeared. She didn't look me in the eye, just took the IV bag and attached it to a pole bristling with hooks. The paramedic who had inserted the IV in the ambulance spoke for the first time. "I hope you'll be okay, miss."

And that's when the tears began. It was out of my hands now. I began to wish I'd gone to the apartment after all. I'd be in my bed by now. I'd be clean and holding Blue Bear, the memento from my other life.

I forced that thought away. Away from Jim and the memory of the carnival.

I closed my eyes.

The nurse left without speaking.

I lay in something like a cubicle. Trauma, I supposed. Trauma. Just like in a movie.

I drifted away. My stomach felt a little calmer. Maybe they put something in the IV to make me feel better. I hoped they did. I wanted to go to sleep and not wake up. Or rather, I wanted to wake up and find it had just been a bad dream.

"Miss?"

My eyes popped open. For a moment, the man leaning over me seemed familiar. Then I remembered. The police officer D. Prine had called. Over his shoulder, I saw another officer, a woman. Thank, God. Thank you, God. There's no way I could tell this story to a man. Especially not one the age of my own father.

The woman stepped up. "My name is Officer Jensen. Do you know where you are?"

I looked at her face. It wasn't unkind. "I'm in the ER," I said.

"I got raped. In the woods. By Preston Stevensen. We both go to UT."

She flipped open a sliver metal clipboard with a lid and started writing. I could see a white legal-size tablet. "Okay," she said. "First, tell me your name."

The other officer produced my purse.

"Marlena Matthews of Window, Texas," I said. "I– I agreed to go on a picnic with him, with Preston. But then he held a knife to my throat and raped me and he hit me with his fist and I lost my phone and my car keys but I had a spare in a magnetic box and I need to call Lana. She'll be worried—"

Officer Jensen held up her hand to slow me down.

I tasted tears and was surprised to find the edge of my sheet wet with them. "Where is my car key?" I looked at the male officer whose nameplate read T. Garza.

He held up my purse. "I tucked it in here."

I reached for it and he gave it to me. I held it against my chest as if it were Blue Bear. "Can I– how can I call my friend? She's expecting me to ca-" But I couldn't finish that sentence. When I imagined myself telling Lana what had happened, my voice disintegrated.

I sensed rather than saw Officer Garza leave the room. Once again, I closed my eyes. "Can I have a drink of water?"

A different voice answered. "I'm sorry, honey. Not just yet."

When I opened my eyes again. A new nurse was the only one in the room. She pulled a stool close to the bed and held out her hand. "I'm Elva Ramsey. I'm your S.A.N.E. nurse."

"Sane?" I asked. "To keep me from going insane?"

She smiled and I felt the weight of the night shift a little. "Sort of." She explained that S.A.N.E. stood for Sexual Assault Nurse Examiner. She held up a box marked Rape Kit.

I closed my eyes again.

Rain.

Mist.

Towering trees.

Thick brush.

Cold.

Dark.

I will do this. I have to go through with it.

She lightly touched my hand with her fingertips. "It will be all right," she said. "I've done this before. Just remind yourself you are not the only one, okay?"

I nodded.

She began by taking pictures of my face, my clothing, the scrapes and cuts on my arms and hands, even my feet. Then she told me to lean my head back. She was extremely gentle when she touched my chin to make me tilt back even further. "I'm sorry," she said. "I have to make sure I document this correctly for your court case."

"What about my neck?" I asked. "Why are you taking so many pictures there?"

She stopped. "You have a jagged cut," she said. "No, don't touch it. The doc said he would be in to stitch it up as soon as I'm finished with you."

I felt my senses slip when she said that. Could it really be that bad? Why didn't I bleed out? Why didn't I die?

"Here, look." Nurse Ramsey turned the camera screen around so I could see. I saw a ragged Z shaped cut on one side of my neck. My shirt was stiff with blood.

"Oh," I said. "Zorro. I didn't know it was a Z." My hand went to my throbbing cheek. My eye felt strange, too. I had to turn my head to the side to see her.

"If it's any consolation," she said. "All these things will heal quickly."

I nodded. What about the other things, I wanted to ask. Will they heal, too? A memory of Jim in his turquoise underwear came unbidden. That had been special, so special. Now this.

Nurse Elva continued to talk and ask me questions. She asked about my medical and sexual history, any medications I was on, like birth control, and if I'd ever been tested for sexually transmitted diseases.

I answered honestly. And tried not to cry.

"You know the officers went directly to school to look for him. The one who did this."

My brain almost exploded. My heart began to pound. "Will they bring him here?" I tried to sit up. What if he saw me? What would happen?

"No, no, no," she put a steadying hand on my shoulder. "Don't worry about that. They will take him straight to the station." She took out a pair of blunt tipped scissors that were bent at a forty-five degree angle. "You're safe here, Marlena. Don't worry. I've got to get those wet, bloody clothes off for evidence." She unfolded a hospital gown and laid it near my head. As soon as she'd finished removing my clothing with scissors, she bagged them in plastic bags. Even my remaining fingernails were clipped and bagged for evidence.

She helped me into the gown. My muscles had stiffened up into hard knots. She explained that she would have to swab my mouth, throat, vagina, and anus for DNA evidence. She tried to be gentle, but when I got up the courage to look at the plastic collection bags, some of the swabs were red.

Next came the pubic comb.

She also swabbed the scratches on my arms and swabbed and took pictures of a bite mark on my shoulder that I didn't even know about.

I felt like a used car.

When I had to turn over onto my stomach, that's when the nausea came. I suspected it was just from the humiliation of it all. Having every part of my body photographed and swabbed felt almost as degrading as what he'd done. It certainly took a lot longer.

"I'm sorry," Nurse Elva kept saying. "You will be all right. I've seen worse, I promise. You will survive this. You will be stronger as a result." She helped me turn back over.

Every part of my body ached.

"Here's the water you requested." She handed me a paper cup of ice water with a bendy straw. It must have been on the table all along.

It was the best thing I'd ever tasted in my life, but as soon as it hit the back of my throat, I started to gag.

Nurse Elva gave me a plastic basin. "Rinse and spit," she said. "Just like at the dentist." She gave me a separate cup of room temperature water with no ice.

I took the second cup and rinsed and gargled and spit and rinsed and gargled and spit again. It took three cups of water before my mouth felt halfway clean. "May I brush my teeth? Please?"

The nurse handed me a small silver blister pack with a single large white pill in it. "Take this first," she instructed.

"What is it?"

"Emergency contraception." She had no expression as she popped the pill out of its package and handed it to me.

I placed it on my tongue and gulped the ice water.

"Now," she said. "Officer Jensen will be back in to finish her report. Is there someone I can call to be with you?"

To be with me? No. Well, maybe Joanna, if she had made it back from her own holiday trip. I wished Lana could come, but she was too far away. She still expected a call, though. "I need to call my friend back home. She's the only one who knew about my meeting with him tonight. She didn't want me to go." I thought back to our previous conversation. "I think she had a feeling something like this would happen." Tears clogged my voice again.

Nurse Elva busied herself with sealing, labeling, and repacking the rape kit. "Is there anyone here in town you would like to call?"

I wiped my face. Cleared my throat. "I could call my roommate. I just—" I turned my head away as a new freshet of tears came. "I feel so stupid. Why did I go? I didn't want to go—"

Nurse Elva patted my leg with one hand while she pulled the phone over with the other hand. "Here, do you know the number?"

I nodded, although I really had to stop and think about it. I had the numbers stored in my cell phone. I never called them from memory.

Joanna answered on the first ring.

I took a deep breath and told her I had been raped.

"Was it Preston? He acted so weird in the parking lot that day, trying to force you to go to breakfast."

"Yes," I said. "I'll tell you more later, I just wanted you to know why I wouldn't be home tonight."

Joanna made me tell her the number of my trauma room. "I'll be there in ten minutes," she said. "Do you want me to call your mom or dad?"

I assured her that she didn't have to come down, that I would be fine. "I'll call my folks," I said. "But I appreciate the offer." It made me feel much better knowing she would be there if I needed her.

The call exhausted me. I lay back on the bed and made my fingers dial Lana's number. She answered immediately. "Marlie! Why are you calling me from a hospital number? Are you all right?"

This time, I couldn't say anything. I could only sit and blubber. Nurse Elva took pity on me, took the receiver from my hand,

and explained to Lana what had happened. She didn't go into detail, of course, and as soon as I pulled myself together, she patted my shoulder and handed back the phone.

"Lan?" My voice threatened to collapse again. "I'm so stupid. I should have listened to you." I couldn't say anymore.

She said, "I'm putting stuff in my overnight bag. I'll be there in a few hours. Can I call your mom?"

"No. I'll call her. You know you don't have to come. They're only keeping me for observation. I'll be released tomorrow."

"Stop talking," Lana said. She'd been my best friend and confidante for so long she could get away with saying things like that. "You sure I can't call your mom? She might want to ride up with me."

I shook my head, thinking of my mother's face if she saw me like this. "No," I said. "Don't tell her. She has too much on her plate right now taking care of my dad. I—I'm going to call Carrie first."

Lana sighed. "Okay. But I don't like keeping secrets. If you or Carrie don't tell them before I get back, then I will." She hesitated and I could hear her opening drawers and rattling clothes hangers. "Should I call Jim Allan?"

"Oh, my God, no. Please don't do that. He wouldn't understand why I went with Preston. I have to tell him so that it will make sense."

"All right," she agreed. "But like I said, I don't like keeping secrets."

"Don't worry. If this goes to trial, everyone will know every little detail." The thought made me nauseous. I had to grab the plastic basin again.

"I'm hanging up, now," Lana said. "I've got to fill up my car and then I will be on the road. You just rest and do what the nurses tell you, okay?"

"Thanks, Mama Bear." I tried to joke like before, but this

time it came out all wrong and I really did throw up. Afterward, I felt a little better.

Nurse Elva gave me a wet cloth to wipe my lips, and then she opened the curtain. Officer Jensen was leaning on the counter at the nurse's station, drinking what appeared to be a cup of coffee. Apparently she'd been waiting.

"Now, I have to go," Nurse Elva said. "I know you are hurting in more ways than one." She paused until I looked at her. "Promise me you won't beat yourself up over this." She held the rape kit box under her arm. "You did nothing wrong." She stuck a business card into my palm. "This is the number for the Rape Crisis Center. Don't lose it. They have wonderful counselors there."

"Thank you." I squeezed her fingers.

She squeezed back. "You *will* be okay. Different. But okay." She made me look her in the eye again. "Do you hear what I'm telling you?"

I nodded, but I didn't really understand.

"You will be changed. But it's not a bad thing. Don't let this define you."

Oh. Okay. Now, I understand. She's trying to prepare me to fall apart. Or not fall apart. "I understand." I wanted to thank her again but Officer Jensen was there, taking control of the box, opening her silver clipboard.

"Just a few more questions," she said. "We'll compare your statement to his statement, get a DNA from him, compare it with this," she indicated the box with a nod of her head, "then we'll go from there."

I took a deep breath and told her everything, beginning with how he'd shown up at the apartment that one morning, how mad he'd gotten, how I'd thought I would be safe meeting at the restaurant, then the slashed tires, and everything else.

As I spoke, her mouth grew thinner and thinner until her

whole face had hardened. After I told her that my phone had gone missing, along with my key ring, which held my car keys and apartment key, her head came up.

"Could he have them, the keys?"

I nodded. "He could. He was chasing me when I lost them."

"Your roommate will need to get the locks changed. The university maintenance department will do it." She wrote something else in her note pad. "Of course that needs to be done immediately." She looked up when Joanna entered the curtained cubicle as if on cue.

"Oh, Marlena."

I burst into huge braying sobs that threatened to choke me to death.

She crossed the small room and leaned down, taking me into her arms, pressing her lips to the top of my head.

"Thank you for coming," I said. "But you have to go back and get the locks changed."

I retold the whole story, with Officer Jensen interrupting from time to time for clarification of details. I ended by showing them my broken, bloody nails and fingertips from where I'd had to scratch the spare key out from under the wheel well.

Joanna clasped my fingers gently. "I never guessed he would do anything like this or I never would have taken you to the gallery that night. I am so, so sorry."

I shook my head. "He set me up. I tried to be careful, meeting him in a public place, but he arranged it so I'd have to go with him." I patted her hand gently. "I'll be okay. I will." Deep down inside I believed it. Later, in the coming months, it would become much harder to remember that feeling. Especially when I had to face him in court.

15

PRESTON

Across town, in his private apartment, Preston Stevensen lay back in a frothy bath scrolling through Marlena's phone. He didn't care if it fell in the water. He'd already washed his hair and his body, burned his bloody clothes in the fireplace, and when he finished with his bath—and with destroying Marlena's phone—he would scrape out the ashes and take it all down to the lake for a little midnight boat ride.

His dad had made sure he had a ski boat on an electric lift. He'd always given Preston over-the-top gifts to make up for the fact that he couldn't seem to stand being in his presence. Preston had figured that out by the time he turned twelve and found himself living in boarding school.

He wiped water from his eyes and scrolled through Marlena's messages.

When he came to the ones from Jimmy Allan, a red fog fell over his vision. It made him wish it had taken her longer to die. After he'd cut her with the knife, she'd gone slack. Just like the other girl. Only that girl hadn't fought back. She'd died with a gurgle. It had been so easy.

Preston liked the fact that the first one would have been Joanna's original roommate. It felt like symmetry. It made things make sense. Fate, or some crap like that.

Now if he could only come up with a plan to get to Joanna, too. She was a tricky one, very self-possessed. Unfriendly. Didn't seem to trust a soul. Getting her in his car would take a lot of work. But worth it, totally worth it.

He had a sudden urge to get all the evidence gathered up. He'd flung the knife and campfire starter into the lake when he crossed the bridge coming back to the apartment complex, but now he had to get rid of this phone and her keys.

His finger poked at the tiny keypad on her phone. Some of her text messages were quite intriguing. Might as well have a little more fun, he thought.

"Jimmy," he wrote in a reply to one of her texts. "I'm sorry. We can't see each other anymore. Please don't try to contact me. We had a great weekend, but I'm in love with someone else. I was wrong to think I could forget him that easily." He pressed send and then opened his hand and let the phone fall into the bath water. "Oops."

He stepped out of the tub, dried quickly, then took the fireplace scoop and scraped all the ashes and bits of unburned clothing into the metal ash can. He retrieved the phone from the bottom of the tub, pried it open, removed the battery and SIM card, then he carried everything down to the boat slip. It took only a few minutes walk.

The boat started right up. Once he got rid of all the evidence, there would be nothing to link him to Marlena's death. The authorities would think it was another random rape gone too far. And if they found his DNA on her, he would just convince them they'd had a "date" after he happened upon her with the flat tire. The guy in the garage would be able to corroborate the fact that they'd been together willingly. Piece of cake, he thought rubbing the slight lump at his temple. No problem.

When he arrived back at his apartment after disposing of the evidence, Preston was stunned to find a note on his door telling him to contact the campus police department.

Preston ripped the note in half and threw it in the garbage. Then he took a damp towel, cleaned the inside of the fireplace, and tossed it in the washing machine with the other towels from his bath. He hadn't tried to burn his leather sneakers, one of those he had tossed out the car window doing seventy down the highway on the other side of town. The other one had gone into a dumpster on a rural road on this side of town. He'd been a very busy boy. But in the back of his mind a question:

Had her body been found already?

Impossible.

On the other hand, what else could explain the cryptic note on the door?

16

HOME

Lana was sitting beside my bed the next time I woke. True to her word, she'd made the four-hour trip in about three. When she first saw me, I think she cried even more than I did. The nurse had to reassure her I would be all right. Of course I hadn't been able to warn her about how I looked when I spoke to her on the phone. And I didn't have my own phone so I couldn't snap a pic and send it—although I guess that wouldn't have been in good taste anyway.

She sat beside me in a straight-backed chair until Joanna came back. "The locks have been replaced," she said. She tried to make Lana go back with her, but Lana insisted on staying in the room with me. The nurse showed her how to fold out the chair into a recliner-bed, and then she brought her a pillow and a white hospital blanket.

They kept me the rest of the night and part of the next morning for observation and then the doctor released me with a prescription for a mild pain reliever.

Joanna had ridden the bus to the hospital so that she could drive my car home for me. Lana followed us in her car. It felt strange being back in my car. I thought it was very kind of

Officer Jensen to bring it to the hospital parking lot. The police had confiscated my bad tire—the one I hadn't had a chance to repair—so they could compare the slash marks if they ever found the knife Preston had used on me.

We pulled into the parking space nearest our apartment door and prepared to get out. Parking spaces were not assigned at our complex, but if you didn't have the University Parking ID on the windshield you could get ticketed or even towed. The complex tried to take care of their students. Visitors were expected to park on the street.

Of course I was glad Joanna parked as close to the door as possible. In the back of my mind, Preston lurked around every corner. After leaving the hospital, I used Joanna's phone to call Detective Lapuli. She—being the organized individual she was —had actually entered his info into her phone from his business card. She had the great idea to call him.

"He's already investigating a possibly-missing student who should have been my roomie. Don't you think he'd be interested in this as well?"

I had no idea if he'd be interested, but I didn't have the energy to discuss it. Joanna acted as my brain at that moment. Whatever she wanted me to do, I would do.

When I told the detective everything that had happened, I also gave him a little history of how Preston had become something of a stalker when I stopped going out with him.

"I'm glad you called," he said. "It's probably just another coincidence, you getting hurt, Mariah Leathers going missing, but it's worth a look. Nothing ventured, nothing gained as the old saying goes."

After expressing his sympathy for my plight, the detective put me on hold and did some checking. I couldn't believe it when he said Preston had turned himself in willingly at the request of the officers who had left the note on his door. "But here's the bad part," he went on. "Even though they took him downtown, the kid bonded out almost before his paperwork was complete. He didn't even call his parents to come and get him. He actually had his own attorney."

I told him how wealthy Preston's family seemed to be. "But he's an absolute monster," I said. "He really tried to kill me in those woods."

"I'm going to visit the city police and the chief of UTPD to make certain they know I'll be investigating your case as well." Rustling some papers, he said, "Detective Smith is the one handling it at the moment, but since it's early, I know he won't mind if I lighten his load." He cleared his throat. "You call me anytime. We will look at getting a restraining order right away. I'll also take a look at all the evidence."

I thanked him profusely. Even though he had struck near panic into my heart when I came upon him outside our apartment door that day, having him on my side now seemed like a very good thing.

Joanna unlocked the door and handed me my new key. "I am so sorry this happened to you. I wish I could kick that prick right in the ba—"

Her diatribe was interrupted when Lana said, "That makes two of us."

I smiled. "I am so fortunate to have you two in my life."

Lana hugged me, and then spontaneously hugged Joanna, too. "And I'm glad you've got Joanna here since I'll have to leave soon."

I crossed the threshold first. Once inside I turned to them. "Okay. That's enough now. I'm not an invalid. I'm fine. I'll be fine." I think I kept the tears out of my voice pretty well. Only Lana, who'd known me since grade school, gave me a second look, checking, I suppose, to see if I would fall apart after making my bold statement.

Joanna broke the tension. "You're right. I know you're strong. It's just..." she looked at my face. I don't think she meant to, but her eyes went there anyway, only for a second but it was enough.

I sighed. "I know. I look like hell. He really did a number on me, didn't he?" You should see the other parts, I thought. You want to know about bruises, and cuts? This face is nothing.

But I didn't say any of that. I didn't want their pity, or anyone's pity. I just wanted to get back to normal. If there was such a thing.

"So," Joanna said. "I'm going to Dos Tacos for takeout. What'll it be? Soft or crispy?"

I caught Lana's confused expression. "Dos Tacos only serves tacos and the trimmings. But they have two kinds, soft shell or crispy—thus the name." I looked at Joanna. "I'll have soft veggie, please." It seemed like a good distraction.

Joanna nodded. "And a large diet Coke with vanilla?"

"You know me too well. How about you, Lan?" I pulled out my wallet to give Joanna some money. "Thank God he didn't get my purse." I thought of all the things I would've had to replace like my driver's license, social security card, student ID, my one and only credit card. "I guess I'll go to the phone store today."

That did it. Thinking of my phone and the thousands of photos, notes, and contacts I would never be able to replace made my emotions spiral out of control. "Do you think my stuff is in the cloud? I mean, do you think it can be downloaded to a new phone?"

Joanna nodded. "I'm sure it can if you backed it up to the cloud in settings."

I sniffled. "Believe it or not, I think I did." I fumbled a tissue from a box on the coffee table.

"Whoohoo!" Lana said. "I'm proud of you, girlfriend." She sat down on the sofa and pulled out her own device. "I'm going to do that on my phone right now. I've never bothered before."

I thought of her night with Dash and how this could have easily been her instead of me. Did we all need to start carrying a weapon when we went out with a new guy? I thought how satisfying it would have been to pepper spray Preston when he'd thrown me to the ground.

"Too bad the police couldn't track it. They tried, but the battery must have already been removed or damaged in some way." An image of Preston lounging against his car in the parking lot the morning I stepped out for a run wiggled its way into my brain. It was immediately replaced with an image of his thunderous face looming over me, the knife coming closer—

"Honey?" Lana touched my shoulder.

I looked up, surprised to find myself sitting on the other end of the small sofa near her.

She held her phone toward me. "I just asked if you would like to use my phone to call your mom now?"

I glanced around our small, neat apartment. Apparently, Joanna had left and I didn't even notice. "Call Mom?"

Lana nodded. "You know you have to tell her at some point. I mean, if you don't, someone else might. What if she's already trying to call your phone?"

I stared at her. "Oh. I didn't think of that."

Her next words came out kind but firm. "Did you call Carrie at least?"

My eyes sought the floor. I didn't want to lie to her, but I just couldn't seem to make myself tell Carrie or my mother. No matter what anyone said, I felt so ashamed I couldn't stand the thought of them knowing.

Lana stood and took my hand. I saw her frown when I winced.

It hurt to stand. Every bone and muscle in my body hurt when I moved.

She pulled me to my bedroom and stood me in front of the

full-length mirror on my closet door. "Look." She actually put her hands on the sides of my head and made me look at my reflection. "He did this. He hurt you. Almost killed you." She tilted my chin up so I was forced to see the bandage covering half my neck and throat. "You will make him pay. I doubt if you're the first one he's done this to, probably won't be the last either. You have to stop him. But to do that, you will need your family."

Tears were suddenly streaming down my face, sluicing across the bandage at my neck, highlighting my swollen cheek and black eye. My fingers went to my mouth—my smashed and bruised lips—and touched them gently. She's right. He did this. That bastard.

"You're right," I said. "I can't let him get away with it, but—"

Lana pulled me to the bathroom and turned on the shower to let it warm up. "But what, sweetie?"

"But what's to keep him from coming after me again?" I heard the dread in my voice. I'm sure she did, too.

She wrapped her arms around me. "He can't come near you. The detective said he's getting a restraining order, remember? If he comes within a hundred feet of this place he goes straight to jail, no pass go, no collect two hundred bucks, and no bonding out."

I nodded. "Yeah. A piece of paper. Sure. That will probably work."

Lana took my soft brush from the counter and began to brush my hair gently.

"Ow!" I couldn't help it. "Sorry. He—um—he pulled some out."

"Oh, dammit, I'm so sorry. I can't—is there anything I can—"

I took the brush from her hand. "You've done plenty. More than enough." I smoothed the bristles down the length of my hair. "I'll take it from here." I ushered her out of the small room. "I'll be all right, I promise."

When she went out, I closed the door, leaned my back against it, and let the tears flow once more. I'll be all right. Sure. Sure I will. You bet.

I looked down at Lana's phone in my palm. Then I reached into the shower and turned off the faucet. This could take a while. I pressed Carrie's number from memory. When she answered, I took a deep breath and began to talk.

Carrie didn't interrupt except when I went too fast for her to understand. Mostly, she simply listened and cried.

"Oh, Sis," she said at last. "I can't believe it. I'm so sorry—"

"No," I said. "Don't be. It isn't pity I want." I closed my eyes. "It's— I only want—" But I couldn't say what I wanted. It was too simple, too ridiculous, too impossible. I wanted to turn back time. To yesterday. To Jim. To Window. To anytime before the picnic with *him*.

Carrie told me not to worry, that everything would be okay. Easy words to say, but before we hung up, she made me promise to call Mom. "If you don't, I will," she muttered. It sounded pretty close to what Lana had said. So I told her I would call Mom immediately. And I did.

She took it much better than I expected. She didn't break down or anything. "I need to come up there," she said. "You need your mother."

"It's okay, Mama. I promise. Lana and Joanna are taking care of me. But what would you think if I took the rest of this semester off?" I don't know where that idea came from, it just occurred to me out of the blue.

"I think that might be a good idea."

I inhaled slowly. "Me too. I just can't imagine going to class right now. What if I saw him on campus? Besides, I wouldn't be able to concentrate. And there's no way I can go to class until my neck and face heal. Meantime, I can help you out with Dad."

Mom sighed. "Only you would think of us at a time like this. But seriously, I don't want to see you give up completely. Maybe you can continue online or something."

"Maybe I can. I'm not giving up. To tell you the truth, I'm just afraid to be here right now. I see his face around every corner." The truth came out. Plain and simple, the way if often does to your mother.

"I'm coming to get you sweetheart. Or better yet, just pack your bags and come back with Lana."

"I will," I said. "That's exactly what I'm going to do. Thanks, Mom. Don't worry. I'll see you tomorrow."

After we hung up, I called Carrie back and told her the news. She sounded as relieved as I felt. Then she had an epiphany. "Come to Denver instead," she said. "I won't take no for an answer. If you go back home, you'll never get back to school. You'll be stuck there, taking care of Dad while Mom works. She won't intend to take advantage of you, but she will be afraid to let you go. Especially if you look as bad as you say."

I told her I'd think about it and call her back. Then I turned the shower on, laid Lana's phone on the counter, and shed my clothes.

I'd been dreading this and looking forward to it all at the same time. The water was warm, not too hot, and it felt wonderful on my back and on my shoulders. The bandage on my neck had been covered with a clear plastic wrap that looked like the same stuff Mom used to wrap my sandwiches in when I was a little girl. I couldn't feel the water there, thank goodness, but everywhere else it felt wonderful. Even on the sore spots on my scalp. I closed my eyes and the water brought it all back...

Rain.

Mist.

Towering trees.

Thick brush.

Cold.

Dark.

I opened my eyes, willed away the images, and then soaped and washed my entire body three times over. Afterward, I carefully washed my hair and rinsed with lukewarm water. I didn't close my eyes again.

When I finally stepped out, the water had run cold but my body felt almost like my own again. Oh, who was I kidding? I hurt all over. My scalp shouted with pain and my skin stung in all the raw, scraped places. I didn't feel normal, and I suspected I never would.

When I tried to remember the fun Jim and I had experienced that night after the dance, exploring each other's bodies and reveling in the pleasure our hands and lips created... I couldn't do it.

I couldn't bring it to my mind at all.

Wrapping my wet hair in a towel, I slipped on my fluffy robe and tied the belt around my waist. I was determined not to show anyone my pain, not even my two best friends.

17

PLANS

By the time I walked into the living area, Joanna had returned with the food. "I called Mom." I handed Lana her phone. "She thinks I should come back home with you." I took a flour tortilla and layered grilled veggies down the center of it. It occurred to me it was the first thing I'd eaten since the one bite of pizza—

My mind slipped away from that image. I could barely stop myself from gagging at the smell of the beautiful red and green peppers peeking out of my folded tortilla.

"Not return to school?" Joanna asked, bringing me back to the conversation.

I shook my head. My towel-turban threatened to fall off. I grabbed it with one hand, balancing my taco in the other. "Look at me," I said. "It will take weeks for these bruises to heal, and well, to be honest, I can't imagine seeing Preston. I'm not going back. I can't. I'll transfer somewhere else, or something."

Lana took her taco to the island separating the small kitchen from the living area. "Marlena..."

I looked at her, waiting.

"I have to leave today." She dipped a chip into the scoop of guacamole on her plate. "I have a big test tomorrow. Of course you can follow me home tonight, but you have to get that other new tire mounted. And what about that?" She pointed at the bandage on my throat.

My hand went to the plastic covered bandage. "What about it? It's one of the main reasons I can't go back. There's no way I can explain what happened without telling the story over and over and he's bound to be there, you know?" I glanced toward the open blinds at the window. "In fact, he could be sitting out there right now, watching us."

Silence enveloped the room as we all looked out toward the parking lot. "Carrie wants me to come to Denver. Maybe that's what I should do. I could stay in the house until this," I touched the edge of the neck bandage, "comes off. You're right, it invites more attention than anything."

Lana shook her head. "No, no, sweetie. That's not what I meant. I agree, you should come home or go to Carrie's like she wants. But what I really meant was, the nurse said you should come back tomorrow and get the bandage changed."

Joanna nodded. "That's right. She did." She took a bite of her crispy taco. "Maybe you should wait to leave after that."

I sat on the sofa and placed my plate on my knees. "I don't– I can't." The words dried up in my throat right along with the suddenly too-thick tortilla. "I'm afraid to go out by myself." I stared down at the taco as if it had some answers.

Both girls set their plates aside and came to sit beside me on the sofa. "You won't be alone," Joanna said. "I'll take you to the hospital tomorrow, then I'll help you pack and take you wherever you want to go."

I buried my face in my hands. "I'm sorry. I can't believe I'm so scared. I just feel so defenseless, even just sitting here. Just knowing he's here, in the same town, at the same school, maybe even on the same street—"

They wrapped me in their arms and vowed I wouldn't be alone, at all.

Then Lana took her phone into the other room and redialed my sister in Colorado. Together they came up with the plan that I would go there as soon as I got my bandage changed the next day. I guess she didn't know I could hear her through the door.

"She's really frightened," Lana told her. "And I don't blame her. You can't believe how he beat her up."

I looked down at the floor so I couldn't see Joanna's face. Then I heard Lana's voice again.

"Yes," she said. "He's out on bond. For all we know he might come after her again, restraining order or not."

Even with my girls right there beside me, I'd never felt so alone in my life. When Lana came back out of my bedroom, I went inside, opened one of the duffle bags I'd brought back from Mom's, dug out my clean pajamas—the ones Carrie had given me when I started school, the ones covered with dancing cats to match my robe—and slipped them over my head.

My right arm would hardly rise above the level of my shoulder. I'd had quite a time washing my hair with one hand, but I knew the pain would be even worse tomorrow, and the next day. That must have been the arm I was fighting with, the one that found the wine bottle, the one I'd used to punch and hit and scratch—

I consciously stopped my mind from going there. Again. I needed to put it out of my head. Tomorrow I would have to decide whether to go south to Window and my Mom's house, or north to Denver where Carrie and Dix ran their own small real estate agency. Regardless of what Lana and Carrie had discussed, I still wasn't sure which place would be best.

Window would be closer to Jimmy. But did I want him to see me like this?

After getting my pajamas on, I went back to the kitchen to

help the girls clean up the remains of our brunch. When I walked in, they stopped talking but still stood with their heads together.

"It's okay," I said. "Whatever you two are discussing, you don't have to hide it. I'm sure it isn't anything I haven't already thought of."

Joanna turned and placed her hands on the edge of the small island. Her posture said it was something serious. "Lana is about to leave, but I'm going to take you to the hospital tomorrow. I'm not going to leave you alone."

Lana interrupted. "I can call and tell the instructor I have to reschedule my test if you need me to. I don't want you to think I'm deserting you."

I shook my head. "Of course not, Lan. You need to go home right now and take care of business."

"But I remember how you and Jimmy took care of me that night Dash scared me so badly."

I couldn't respond to that. I wanted nothing more than to call Jim Allan and tell him what had happened. Ask him to come and get me, rescue me, make me whole again. On the other hand I wanted nothing more than to pretend I'd never met Jim at the carnival that night. That we'd never even fallen in love—or lust—or whatever it was we'd shared. After all this, I could hardly believe it had even happened. Now it felt like nothing but a dream, a sweet, aggravating dream from another lifetime.

How could I ever tell him about this, or let him see me again, or touch me, or kiss me?

Those thoughts helped me make up my mind on where to go.

I couldn't imagine the look on Jimmy's face if he saw me like this.

18

JIMMY

J im was sound asleep when the text came on his phone. If he hadn't been so worn out from the long horseback ride into the mountains with his dad followed by the three-hour drive back to school, he might have heard the tiny *ding!* right then. It probably would have awakened him the way it usually did.

But that ride, on top of the wonderful time he'd spent with Marlena, had given him the best sleep he'd had in a long time.

Then the morning had come.

As always, he'd showered and dressed then headed to the dining hall at Sul Ross's University Center for breakfast.

Over scrambled eggs and biscuits, he looked at his phone, delighted to see Marlena's name in his message alerts. But when he read the text, his scrambled eggs turned to sawdust in his mouth.

Jimmy laid his fork beside his plate with careful deliberation. The words danced before his eyes. It had to be a joke. A bad joke. He thumbed the screen to turn off the words, and then he simply sat for a moment, as if in a trance.

After appearing to study his congealing breakfast, Jimmy

finally stood and walked to the nearest garbage can. He scraped the food into the trash, carefully placed the heavy china plate and flatware back on the red plastic tray, then slid the entire thing into the half-window where a student would pick it up and load it into the industrial dishwasher with the rest of the breakfast dishes.

He glanced back down at the phone in his hand as he strode across the dining hall in his well-worn boots and TCA—Texas Cattlemen's Association—cap. He'd been on his way to class, but now he couldn't imagine sitting in a lecture hall pretending to listen to a professor talk about the economics of ranch life. Right now he couldn't see himself doing anything but getting out. Getting away. Going someplace where he could think.

He stalked outside into the gorgeous fall morning. The air was crisp, cold, and still. He passed a couple of girls he recognized, but he didn't notice their hands raised in greeting. His roommate, Daniel, had left earlier this morning. Jim had told him all about Marlena when he got back last night. Now he felt like a fool. But Dan wasn't around now. A rodeo cowboy, he always had to be up early to feed animals and clean stalls.

Animals.

That's what he needed. Animals and fresh air. Mother Nature. Open country. Big Red would probably welcome a day out of his stall, too.

He crossed from the dining hall to the parking area where he'd left the Camaro. It was quite a trek from his dorm room in Lobo Village to the dining hall.

When he clicked the remote to start the car, he glanced at the message again. It didn't make sense.

Once inside the still-warm Camaro, Jimmy decided it had to be a mistake. A joke like the "Who is this?" message she'd sent him that first night.

Engine running, he looked at it once more, and then he hit

the reply bar to respond. "Hey, Mar," he typed. "Just got your message. I know you have a weird sense of humor, but still... let me know this is your idea of a joke. K?"

His thumb pressed send before he could overthink it and back out.

Then he waited.

For a few seconds he did nothing. Just sat behind the wheel. What'd I expect? An immediate reply? He looked back at the message to see when it had been sent. Last night.

What was she doing when she sent it? Was she out with the other guy? Did they spend the night together? Were they together now, having breakfast, going to class, sleeping late? She'd said *she had never*. Had that been a lie?

Jimmy shoved the gearshift into reverse and stopped short of slamming his foot down on the accelerator. Anger flooded his brain, but he wasn't a kid anymore. He wouldn't take his feelings out on his car. That would be stupid. Instead, he let the tears of frustration fall, and then he drove out of the parking area and onto the highway leading to the stables where Big Red lived.

After the tears dried, the questions remained. Had she used him? Why would she do that? He'd considered himself a good judge of character. What they'd experienced had seemed real, especially when he'd gone to her home, helped her dad, then Lana. And Dash. It seemed he couldn't do enough for folks. And this was his reward? This was how he was repaid?

The Camaro hit ninety. So much for getting control of my emotions, he thought. For a moment Jimmy considered forgetting everything and just driving. Head north and keep going. He could pick up ranch work in Wyoming, or North Dakota, nearly anywhere. He had ranching in his blood. No reason he couldn't take off and go someplace where no one knew him. He'd never felt so used, so ruined, so *destroyed*. The message said she loved someone else.

The sign for the stable appeared on the horizon.

His foot automatically came off the gas and the car slowed. Big Red. The rangy bay his dad had given him on his twelfth birthday. He'd broke the two-year-old to saddle all by himself. Not by starvation and intimidation but through gentleness and patience. He thought of himself as something of a horse whisperer. His dad had been downright amazed. Big Red had been one of the main factors in Jimmy's decision to attend Sul Ross. He couldn't imagine living someplace where he couldn't keep his horse nearby.

He turned onto the gravel drive. When he lowered his window, he could hear the familiar whinny. No doubt the old horse had spied the car coming up the long lane.

Before he exited the vehicle, Jimmy glanced at his messages to make sure he hadn't missed a new one coming in. But there was nothing. It felt as if his reply had gone into the void, into the ether, into the nothingness that seemed to have taken over his whole world.

He still couldn't believe the awful words in her text. They'd had such a connection, such a wonderful night. She was the girl he'd been looking for. "I'm sorry," the message had read. "We can't see each other anymore. Please don't try to contact me. We had a great weekend, but I'm in love with someone else. I was wrong to think I could forget him that easily." His anger felt like a live thing in his gut. He got out of the car, took leftover supplies out of the Camaro's trunk, greeted Big Red, unhooked the stable half-door, and went through the procedures that were ingrained in his DNA.

First the blanket—*not* the one he'd shared with Marlena, that one he'd left in the Camaro—then the saddle, then the bit. He considered halter only, but he wasn't sure where he was going. As much as he trusted his horse, it would be more prudent to have complete control. He would take the halter though. If he decided to camp a few days, he would need it to give Big R's mouth a rest.

Next, he took a feedbag and enough feed for a day or two. Grazing was not encouraged in the park. He had a vague notion he would head down to the canyon, his favorite spot in the world aside from his parents' ranch. It was all part of Big Bend National Park and he knew where every creek and water hole existed for miles and miles around. He needed to get out there. It was almost like his church.

He tied on his rolled up sleeping bag, a thin waterproof poncho, a bag of beef jerky and trail mix plus a water bottle and some purifier for streams. It was all stuff he had leftover from a trail ride with Daniel right before the Thanksgiving break. "C'mon, Red." He led the bay from his stall. "We need a little religion, don't we?"

The big horse snuffed in the crisp air. "Be winter, soon," Jim said aloud. "Just a few more weeks." He thought of how he'd already been looking forward to the winter break, seeing Marlena back in Window for Christmas. He'd even thought of giving her a ring—oh, not engagement, not yet, but something, some token of his undying love—Jimmy snuffed in an unconscious imitation of his horse. Undying love my ass, he thought.

Before closing the stall door, he reached inside and removed his old Stetson from a nail just inside the door. He only wore it when he was at home on the ranch or out on the trail. He only wore it to keep the sun off his face and the back of his neck. Or by the looks of today's sky, to keep the rain from going down his collar.

Settling the hat on his head, Jim hung his TCA cap on the nail and closed the stall door. He wanted to pull his phone out and look at the message again, but if she had replied, he would have heard the alert.

He resisted the urge, left his phone in his pocket, and

climbed on his horse. The stable backed right up to the national park. In no time the two of them were miles down the trail.

That's when he realized he hadn't brought his solar charger. In light of that, he made a quick call to his advisor and left a message telling her there had been a little crisis and he would be away for a few days. He wasn't worried about his classes; they were all reviewing for semester finals, which would start next week. Jim knew they weren't going to be a problem.

After that call, he phoned his dad and told him his plans. "I'll be out of touch," he said. "Forgot my solar charger." He knew his dad wouldn't worry. The man had raised him to be self-sufficient.

"Take care of yourself, boy," his dad replied. "Call me when you get back."

"I will, Dad. I'm already looking forward to Christmas." Jimmy allowed Big Red to meander along as he tried to decide whether he should use his last iota of battery life to call Marlena.

Her message had said not to contact her, that her decision had been made, and he'd already sent one text in spite of it. Why even bother to call? He stared down at the little phone in his hand, looked up at the stubby oaks and junipers, threw caution to the wind and stabbed her name on his contact list with his forefinger.

The phone rang three times and cut off. It didn't even go to voicemail.

Jimmy was perplexed. He'd never had that happen before. Unless she had blocked him. He had no idea what that would sound like. Without thinking, he tried it one more time. She couldn't have been that fake. They'd spoken of love. They had made love. It had been wonderful, everything he'd ever wanted and more.

The phone rang three more times, and then cut off just like before. This time, his battery showed 0%.

Jimmy swiped his finger across Marlena's name and deleted her completely. Then he touched Big Red's ribs with his heels and the leggy horse sprang into a gallop.

The wind dried the tears on his face before he even felt them fall.

19

DOUBTS

That night we went to bed early, but I could not sleep. Joanna asked if I needed anything and I assured her I would be all right. I think she would have slept in my room with me if I'd asked, but of course that would have been silly.

I opened my computer so that the screensaver came on. Lowering the brightness, I turned my face away from it so that only the glow of the screen fell across my bed. I set the timer to stay on for an hour, but every time I dozed off I would jerk myself awake, certain he was chasing me through the cold, dark forest.

Once I awoke feeling as if I were wrapped in fog, not a fine mist but a curdled-milk fog. One of my legs had gotten cold out from under the blankets. I thought about the prescription I hadn't bothered to fill. Would it help me sleep, or was it just for pain? Maybe it did both.

It didn't matter now, not in the middle of the night, but perhaps I should get it filled before I left town. I knew I would be safer in Denver, but I might still need something to help me relax and rest. I couldn't wait to get away from Austin.

Eventually, I left my bed and went to the living room, turned on the small TV there, and curled up on the sofa. I wrapped myself head to toe in my blanket and dozed in and out, my face turned to the door, my line of sight encompassing both the window and the door.

I'd made a stop on my way from my room to the living room. Now, concealed beneath my blanket was the largest knife in our tiny kitchen. For the first time in my life, I wished for a gun. I knew in my heart I wouldn't be able to defend myself against him with a knife, just thinking about it made my neck throb—which I recognized as a purely psychosomatic response—but we didn't have a gun, and we didn't have a baseball bat. We didn't even have a hammer. The only tool we possessed was a pinkie-sized screwdriver with a magnet on one end.

The knife seemed better than nothing. At least I had something to hold on to.

If necessary, I would use it to the best of my ability. I swore right then and there that I would never be hurt that way again. Instead, I would go down fighting—life or death—all the way. Never again would I simply lie down and let a man—or anyone—do to me the things he'd done. It never occurred to me that I'd actually saved my own life by doing that very thing. By pretending to be dead. I couldn't possibly have overpowered him, even though I'd tried by hitting him with the wine bottle. Once I realized that—with the help of a therapist weeks and months later—that's when I finally began to heal.

But on this night, I simply lay there, courting sleep by the light of the TV, thinking of my two best friends. We'd sent Lana on her way home earlier in the afternoon with promises to stay in touch through Joanna's phone. "I'll get a new one tomorrow," I promised. "Before I head to Denver." But when I thought of actually going into the phone store, I wondered if I'd be able to make myself do it. I couldn't imagine walking in and watching people's faces try to mask their shock at my appearance. Even the anticipation of going to the hospital tomorrow was almost more than I could handle.

I thought of layering on makeup so the cuts and bruises weren't so noticeable, but I couldn't stand the thought of having to scrub it all off later. The bruising, especially around my eye, proved extremely painful to the touch.

The best thing I could think of would be to simply wrap a scarf around my neck and wear the biggest pair of sunglasses I could find.

With that little bit of a plan in mind, I finally dozed.

I woke twice more with the feeling of someone staring at me the way he'd done in the forest when I thought I'd got away but he had actually been right behind me. After the second time I awoke, I gave up and went to the kitchen to make coffee.

While it brewed, I went to the closet, took out my duffles and my overnight bag, and started repacking. It didn't take long. I'd barely unpacked anything. The clothes I'd worn to meet Preston were now in an evidence bag at the Police Department.

Tomorrow I would find a couple of boxes for my books and the few things I wanted to take from the kitchen and bathroom.

At last I went back to bed, Blue Bear in my arms, and fell asleep surrounded by my luggage.

THE DRIVE to Denver felt surreal. I blared music and talked on my new TracFone the whole way. Joanna had tried to get my iPhone replaced, but they wanted a police report for the insurance, and it wasn't ready yet. They assured me I could take care of it in Denver when I received a copy of the report.

So Joanna went to Walmart and bought me a phone out of

her own pocket. Of course I tried to pay her but she wouldn't let me. She said I could take her out to dinner when she came to visit me later. I think we both knew I'd never be coming back to school in Austin. I couldn't walk across the parking lot without holding on to her arm. I felt like a brittle old woman terrified to even be outdoors.

I didn't argue at all when she took it upon herself to take my car in to get another tire mounted. Now I knew for certain I could never repay her.

I also had to promise her I would contact the Rape Crisis Center in Denver, and I did promise. I knew I would need help. I couldn't imagine going to school, or anywhere, with this feeling of vulnerability clinging to me like a second skin.

Carrie was thrilled I was coming to her house. Mom and Dad were, too. They thought I should get as far away from school and from *him* as possible. I'd thought of going back to Window, but I couldn't stand having the whole town know why I had to come home. I didn't feel ashamed because of what happened, but I did feel completely stupid for putting myself in the position to allow it to happen. I told Lana I was ashamed that I hadn't been smart enough to prevent it.

Upon hearing that, Mom tried to reassure me I had no reason to feel that way, but when she couldn't change my mind, she started investigating rehab hospitals for Dad in the Denver area. There were way more opportunities there than in our tiny hometown.

She wanted me to send her a picture of my face when I got my new phone, but I lied and told her my cheapo phone didn't have a camera. If she'd seen me, she would have freaked out. I didn't want that. Nor did I want her to see her youngest child looking like a human punching bag.

I withdrew from school over the phone. My advisor didn't try to dissuade me. She took care of everything. When she asked where to send my transcript, I gave her Carrie's address. "But please, keep that confidential. He still goes to school here and I don't want him to know where I'm going."

That gave her a moment's pause. I guess knowing a violent rapist walked among them would give anyone a second thought. It didn't seem right for him to be free to come and go as he pleased while I was afraid to walk down a public street in broad daylight. She agreed to keep my new address private.

I sent Jimmy a message telling him I might not be home for Christmas after all. I purposely left it vague because I hadn't decided what I would tell him yet. I didn't want to keep him in the dark, completely, but I also didn't want to lose him.

Selfishly, I wanted to put him on hold. So far I'd told only my closest family and the two friends who were helping me survive. What could Jimmy do, way down there at Sul Ross? It would be an unnecessary worry for him. After I'd healed a bit, I'd be ready to see him. Maybe if my face looked better, he could make a trip to Denver over the Christmas break. But I didn't tell him that. It was simply a vague idea in the back of my mind.

My drive to Colorado would be long. I'd have plenty of time to call him once I got out on the highway, away from town. When I could breathe.

Joanna followed me out of Austin on 183. She followed me all the way to the town of Lampasas where we pulled over at a truck stop for coffee. I had weathered the hospital okay, changing the bandage had only taken about an hour, but getting out at places like this, where folks weren't expecting to see a person who looked like me, that was a new kind of torture.

Of course Joanna traveled along with me, but it was a long way to the halfway point of Lubbock, Texas. On the phone that morning, while sitting at the hospital, waiting for the doctor,

Carrie had informed me that Dix wanted to bring her at least halfway. We would meet somewhere, have a bite to eat, and then she would get in my car and drive the rest of the way with me. Dix said Lubbock was close to halfway between Austin and Denver.

I hate to be that much trouble, I'd protested, but they wouldn't hear any more about it. "I want to come all the way. I could get a flight out this evening," my sister had said. "Then I could drive you all the way here."

I'd vetoed that. I couldn't wait to get out of Austin. It was tainted. The place I'd fallen in love with as a junior back in high school, when I first did the college tour, the place I'd longed for all my senior year, had been ruined. I would never be able to walk the beautiful campus again. Not now. Not safely. Not as long as Preston walked free. I think the loss of my dreams hurt almost as much as the physical wounds. Maybe even more.

I told Carrie I would see them in Lubbock. And of course I gave her my new phone number.

JOANNA and I stood in the Lampasas truck stop parking lot, preparing to part ways. She made me promise to keep in touch. "It's still a few hours to Lubbock. Are you sure you're able to make it that far by yourself?"

I hugged her. "I'll be fine. Now that I'm away from Austin, I feel so much better. There's no way he could know where I'm going."

Joanna stared at me with a worried look.

I rushed to put her mind at ease by directing her thoughts to something else. "I hate that you have to get a new roommate." We were standing outside my car. I had the engine running. I was ready to go. I found myself making small talk to keep from leaving. I didn't really expect her to respond.

But she did. "I have something to tell you," she said. "Detective Lapuli called a few minutes ago while you were in the bathroom. He wanted me to tell you to call him from your new phone, but I think I'd better go ahead and tell you what he said first."

I waited, unsure I wanted to hear it.

Joanna continued. "Mariah Leathers, the girl who should have been my roommate?"

"Yes?" I was a little confused. "What about her?"

Joanna shook her head. "They found out she had told a friend she planned to meet some guy that lived near her and follow him back to school in Austin." Her face clouded like an impending storm. "They were both returning students."

"Oh, no. That certainly puts a new spin on things, doesn't it?" I touched my throat, and my swollen cheek. "I guess I'll call the detective when I get on the road again. See what else he wants to tell me."

Joanna nodded. "There's more."

My mind raced with questions.

But before I could ask them, Joanna said, "They found her body just off Green Bay Trail near Glencoe, Illinois. It's a wealthy suburb of Chicago." She rubbed at a spot on my window. "Glencoe is Preston's hometown."

I gasped so loudly a couple walking across the parking lot turned to see what had happened. I smiled to let them know we were all right. Then I said, "Did Lapuli tell you that?"

"Yes. And then I googled Preston's name along with the town of Glencoe and some articles popped up about his family. His dad's a very well known cardiologist."

"Oh, my God. That's unreal."

"That's not all. I also researched 'unsolved rapes' around Glencoe and there have been quite a few—"

"Wait, she was raped and murdered?"

"Yes." Joanna's voice grew softer and softer. "Raped, and murdered. Throat cut. The only difference was, her hands were bound with those plastic zip tie things."

Once again, my hand went to the bandage hidden beneath my scarf. "You don't seriously think—"

"Actually, I do. And so does the detective." Her teeth were clenched tight. "It's way too coincidental. The girl went to meet some guy, someone she trusted enough to follow across the country, and that was the last time anyone saw her until they found her body." Joanna had nearly rubbed a hole in my driver's side window by now. "Her cell phone made it to school, but she never did. No one knows who she met, only that he told her he attended UT also."

"That's not—I mean it can't—" The possibility that it might be Preston blew my mind. But I had to consider it. "I'm glad you told me. I—I think I'll call Detective Lapuli now. I need to give him my new number anyway." I thought back to how he had told me someone kept texting Mariah's parents from her phone right up until her mother called the school. I made myself inhale deeply. "Do you think Preston had her phone? That he was pretending to be her by texting her parents?"

Joanna leaned forward. "After what he did to you, I truly believe that is exactly what he did. Here," she held out her open palm, "let me have your phone and I'll put in Lapuli's number for you."

I gave it to her. "I think you're right. He is one sick individual. That poor girl, and her parents. How horrible to find you've been texting with your daughter's killer for months."

"Yes." Joanna handed back my phone. "That's serial killer sick."

I nodded and gulped my takeout coffee. It was already cool. I knew it might be nothing but a coincidence, but for the victim to have been registered to move into the very apartment I'd just left, and now to find out she'd been raped and had her throat slashed, and to hear that her body had been left in a wooded area, those were too many coincidences. Way too many.

The parking area suddenly felt exposed. I wanted to get in my car and go. I would have given my right arm if Joanna had been travelling all the way with me. I knew I would only have to ask, but she was already doing so much—buying me the phone, getting my new tire, following me this far—I couldn't possibly ask for anything more.

We hugged and held on a few extra seconds. "I wouldn't have told you," she said. "But Detective Lapuli said you needed to call him right away. We both want you to be extremely careful, okay?"

I nodded. "I'm going to ask you one more favor,"

"Of course, anything."

I gripped her upper arm so she would look at my battered face. "Demand a new apartment. Don't spend another night there where he might find you. I mean, he might come looking for me and find you there alone."

Her face paled. "I hadn't thought of that. You're right. I will revisit the office. I might even ask the detective to meet me there."

I loosened my grip. "Good. I can't stand the thought of you there alone. Maybe you should even stay with someone or get Antonio to stay with you until you get a new place?"

"That's a good idea. If 'Tonio can't do it, I might ask Sandy Romero. We've been friends awhile."

"Thank you. I won't worry quite as much now." We hugged again. "Call me," I said. "Better yet, come to visit me."

"I will. I promise." She tucked me into the driver's seat and I couldn't help but notice how her eyes skimmed the parking lot. I assumed she was looking for Preston, just like me.

I reversed out of the slanted space and carefully made my way back toward US-183 North. But I didn't pull out until I saw Joanna get back into her car for the drive home to Austin.

As soon as I felt comfortable, I set my cruise control, picked up my phone, and touched Jimmy's number.

The phone rang a few times and probably would have gone to voicemail but I panicked. I didn't know what to say. I hadn't considered that he might not answer. Hadn't thought that far ahead.

He's probably in class with his phone turned off. What will I say if he recalls this number? I might not be home for Christmas because I was raped and beaten and left for dead. Oh, and by the way, he cut my throat, too. Yeah. That's something you want to tell your new love on the phone. You bet.

I shook my head and tossed the phone into the cup holder. Then I picked it back up and looked at Jimmy's number to make sure I'd pressed the correct one. This is stupid. I'm just going to call back and leave a message telling him I have a new phone and that he can call when he has a chance. I have to tell him something.

But just then my phone trilled. It was Detective Lapuli. Joanna had called and given him my new number in case I forgot to call him. She probably remembered how long it took me to call Carrie and my mom the day before. I told him my plans and what Joanna had said. He confirmed everything she had told me.

"I'm glad you're leaving town," he said. "I think it's the best thing you could do right now."

I felt both angry and hurt when he said that. I was the victim here. Why should I have to run away while the monster roamed free to do it all again? I thought he should still be in jail. Without bond.

Before we broke our connection, I came right out and asked the detective if Preston was under suspicion for Mariah's death.

He hesitated for a moment. "It's like I told Joanna, I can definitely see the similarities between your case and hers. And I've made certain Detective Andrews in Chicago is aware of it, too."

"Will you look after Joanna, and make sure she stays somewhere else, or has someone stay with her?"

"Of course," he said. "I'm taking this all very personally. There are too many loose ends here. And Miss Matthews?"

I waited. I wanted to tell him to call me Marlena, but I assumed this would be the last time we ever spoke so what difference did it make?

"Since you will be so far away, are you still planning on pressing charges against him?"

My hand gripped the phone tightly. "Charges? Well, yes. I told the officers at the hospital I would definitely press charges."

"Good," Detective Lapuli said. "Not that you have to. The state will do it if you don't, but it's better for the victim to be the one. Carries more weight."

I nodded. "I'll press charges, don't worry. He cannot get away with this."

"Then I'm sure we will be in touch before the trial. Until then, take care of yourself, and call me if you need anything."

"Okay. I will." Stunned, I put down the phone. This had just got real all over again. I'll have to tell Jimmy. There's no way around it.

I'll be brave. I'll just tell him what happened. I'll make sure he understands I didn't go with Preston because I wanted to. I'll tell him about the tires and the nonexistent restaurant reservation, and I'll make him understand it was all out of my control.

But will he?

Will he understand?

I pressed his contact again, determined to leave a message this time, but for some reason no voicemail message came on. The phone just rang and rang and then cut off. That's about right, I thought. I finally get up my courage to tell him and now I can't.

20

DÉJÀ VU

The phone rang and rang. Preston sat back and stared at it until voicemail answered. He pressed the speaker icon and listened, but did not pick up.

"Preston," a man's voice said. "I know you're listening. You're never without your phone. I also know George Mendelssohn bailed you out. What the hell, son? A rape charge? What was it, a frat party gone wrong? Call me, dammit. I don't want to hear from George, I want to hear from you."

Preston leaned back and swigged his beer. He'd been completely blindsided when he had called the police department after finding the note on his door. They had asked him to come in for questioning and then they had arrested him.

The stupid bitch had made it. He hadn't finished her off. He'd been lax, careless. She must've been found by the people whose voices he'd heard.

He looked at the phone on the counter but he didn't push redial, he didn't even pick the thing up. "Nope," he said. "Not in the mood." He chugged the rest of the beer and tossed the empty bottle toward the trash. Fortunately, it hit the mark instead of shattering on the tile floor. "Only time you want to hear from me is when someone else calls you first. Ever think about calling me for nothing sometime, Dad? Or better yet, taking me with you to Switzerland for turkey day? So what if my grades weren't that great? Did you really think I was going to sit here in this empty apartment and study?"

He stood suddenly, grabbed the phone, and deleted the message. Then he walked—unsteadily—toward the living room.

His private apartment was much nicer than the student residences where Marlena and Joanna lived. Stupid little twat wouldn't go skinny-dipping or even have breakfast with him, had to be forced into a simple fucking picnic. Piece of trash, that's all. Tough, though. If it hadn't been for the partiers on the other side of the lake, he would have made certain he finished the job, and disposed of the body. Then he wouldn't be in this mess.

A rape charge, Dad? She's lucky she could make any charges at all. Not that they will stick. He'd been careful. No one could dispute that it was consensual. Who was she anyway? A nobody. No one would take her word over his. Not once he had his frat boys on board. And once the charges were withdrawn—and he knew they would be—then she wouldn't be so lucky. No sir.

She wouldn't ever be that lucky again.

"I can guarantee you that, Dad," Preston said to the empty room.

JIMMY TOOK Big Red deep into the canyon. Near dusk he decided they'd gone far enough. As the sun touched the canyon rim, he built a small fire. He was now on private land, and he'd gotten permission to camp there last year. He ate some beef jerky, drank a cup of water, fed Big Red and let him graze, and then he crawled into his sleeping bag. At the last second, he pulled out his phone to check for messages, but it was only habit. The battery had absolutely no charge.

He shoved it deep into his saddlebag and put it out of his mind. As long as he stayed on the move, Jim could forget what happened, but as soon as he stopped, everything came back to him in waves. He put the fire out and fell asleep wondering how he could have been taken in so easily. He drifted off, vowing it would never happen again. His heart was broken and his ego was bruised. It would be a long, long while before either of them began to heal.

I STOPPED at a roadside rest area. Texas does those best. This one had wagon wheels supporting cement picnic tables and benches. The bathroom was open and airy. I inspected each stall by looking under the door at the feet before selecting the one I would use. Once I felt safe, it took me about two minutes to urinate and wash my hands before hurrying back to my car.

The entire time I was outside, walking to the restroom in my giant sunglasses, inspecting the stalls wearing my filmy scarf, washing my hands, trying to quell the shakes, I felt like the proverbial bug under a microscope, or a rabbit out of its hole.

Run, little rabbit, run.

When I dove back into my car, my hands were still shaking. I locked the doors, started the engine, and gripped the steering wheel tightly. My knuckles went white as I forced myself to breathe deeply and slowly until the panic abated enough that I could move the gearshift into drive and pull away from the curb.

I drove carefully and deliberately, knowing my mind wasn't fully on the task at hand. Knowing I had to concentrate in order to get past this aftermath and get on with my new life. My right hand kept creeping to the fresh bandage on my throat. My left hand controlled the steering wheel.

Get on with it I thought. Just get on with it.

Once back on the road, my panic abated and I began to relax. The rest of the drive to Lubbock went by without a hitch. I kept a close eye on my mirrors, though. I had to. Self-preservation had replaced naïve as my middle name.

At last, I made it to the Cracker Barrel Restaurant and there sat Carrie and Dix on the iconic front porch. Just like they'd said they would be.

As soon as Carrie saw my car turn into the parking area, she stopped her rocking chair, stood, waved, and then loped toward me across the tarmac. "Marlie!"

I could read my name on her lips even as I eased into a parking space. I turned off the engine as she opened the door and dragged me into her arms. "Marlie, Marlie, honey." That seemed to be all she could say, and then we were hugging and crying and she was patting me and touching my wounds ever so gently.

When we finally broke apart, I saw my beloved brother-in-law, Dix, standing near the entrance to the restaurant, hands in his front pockets, eyes cast down toward the wooden floor of the porch. He glanced up and smiled, waved a little wave, but he seemed out of place, as if he didn't quite know where to look.

"Do you want to get something to eat before we take off again?" Carrie asked.

My hand went to my throat, to the bandage. I took off my sunglasses.

Carrie inhaled sharply.

I reached back into the car and retrieved the scarf to wrap around my neck. Then I felt a momentary lapse in courage. "Should we?" I asked.

She nodded, but it was hesitant. "If anyone asks, we'll just say car accident. They'll never know the difference."

That sounded reasonable. I wondered if I should keep my sunglasses on inside the restaurant. I wasn't sure I could tolerate people staring, but I didn't want to deny Carrie and Dix dinner after all they were doing for me.

My stomach churned with anxiety.

Cracker Barrel restaurants are built to resemble old-fashioned general stores. When we stepped inside, country music played on the overhead speakers. It was also promoted and sold on CDs near the checkout counter. My family always stopped at the Cracker Barrel chain of restaurants when we travelled.

Mom and I often joked we would go there for the smell of the place if nothing else. The scented candles and potpourri on display mixed with the odor of home-style food being prepared in the kitchen. A crackling fire in the huge stone fireplace made it feel like an old country version of paradise. In addition to the lure of the food and the simple ambiance, the three of us had always loved looking through the decorative seasonal items on display.

No shopping this time, though. I walked with my head down and my scarf pulled close. The hostess put us at a table in the corner and that made me feel a little less self-conscious.

Somehow, we made it through the meal. Dix had glanced at me and smiled as he hugged me gently, and then he hadn't looked at me again. I also noticed how the eyes of the servers, the cashiers, even the other patrons, would land on my bruised face and the bandage peeking over the edge of my scarf and then slide away as if I were coated in oil.

After we finished our meal, Carrie led me to the door and we hurried out while Dix stopped at the counter to pay the bill.

We were already in my car when he came out and instructed us to follow him to the nearest convenience store so we could all fuel up before setting out again. Then he handed Carrie a Cracker Barrel sack with a package of fireplace lighters inside. "That cozy fireplace reminded me we needed these at home," he said.

A sensation of horror and revulsion washed over me.

Click, whoosshhh.

No one knew how Preston had threatened me with one of those long-barreled lighters. No one knew because I'd blocked it out. Of all the horrible things he'd done, threatening me with the lighter had been pushed to the back of my mind. Now, I remembered. If my hand hadn't found the empty wine bottle at that moment, he would have lit my hair on fire. Just seeing the package brought it all back.

I averted my eyes and concentrated on not screaming.

When I looked back at Carrie, she had put the sack in the back seat and started fiddling with the radio dial. "Gotta get all set up before we take off," she said.

I nodded as if I agreed. Right then, music was the last thing on my mind.

We followed Dix to the gas station and filled our tanks. Actually, Dix filled both of them at the same time. Such a sweet guy. My sister had really hit the jackpot when she found him.

Once we were underway, Carrie called Mom and the three of us discussed my plans and, in a roundabout way, about what had happened.

That's when Mom told me she'd found a great rehab hospital for Dad in Denver, along with a nearby assisted living complex for both of them. And so it was settled. I would stay with Carrie and Dix and think about whether I would transfer to a college in Denver, or near there, or whether I would do something else.

I didn't want to think about it, but I knew I would have to make some decisions eventually. Carrie assured me I did not have to do anything right away except to heal and then find a therapist to help me deal.

We didn't mention court, or charges, or anything having to do with Preston. I'd got away from him and now I was safe, that's all that mattered.

THE NEXT MORNING, Jim built his fire before the sun rose. He'd decided not to let Marlena ruin his life. He thought he'd found his future, but obviously that had been wrong. In light of that he would just have to make a course correction. Back to square one. Continue on with the original plan but watch for other pitfalls.

The only thing he wanted to do differently was to travel. Before—or if—if he ever gave his heart away again, he wanted to see the world, the Amazon Rainforest, the Great Pyramids, the Tower of London, or even seek out Snowy River in Australia, find out if the old cowboy poem his dad recited to him told of a real place. Experience some of the things he'd only read about. Then maybe he'd be ready to settle down. He didn't know if he'd want to rebuild his granddad's house now or not. That could wait. There was no hurry. Not now.

21

DENVER

Once upon a time, a girl holed up in her sister's house after a traumatic event that changed her whole life. It even changed her outlook on life. Where once she'd been optimistic and full of plans, after the event she became pessimistic, paranoid, and angry. Depressed? Who wouldn't be?

Christmas came and went. The unfamiliar Colorado snow was magnificent. A white Christmas. Every desert-dweller's dream come true. I tried to be excited. I tried to take part in the celebrations at Dix and Carrie's house, trimming the tree, going to midnight services on Christmas Eve, but it was no use. Everything felt muted. Wrong. I couldn't seem to find the Christmas spirit anywhere. I just wanted to sleep.

One bright spot came when we learned that Mom and Dad would soon be living nearby. Mom had found an assisted living apartment very close to a top-notch rehab facility in Denver. She seemed so strong, dealing with Dad and the move and my problems all at the same time. I knew I should try to be more like her, I simply didn't know how. Maybe after a few more months of therapy I told myself. Maybe then.

After about three months, Carrie had stood as much as she could stand. She marched into my room at eight o'clock one morning. "Get up," she said.

I rolled over and squinted at the clock. "Okay, Sis. Have you had breakfast? I could make some waffles."

Carrie pulled my blanket down. "We'll get breakfast on the way to the office. It's time you got back in some kind of routine."

I wanted to pull the pillow over my head and tell her to mind her own business, but I knew it would do no good. My therapist had been saying exactly the same thing for the past few days. My face had healed, bruises having faded to green and yellow before they finally disappeared. Even my mark of Zorro had nearly healed. It would scar, a little, but the doctor had given me some sort of miracle cream to rub on it and I was surprised at how good it looked.

"You're right," I said. "Let me grab a quick shower. I won't even wash my hair."

Carrie laughed at that. "Good. I'll tell Dix to go on ahead and we'll bring the donuts."

I smiled for the first time in a while. I'd only recently got the news that my second HIV test had come back negative. I couldn't believe it took so long to get the results. All the other tests for sexually transmitted diseases had been negative, too.

A huge weight slipped off my shoulders when I received that news, a weight I hadn't even realized I'd been carrying. In retrospect, it was a real blessing. If I'd had to be treated for something like that on top of everything else... it might have been too much to bear. It might have broken me.

Out of the shower, I toweled off quickly. Maybe I should start those self-defense classes the therapist told me about. I'd taken her advice on the Xanax and it had helped with my anxiety and insomnia. I'd also taken her advice about trying meditation. Somehow, I had to learn to let go of my rage. Maybe her self-defense advice would help with that, too. One day she'd been called out of the office during our session and I'd chanced a look at her notes. "One episode away from a total breakdown," she'd written.

That floored me. I thought I'd made so much progress.

Now, I pulled on work clothes, soft knit pants and a button front blouse, and grabbed my favorite sweater off the chair beside the bed. I didn't feel strange wearing it the way I'd worried I might; instead, it turned out to be just the opposite. It felt comforting, a sort of badge of what I'd survived.

After spreading up the comforter, I fluffed my pillows and placed Blue Bear between them in his usual place of honor. Even though I still hadn't heard from Jim, I slept with the stuffed bear every night.

Carrie and I went through the drive at Dunkin' Donuts and got coffee and pastries for the office. "We can't make a habit of this," I said. "I don't even want to think about how many calories—"

Carrie bit into a cherry glazed. "And how much *fat*," she sputtered.

I laughed at the hot pink icing that ringed her lips. "You look like my big sister," I giggled. "When we were eight and ten years old!"

She stuck her tongue out at me before licking her lips and wiping them with a napkin. Then she popped the last bite into her mouth and followed it with a sip of black coffee. "Ahhh," she said. "That's the way to start an amazing day."

I laughed again, delighted that I felt good for the first time in months. Later, black clouds of depression would crash down on me again, especially late at night when sleep wouldn't come. But things were getting better.

The first few weeks I would put my bedroom TV on and tune it to a documentary channel. But sometimes the flashing of the changing scenes would wake me at the instant I dozed off.

Eventually I cut that out and stuck to over-the-counter sleep aids, the Rain Sounds app on my phone, and reading. The books helped most of all. I read late into the night only stopping when my paperback would fall over and hit me in the nose. Sometimes I didn't even turn off the reading light. It made a soft glow behind my head. That didn't bother me at all.

Now we were going to work. It felt good to say that. It felt good to be back among the living-working-*normal* population.

But even after the light-hearted beginning, that first day turned out to be tough. Every time the door opened, I imagined he had found me. However, after a few days I began to believe things would be all right. "He's in a whole other state," Carrie said, watching me panic every time a new person entered. "He's not here, it's fear causing you to feel this way." We both agreed I had to start the self-defense classes as soon as possible.

And so I did.

My therapist directed me to a class sponsored by the Denver Police Department. For the first week, I only watched.

The day I saw a grandmother take down an opponent half her age, I decided I'd seen enough. I enrolled that day. The course lasted six weeks. By week three, neither Dix nor Carrie had to drive me. I felt brave enough to drive myself. I'd recently learned about equalizers.

After the self-defense course, I bought a gun, a Smith & Wesson .38 revolver. My next few weeks were spent attending Concealed Carry classes and going to the shooting range. I vowed never to be helpless again.

I began to seriously enjoy going to work with Carrie and Dix, helping them out with paperwork and online filing and research. My favorite part was doing research, looking for new listings, checking the status of current listings, and doing call backs for people who left messages while Carrie and Dix were with clients. It made me think I might have a career even if I couldn't return to school yet. I knew I would never return to UT Austin, but maybe I could do this. Maybe I could get my own real estate license.

During these weeks and months, I heard nothing about my case against Preston. I wondered if it had somehow been dismissed. I called Detective Lapuli and he assured me they were still gathering evidence to present to the District Attorney. A few days later, Assistant District Attorney Andy Montoya called me back. He said he would be in charge of prosecuting the case.

I asked if they had a court date scheduled. He assured me they did not. "I'll let you know when we do," he said. "I will want to go over everything with you as soon as we have a date." He hesitated. "Especially since it's been awhile."

I started to say something but he wasn't finished.

"I would suggest you make a journal so that details don't become lost to time."

"That's a great idea," I agreed. "I've actually had a journal going for some time now. It was one of the coping tools suggested by my therapist at the Rape Crisis Center."

"Excellent," the attorney said. "We've found it to be helpful with all kinds of witnesses and victims."

I thanked him for his time and ended the call. Then I immediately called back. The word "victim" had reminded me of something else I should've asked.

When I called back, his secretary answered. "He's on another call," she said. "May I take a message?"

I asked, bluntly, whether I still had a restraining order against Preston. She assured me that I did, and that I should keep a copy of it in my possession in case any problems arose. When she said it like that, it sounded like routine business. But I knew if a problem ever did arise, it would be because he had found me, and my life would be in danger. There would be nothing routine about that.

I visualized my .38 and my other equalizer, a stun-gun flashlight. It appeared to be a simple flashlight, but if I pushed the on/off switch backward it would deliver a tremendous jolt of electricity to anything it touched. My instructor had suggested it. He also showed me how to make sure I touched any would be attacker in the most vulnerable area possible: groin, throat, face, or chest. Don't hesitate, he'd said. Hesitation can get you killed. He didn't have to convince me of that fact. Nor did I think I would have a problem using it.

Of course it was easy to think about those things in the broad light of an ordinary day. The real test would come if I ever saw him again. But the instructor said it was good to play scenarios over and over in my mind. Follow them to a final conclusion, he'd said. It's like an athlete visualizing a winning play. You go over and over it in your mind, then when the time comes, memory takes over and does all the work for you.

That's how you survive, he told me. That's how you survive.

I asked the attorney's secretary to send me a copy of the restraining order as soon as possible because I couldn't recall whether I'd ever had a physical copy.

I'd begun to think of myself as a caterpillar emerging from her cocoon, different in every way from the girl who'd been too timid to hurt Preston's feelings by refusing to go on that ill-fated picnic. Now, if I ever felt threatened by him again, I would not worry about hurting his feelings, I would do whatever it took to defend myself.

Time and time again, men would ask for my number, especially out at the shooting range. I had no trouble turning them down. I didn't feel I had to make polite conversation to spare their feelings either. I simply said no, I'm in a relationship.

Of course I wasn't in a relationship. Not anymore. I hadn't heard a word from Jimmy. I could understand why he hadn't been able to call me. I'd lost my phone in the woods. But why hadn't he tried to contact Lana? Or my parents? Did he even realize they had moved away from Window? Didn't he wonder about me the way I wondered about him? It felt like he'd dropped off the face of the earth.

Lana wanted to find him for me. She said she drove past his house once—no small feat since his folks lived on a ranch—but she didn't see his car. Nor even his old red pickup. I told her it was probably parked in the barn. Don't worry about it, Carrie said. If it's meant to be, it will be. Mom agreed with her.

I liked the sound of that, too. Leave it up to God and the universe. Fate. It took the burden off my shoulders and let me concentrate on pushing forward.

For months I had been so focused on getting better, finding my inner strength—surviving—that romance had been the last thing on my mind. There just hadn't been room for anything else. Maybe that's the way it had to be.

22

COURT

F inally, the time came to go to trial. Even though I'd emerged from my cocoon stronger than ever, I still didn't know if I could make it through this. It had already been six months after the fact when ADA Montoya called and interviewed me on the phone. And that had been three months ago. As we talked, I would read from my journal when I couldn't recall certain details. I told him I'd gathered up the pieces of my life as best I could, but if I had to, I would take a few steps backward and relive it all again.

I didn't say as much to ADA Montoya, but deep down I resented having to dredge it all up again. I resented having to see *him* again. I resented having my new life interrupted—but what choice did I have?

In truth, I was terrified. Even with my newfound confidence, I didn't want to have to face him. My counselor had said it would be this way. She said it would seem as if the justice system took his side. I thought I understood what she meant. But I didn't. That would change soon, though.

After talking to Montoya, I almost backed out. Told myself I should just forget about it. Chalk it up to stupidity, to experience, to hard lessons, to life. I lived. Maybe that should be enough. Did I really have to face him again? I began to have tremendous doubts. Especially after reading through my journal. That in itself was an exercise in despair.

I *wanted* to back out, but I knew I'd never forgive myself if I let him off the hook without a fight. So I gathered my shredded and rebuilt courage, held my head high, and made my plans. Of course Mom and Carrie wanted to go with me. They would lend me their courage. We had to travel all the way back to Austin where the charges were filed. That was the hardest part, thinking about going back to where it had happened.

Finally, the day came. Carrie drove, Mom rode shotgun, and I stretched out in the backseat. A caregiver stayed with Dad, and we left Dix home to run the office. No one could say how long the trial might last. Joanna would be there. She had been called as a character witness.

MOM and I perched on the church-like pews in the hallway outside the courtroom. She touched my hand. "Are you all right?"

I shook my head. "Think I'm going to be sick." I jumped up and hurried toward the bathroom down the hall. And there he was. Preston. Just like that. Getting off the elevator with a silver haired couple I assumed were his parents. From the corner of my eye, I saw a sign pointing toward the stairs. I quickly turned that direction instead.

Joanna must've seen him. The next thing I knew, she materialized right beside me on the stairs. Carrie appeared on my other side. "That's him? That's the rapist?"

I nodded. Tears of panic filled my eyes. "I can't," I said. "I can't do this. Not in front of everyone. I can't tell with him sitting there, smirking at me—"

Joanna shook my arm none too gently. "Look at me," she said.

I did. She gave me no choice.

We stood there in a swath of sunlight coming through the tall stairwell window, Joanna on one side, Carrie on the other. Joanna's tone of voice shocked me almost as much as her physically shaking me. At least my nausea had abated. For a moment, I could feel the warmth of the sun on my face. "Jo?"

Her lips were clamped into a thin hard line. "You can't be thinking of letting him get away with this?"

I let my gaze fall to the marble stair beneath my feet. That's exactly what I'd been thinking.

"You aren't the only one," she said. "Besides, he didn't just rape you—that's bad enough—he also tried to kill you. He stabbed you in the throat. Now, I know your attorney has coached you on what to say when they ask you, but I'm telling you now, you see an opening, you tell it like it is. I don't care what the attorney says." Her eyes flashed. I'd never seen Joanna so angry. "This is your life. You get it? Your *life*." She let go of my arm as if she'd just noticed how hard she'd been squeezing. "Sorry. I just—I wish I could get up there for you."

I grabbed her in an awkward hug. "You are. When they call you for a character witness and to tell about the fit he threw in the parking lot that day."

She nodded. "I'll tell them exactly how he frightened us that day."

Carrie had stood quietly during all this. At last she said, "We're all here for you, sweetie. If you get up there and feel panic coming on, just look at me, okay? Look at me. I'm not afraid of that prick." Her voice was pure steel.

"Okay. I will. I will talk to you and no one else. That might help, 'cause, sis?"

She looked at me.

"It was really, really bad. I haven't told anyone everything. You're going to hear some things he did that were so vile, so evil—"

"Don't worry about it. We're grownups. You just do like Joanna said. You tell it like it happened. Tell it *exactly* the way it happened. You have nothing to be ashamed of, honey. He's bad. He can't be allowed to get away with it—Jo is right—it's nothing short of a miracle that you are still with us." She put her hand up to stop me from responding. "I know. I know. The lawyers might focus on the lurid details of the rape, but what it boils down to is this: he tried to kill you. He needs to go to prison for life."

My attorney appeared at the top of the stairs. "Ready?"

`I couldn't speak.

He came down the few steps and took my arm. "Are you all right?"

Carrie stepped aside so he could usher me back up.

I nodded. "I think so. No. Not really, I feel like I'm going to puke or pass out. Maybe both."

He stuck his hand in his jacket pocket and pulled out a peppermint.

Seriously?

He must've seen the look on my face. "I know. Seems like nothing, but trust me. I've done this a hundred times. It will help soothe your stomach and give you a minty burst of courage."

My eyes went to his face to see if he was joking.

"For real," he said. "Trust me."

He smiled and it reminded me of a picture he had on his desk, a picture of him with his daughter and grandkids. Maybe it would be all right.

But it wasn't all right. It wasn't all right at all.

Preston stared at me.

His parents stared at me.

Two boys I'd never seen before stared at me.

My mom looked straight ahead, clasped my hand briefly over the wooden divider that separated the attorney's box from the spectators, and tried to pretend everyone in the room wasn't staring at me.

Then his attorney stood and walked to the jury box to give his opening statement. He wore a three-piece suit the color of pewter. It matched his flawless hair. When he moved, his suit jacket swung open so that his buttoned-up vest showed through in flashes. His whole demeanor cried money.

He walked down the front of the jury box, his well-manicured hand sliding the length of the rail as if he were deep in thought.

When he got to the end of the rail, he turned on his heel and pointed at me. "That girl!" His voice boomed, making us all jump in our seats. "Wanted to get her hooks into a wealthy young man and failed. Now—" he lowered his arm and turned his back on me to speak to the jury. "Now, she wants to cry rape. Hah!" He looked back at me. "There was no rape. Consensual sex in the woods, that's all. It may have been a little rough—my client says she likes it that way—but there was no rape. Just sex games. You chase me, I run, you catch me, we do the deed." His voice trailed off as he neared the end of his statement.

My nausea came roaring back. What would happen if I puked right here on the table?

Montoya offered me another peppermint and I grabbed it with gratitude. He'd told me it to expect this. He'd warned me of his opponent's strategy to tear me down and make me look like a money-grubbing slut, but nothing could prepare me for this all-out onslaught. I was a good girl. Jimmy had been my first. My one and only.

His attorney went on to say the whole thing had been my idea, a rape-fantasy game I talked Preston into playing out in the woods. He said the idea had first been mentioned at a frat party and the two witnesses—he indicated the two boys sitting behind the defense area—would testify that I had tried to entice them to play along, too.

He strolled back to his table with the air of a gladiator.

He'd done his best to destroy me.

I felt terrible. Abused all over again. My stomach churned, my head pounded, and my face felt like it was on fire.

ADA Montoya rose slowly. He approached the jury box with reverence, greeted the members with respect. His brown suit was nice but not flashy. His jet-black hair appeared to be thinning a little, right on top. He looked like a kind man, one who would stand up and offer you his seat on the subway.

He told the jury they should expect to see and hear all the horrific details of the rape and attempted murder, and that in good time, he would also allow me to describe, in my own words, the nightmare that had almost ended my life.

His voice remained stern as he told how Preston had slashed my tires and tricked me into going with him. Then he shrugged and said how I had been so grateful to him for fixing the tires, I went with him willingly, but that had been the end of my cooperation. He reiterated that I was lucky to be alive. And then he told the jury they would see pictures of my injuries, of the knife wound across my throat. It made me hopeful, the way he kept saying it. The way he got the attempted murder in there right away.

After his speech, he sat down beside me and patted my arm reassuringly.

Maybe it will be over quickly, I thought.

But the prosecutor had other ideas.

He called the two boys to the stand. They both lied and said I'd tried to get them to play the horrible hide-and-seek sex game. Said I told them, "the more the merrier."

Montoya cross-examined them. He tried to trip them up, expose their lies, but they were steadfast in their made up stories.

Several other witnesses were called to testify to Preston's stellar character. I'd never seen any of them. Most were from his childhood, from the church he'd attended with his family years ago.

I couldn't believe the number of character witnesses they called.

Then Mr. Mendelssohn, his attorney, called Preston to the stand. He told the same story as the frat boys, except he looked right at me when he told it. He even went so far as to say there was never any mention of eating at Double Dog Dare Ya, and that I'd ruined my own tires to get him to help me out.

Somehow his attorney wove all of Preston's statements into a fictional tale involving me—my small town background—and my overwhelming desire to snag a rich boy into marrying me by using these twisted sexual escapades.

It sounded so ridiculous I thought there was no way the jury could believe a word of it.

But some of them did believe him. I could see it in their faces.

When it was Montoya's turn to question him, he asked Preston about all the times he'd been seen outside my apartment, all the times he'd shown his temper when I wouldn't do what he wanted, and he asked him why I would have gone to the hospital if I had just been playing some kind of game.

Preston looked into my attorney's eyes and smiled. "I never went to her place unless she invited me. As for the sex games in the woods, I can't say why she drove herself to the hospital." He glanced at me. "Maybe I played the game better than she expected."

My attorney turned toward the jury and shook his head. "Do you expect any of us to believe that, Mr. Stevensen?" He glanced back at Preston as he said it. "Are you so delusional you believe it yourself?"

Preston raised his hands, palms facing upward, in an I-don't-know gesture. "Some people are just really into S&M," he said. "And some only think they are." Then he looked at me again and his smile widened into a grin.

"I believe you are describing yourself, Mr. Stevensen," Montoya said. "Thank you for telling us that. It explains a lot."

He turned back toward the jury box, still shaking his head.

Preston's smile faltered.

"I have no further questions, Your Honor."

When Preston returned to his seat, his attorney leaned over and whispered something in his ear. Preston's smile not only faltered, it disappeared completely.

What an ass, I thought. Surely everyone can see through his lies.

But it didn't work out that way.

Some of them still seemed to believe him.

The trial lasted three days.

The second day, it was our turn to call witnesses.

ADA Montoya called Joanna first. She testified about Preston's strange behavior and how he would sleep outside our apartment, how he practically stalked me around campus.

When his attorney stood up to cross examine her, a few members of the jury sneered at him.

My attorney had prepped her as best he could. But when Preston's lawyer asked where she had been on the night of the frat party, the night I supposedly concocted the plan to lure

Preston into the woods, she had to admit she'd been in another room at the house, watching a couple of jocks from her kinesiology class play beer pong.

"And would you say your roommate visited with Preston willingly that night? The night she gave him her phone number and told him to call her anytime?"

Joanna shook her head. "No. She didn't even come in to that party. She only dropped off a friend from her part time job—" But he didn't let her finish the explanation. He simply cut her off and moved on to something else.

"But earlier," he said, "when they went out to lunch, and then dinner, and the party at the lake... were all of those against her will, or did she go eagerly?" He drew out the syllables on eagerly as if to add to the idea that I had been the one chasing Preston, not the other way around.

Joanna took a deep breath. I could see her fighting for control of her emotions. "I wouldn't call it eagerly." She glanced at the jury. "He seemed nice at first—" She tried to tell them how he had changed. How he began to try and control me. How he got so angry in the parking lot that day because I wouldn't go to breakfast, how frightening he became. But she wasn't able to tell anything else.

The attorney dismissed her with a wave. "I have no more questions, Your Honor."

When she stepped down from the box, she shot me a look of apology. I tried to smile, to let her know I understood, but from the corner of my eye I could see Preston. His cruelly curved lips wiped any semblance of a smile off my face.

Montoya called two other character witnesses from my small group of friends at college. Lana also came and testified to my character since we'd been friends forever. Even my old Sunday school teacher made the trip. They all testified that I would never have done what Preston's side alleged.

Just put me up there on that stand, I thought. Let me tell what that bastard did. My nerves were jumping. I was furious and afraid. By the time Montoya called my name, I could barely think. I walked across the room and took the stand, my knees and hands shaking so hard I could not force them to be still. Once again, I prayed I wouldn't faint.

Montoya coaxed me to tell exactly what had happened. Several times the judge admonished me to speak up. I nodded, took a sip from the glass of water sitting on the stand in front of me, and tried to make myself heard.

When I told about running through the forest, tripping, falling, how he kept hissing at me to "run, little rabbit run," I realized my eyes were closed.

I made it a point to open them. I looked at Carrie. She gave me a slight nod and a smile, but I couldn't look at Mom. I chose not to look at Preston or his family, but I couldn't keep from glancing at the jury. I couldn't tell what they were thinking. White, staring faces, clenched lips and jaws.

ADA Montoya apologized as he quietly displayed the pictures of my face and throat up on the big screen. "Tell me ladies and gentlemen of the jury, does this look like someone who enjoyed the rape and attempted murder? Look at her face, her eye, her throat where he cut her with the knife and left her to die." He gave them a moment to examine the photos. A couple of jurors cringed and looked away.

Then he put up the photos of the rest of my body but kept his hand over the projector light for a moment. "I'm sorry to have to show these," he said, his voice quiet. "If you are a family member, you may want to look away." And then he uncovered the light and there were photos of my naked back, my shoulder with the bite mark, my naked hips and legs and buttocks. Every inch of my body had some trauma; some bruise, some scrape or cut. The photos were bits and pieces.

ADA Montoya had tried to protect my dignity as much as possible.

"I'm sorry, Marlena," he looked directly at me, and then he put up a black line forensic drawing of a female body with the extent of my genital injuries marked on it with red marker. "I've got the photos to match these injuries," he murmured, standing directly in front of the jury, looking into their faces one by one. "But I think my client has been victimized enough." He turned at the end of the railing. "I will let you look at them in the jury room if the judge will allow, but I won't put any more on display just now. It was a brutal, planned attack, ladies and gentlemen. Not a game." He pointed toward me. "It's an absolute miracle my client survived."

Most of the jury sympathized with me now. I could tell. There were tears. Some of them scowled at Preston and his family.

When Lucifer got up to question me, it was the same old song and dance. He tried to shake me out of my story, but he wasn't able. The lurid pictures told their own version of the truth.

I didn't bother to look at the jury as I went back to my seat. My wobbly legs felt stronger.

My gut said we had won.

23

THE VERDICT

A fter the second day of testimony, ADA Montoya told me not to get my hopes up. "I don't *think* any jury could look at those pictures of your injuries and not see the truth. But experience tells me not to ever count my chickens before they hatch." He rubbed his chin. "Especially when it appears our adversary has enough money to buy witnesses."

We were in his office.

He scrolled through the contacts on his phone. "I'll have my investigator examine the bank accounts and backgrounds of those two boys. See if they've come into any cash or new cars recently."

That scared me. If witnesses could be that easily bought, then what else could their money do? It made me seriously doubt the entire justice system.

Montoya continued, "I hope they saw through those boys." He touched his chin again. "They really tried to make you out to be quite a—a—"

"A slut?" My voice cracked.

He didn't nod, but his eyes looked down at a folder on his desk.

"I can't help that," I said. "I should never have gone to meet Preston that night, but I really thought it would be one dinner and that would be the end of it." I laughed and it came out so harsh it sounded like a bark. "I wanted to be nice. To let him down easy." I glanced up at the attorney. "What is that old saying, no good deed goes unpunished?"

Montoya sat behind his desk, across from me. "Marlena, sweetie," his tone was fatherly.

"I know what you're going to say—"

"Do you?" He shifted his weight. His expensive leather chair creaked on its rolling wooden base. He leaned forward, elbows on the desk. "I know this guy is a monster. You've said it yourself." He jerked his thumb over his shoulder toward the courtroom. "Maybe all the jurors don't see it yet, but I do. He left you for dead." He sat back. His chair settled. "I really think he murdered the other girl, too. The one near Chicago. There just isn't enough evidence to charge him on that one. Yet."

I began to cry. I could tell he was preparing me for bad news. Drying my tears, I tried to put on a positive face. "Who knows, maybe Detective Lapuli will come up with something and he will swoop in at the last second and arrest Preston for Mariah's murder."

Tears seeped from the corners of my eyes again. I imagined the tracks they were creating in my makeup. I reached for a tissue from the box on his desk. Why did I even wear any makeup? Oh, yeah, because I hadn't slept in days. Because the mirror said I was thirty-nine, not nineteen.

Montoya placed his hands flat on his desk. "I think we've done all we can do." He stood. "I just thought when the jury saw those pictures it would be a slam dunk." He grimaced. "I didn't count on their deep pockets."

Right then, something occurred to me. As much as I liked ADA Montoya, as much as I respected him... had he done all he could do? Should we have known about the false testimony of the frat boys? Should we have had some sort of trap ready to expose them?

Surely this wasn't as bad as it seemed. After all, Preston raped me. He left me for dead. Thank God for the disembodied voices. Thank God his aim with the knife was off. Thank God for my sister and her spare key holder. I'd fought for my life, ADA Montoya was right about that. Why should I have anything to worry about? Even if I had gone with him willingly, that shouldn't matter. He'd tried to kill me. He'd forced me to do things I never would have done in a million years, and then he'd tried to kill me.

No. I wanted to believe we had nothing to worry about. No matter how rich or influential his parents were, no matter how many liars they lined up on the stand, there was no way we could lose. Pictures don't lie.

I dried my face, dabbed at my eyes, held my head up, and followed my attorney into the hall.

"Don't worry," I said. "Anyone with a heart and half a brain will see what he did to me." I tried on a smile. "We'll win this thing. He can't get away with it. He can't."

Montoya patted my shoulder. "I'm sure you're right. Tomorrow, closing arguments. Make or break time."

I took a deep breath. Make or break. It all comes down to a few sentences. Surely the jurors can look at his face, at that smirk, and see his soul. See how black it is, how dead. Surely, those twelve fine folks can see that. "Okay," I said. "Let's go." I walked out of the building and into my new future.

WE DIDN'T TALK MUCH about the case that night. Carrie found an old movie on the hotel TV and the three of us zoned out with nachos and beer. I think the beer helped me sleep.

The closing arguments were what one would expect. More of the same. The defense attorney reminded the jury that I was a slut who had lured Preston to the woods for a game of catch-and-rape. He reiterated the testimony that I'd tried to lure at least two other boys into the same game. He told them that I'd even brought the knife, to make things more realistic, and that when it slipped and actually cut my neck, it was my fault. That I'd freaked out and started hollering rape.

He said I took off and that Preston spent the rest of the night looking for me, to save me. "Folks," he'd continued as a wrap up. "Seriously, look at the two of them." He'd hesitated to make certain all eyes were trained on the two of us. "He's six-three, one eighty-five. She's barely what? Five-foot-five, one twenty? Do you think if he'd taken her to the woods to kill her she would still be with us? Do you? Does it make sense that he would have let her live if his intention had been to take her life?" He slapped his forehead dramatically. "It was a game, people. A silly, sexy game made up by a young woman so desperate to marry a wealthy young man that she would do anything to impress him. A silly, sexy, game gone wrong, that's all."

And with that, he'd spun around, stalked back to his table, and sat down. Case closed.

My attorney had a pretty good poker face, but even so his lips got thinner as he pressed them together. He couldn't argue any of those points. He couldn't shake Preston's friends out of their lie, and he couldn't dispute the fact that Preston didn't kill me, *only* raped and cut me, supposedly at my request.

All he could do was remind them of the slashed tires—Preston had said it was just a prelude to the game—and the horrific pictures and testimony from the nurses at the hospital.

They all agreed it was definitely rape. They were there. They saw me and testified to my pain and my certainty that he would come and finish what he had started.

"Ladies and gentlemen of the jury," ADA Montoya stood directly in front of them, not pacing, non-threatening. "I don't have to convince you of Mr. Stevensen's guilt." He took a slow breath. "The evidence has done that. I've presented to you all the physical proof that my client was brutally raped, beaten, stabbed in the throat, and left for dead. You can't possibly refute the mountain of physical evidence." He pointed to the stack of pictures he'd strategically placed on the corner of the table near my elbow. "All they have is a made-up story that has absolutely no merit."

He looked straight at Preston and his attorney. "Why would my client—a young woman who never had so much as a parking ticket in her life—suddenly go all Girls Gone Wild at the risk of her own life? Does it make sense to you?" he stared at each juror in turn. "Did you listen to her? Did you?"

I don't really know what he said after that. There was one man who wouldn't meet Montoya's eye. He kept his gaze trained on his hands, folded in his lap.

The world fuzzed away. Words slurred into silence and brain fog. In a moment, I felt the ADA sit down in the chair beside me. I looked at his face and it was pale. That's when I knew we were not going to win. Nausea rose. My stomach roiled. I couldn't believe the closing arguments had taken less than an hour. Everything that had happened condensed down to mere minutes.

The judge gave the jury their instructions for deliberating, and then we were out on the steps in front of the courthouse and Montoya was telling me to get some rest and he would call me as soon as they came back with a verdict. "It will probably be tomorrow," he said. "Or maybe the day after that."

Since it was slightly after noon, Mom suggested we get something to eat and go back to our hotel room.

When we walked down the steps, reporters had gathered. Until now there had been only one or two taking notes in the courtroom. Due to the graphic photos, the judge had outlawed cameras during the trial.

"Marlena, Marlena, look this way!" I turned my head toward the voice. A woman with shiny brunette hair held a microphone toward me. Behind her lurked a guy with a camera on his shoulder. "How do you feel about the trial?" she shouted as I kept walking. "Do you feel confident about the outcome?"

My attorney reappeared. He held one hand in front of the camera while giving me a little push in the middle of my back with the other hand. "Just keep walking," he murmured. "No comment," he said to the reporter.

Before this, the trial had been kept pretty much under wraps. I hadn't realized how lucky we were until a second reporter scrambled toward us, microphone in hand. Seeing ADA Montoya ushering me along, the reporter descended on Mom and Carrie. Joanna was smart. She'd slipped out after her testimony.

"Mrs. Matthews, can you give us a moment? How did the trial go, will he be convicted?"

Mom took her cue from our attorney. She didn't say no comment, she just held her hand up between her face and the looming camera. Carrie didn't even give them a chance, she grabbed Mom's arm and rushed them both down the sidewalk toward the parking lot.

When we were even with Carrie's car, ADA Montoya reached over, opened the back door, and stuffed me inside. With a short little salute, he mouthed, "Keep your phone on." And then he strolled unhurriedly toward his own vehicle at the curb. I admired his attitude. Too bad I couldn't act like that.

"Where should we go for dinner?" Carrie tried to sound cheerful as she got behind the steering wheel. Mom slid in beside her and put on her seat belt.

I wasn't hungry, and I sure didn't want to go in anywhere. I opened my mouth to mention visiting a burger drive through again, but from the corner of my eye I caught a glimpse of rushed movement.

Preston and his attorney came down the courthouse steps flanked by his parents and a girl that had to be his sister, the resemblance was uncanny right down to the high forehead and thick, straight brows.

The original reporter had been joined by two or three more, but rather than shy away and hurry down the sidewalk the way we did, Preston and Lucifer appeared to be holding a press conference.

I found myself clenching white quarter-moons into my palms. I closed my eyes but couldn't block out the images of dark trees and cold mist, sharp twigs and invisible roots rising up from the ground; couldn't get away from memory of his furious face hanging over me, his fist smashing into my cheek, his hard knee forcing my legs apart, the knife coming down, and down. The knife coming down, parting the cold mist, the warmth flowing—

"Sis?"

I felt the car lurch to a stop. My eyes came open slowly. For a moment, I didn't know where I was. I looked out the window at a street scene that made no sense to me.

"Are you okay?" Mom sounded alarmed.

I tried to still the fluttery sick feeling around my heart. "I think Preston is doing an interview back there." I closed my eyes again.

Carrie groaned. "Hasn't he done enough? Now he has to get on TV, too?"

"My thoughts exactly." I began to implement the deep steady breathing techniques I'd learned in therapy.

We drove away. I couldn't help myself. I turned and took one last glance at the ugly tableau. Why weren't his parents more upset? They looked positively elegant, at ease, as if they were on vacation—all except for the girl. She didn't look comfortable. In fact, she stood slightly apart, head down, gazing at her phone.

As I watched, she glanced up. Our eyes met, it felt as if our souls met. What an idiotic thought my subconscious whispered. And yet, I still felt it. As if an invisible string connected me to her. Could she know the truth about her brother?

I couldn't look away. Something on her face said she did not agree with this at all. Something said she was not a huge fan of her brother. Something told me she had stories she could tell. What must it have been like to grow up alongside a psychopath like Preston?

Or had I read too much into one glance?

She smoothed her blonde hair away from her forehead and stood a little straighter. But her gaze never left my face.

I tore my eyes away and turned back around in my seat. Gooseflesh coated my arms and legs. What was that? I couldn't help it. I looked back over my shoulder once more before we turned the corner.

She still stared at me through the back windshield.

I didn't say anything to Mom or Carrie. What would I say? His sister is staring at me with a funny look on her face?

On the way back to the hotel we stopped by Burger Barn, got three orders to go, and carried them into the hotel. We were sharing a room with two queen beds. Carrie and I hadn't slept together since we were kids, but we had immediately fallen back into our childhood routines. She took the right side and I took the left. I got the bathroom first—after Mom—and Carrie went last because she loved a soak in the tub while I preferred a quick shower.

Now, we spread our heart-attacks-in-sacks on the round all-purpose table near the window. "What if he doesn't go to jail?" The question had been on my mind ever since ADA Montoya called me back to his office after the closing arguments.

Mom sat in the chair nearest the balcony window. We were on the fifth floor so we had a wonderful view of downtown. Even in November, the view was spectacular. "He won't get away with it," she said. "That can't happen. He's evil." She shuddered. "I studied him the whole time. He has no conscience, no soul—"

"I agree." Carrie opened a packet of ketchup. "He is evil. Pure evil." She stuffed a couple of fries in her mouth and unwrapped our burgers.

I didn't think I could take a bite, but when the smell of fried meat hit my nostrils, I suddenly found myself ravenous. Sipping my soft drink and dipping my fries in the ketchup, I managed to devour the well-done burger in a few bites. Nerves, I thought again. It felt as if this nightmare would never end.

"I hate having to drag y'all through this." I'd never voiced my feelings about everything before, but I had to get it off my chest. "I just want you both to know how much I appreciate you being here with me."

Mom jumped up, came around to my chair, and wrapped her arms around my shoulders. "We wouldn't have it any other way, sweetie. I'm just sorry you ever met that creep. I thank God every day that you survived."

Carrie nodded her agreement.

But I had a couple more things I wanted to say. "It's been awful living in limbo this past year. Waiting for the trial..." I cleared my throat, dabbed at my mouth for ketchup. "Carrie, I just want to say thanks to you and Dix for taking me in and letting me hide. Getting me back and forth to therapy and my self-defense classes. You guys have been everything to me." I looked at the tabletop. This was hard to say, hard to admit. "Once he's behind bars, I think I'll be able to start living again."

Carrie grasped my hand across the small table. "I know you will, Mar. Everything is going to work out, you'll see."

I nodded again. "I've been thinking about that real estate course you mentioned. I mean I've enjoyed working for you and Dix, but I think maybe I'm ready to do more. To get my own license perhaps."

Mom and Carrie both clapped their hands. They reminded me of twins. Since she and Dad moved to Denver, Mom had seemed to grow younger. No longer shouldering Dad's care alone had relieved her of a huge burden.

After we ate and cleaned up, we pulled off our shoes, made ourselves comfortable, and turned on some inane movie.

When my phone rang, we all jumped. "It's only been a few hours," I said. "Surely it's too soon for a verdict." Then I looked at the phone's screen. "Oh. Oh, my God." My fingers shook so badly I could hardly press the answer icon.

"The jury came back," Montoya said bluntly. "Meet me back at the courthouse ASAP. I'll wait for you on the steps."

I broke the connection and tried to catch my breath. My heart began to pound.

"Is it time?" Mom asked.

I nodded.

Carrie pulled me to my feet, we brushed our teeth, put our shoes back on, and together we made our way out to the car with Mom bringing up the rear.

I don't remember the ride to the courthouse. I rode there in limbo. I existed in limbo. The whole past year I had lived in limbo. Now, limbo was about to end.

Reporters swarmed the entrance.

ADA Montoya didn't wait on the steps. He came to the car,

helped me out, put his hand beneath my elbow and led me to a side door I'd never even noticed. Without speaking, we went directly to the courtroom. At the prosecutor's table, we stood and waited for the judge and jury to come in and be seated.

My mind wandered as I tried to avoid looking at the defendant's table where Preston and his attorney also stood waiting. If I let myself think about it, I would go mad. The fact that I had to even be near this madman, in the same room, made no sense at all. He should be locked away like a wild animal in a cage.

I straightened my skirt, smoothed my hair, and then everyone came in and the bailiff told us all to be seated.

The charges were read again.

The jury foreman stood and the judge asked her if they had reached a verdict

The woman's voice trembled. "We cannot agree on a verdict, Your Honor."

Hung jury. Oh, my God. That means he gets off. My mind closed down. The room began to gray. I closed my eyes and grabbed the edge of the table with my fingertips. It seemed to tilt. Someone eased me down to the floor and someone else patted my cheek. I opened my eyes.

All around me, voices were raised in disbelief.

The judge banged her gavel. "Order," she said. "I want order in this court!" She pointed her gavel at the defendant's table. "Will the prosecution seek a retrial?"

"Yes, Your Honor," Montoya said over his shoulder.

She nodded. "Trial will be rescheduled. Defendant is reminded his bond and restraining order still stand." She banged her gavel once more. "This court is adjourned." She leaned over and spoke across the room toward me. "Should I call a paramedic?"

Allowing ADA Montoya to help me to my feet, I shook my head, embarrassed.

The judge nodded. "Counselors, with me, please." She strode behind the bench to her inner chamber. I could see Mom being held back by Carrie. She appeared ready to vault over the half-wall separating us.

My attorney came up with a bottle of water from somewhere. I gulped a few swallows and held the cool plastic to my burning cheeks. I couldn't believe the outcome and my involuntary reaction to it. I could feel Preston looking at me from across the aisle.

"Will he walk out of here with his folks?"

Montoya nodded. "They appear to have very deep pockets."

"Not even more bail?" I didn't understand why he had made bail in the first place, having been charged with attempted murder. And I sure didn't understand this. It seemed as if he had gotten off Scott free.

Montoya shook his head. "The bail was very high when he was first charged, and since he didn't skip out on it, the judge has no reason to change it."

It sounded logical when he said it, but in my gut, I knew he could take off and disappear if he wanted. With pockets that deep, what could possibly keep him from going to some island nation without extradition? I could easily picture him on the beach, a drink in his hand, ogling some innocent girl strolling by in a bikini.

"I'll talk to the judge," Montoya said. "But I don't have much hope—"

"Do I go in there with you?"

He shook his head again. "It will only be a few minutes to discuss a new trial date."

I couldn't help it. I glanced at Preston's table. "What about him? Do I have to stay out here with him?"

Montoya followed my gaze. "I'll make sure the bailiff stays by you, and your family." He turned and nodded at Mom and

Carrie who immediately came around to the table. The attorney stepped aside and Mom sat down in his chair beside mine so she could hug and pat me and make sure I was really all right.

I saw Montoya speak to the bailiff on his way to the door behind the judge's bench. The bailiff looked at Preston's table and then headed directly for ours. Without a word, he took his position at the end of our table near the aisle. Feet apart, with his back to us, he stood statue-like and immovable. Thank you, God. Thank you, ADA Montoya.

In minutes, the two attorneys were back. The new trial could not be scheduled for six months due to a backlog of cases on the docket. Everything else would be the same except a new jury would be selected. In other words, this was like the nightmare without end. In six months, I would have to come back. Do it all again.

"One guy," Montoya said. "One guy said he wasn't guilty and that nothing would ever change his mind."

I remembered the man who wouldn't meet anyone's gaze. "I don't know if I can do this again," I said.

He nodded. "I'm sorry. I can't believe it, but at the same time, I'm not that surprised." He glanced over at the defendant's table. "I wish I could prove they bought a juror and two witnesses."

"I know. How could that man possibly look at my injuries and think I asked for that?" I let that thought trail away. "No. I seriously don't think I can do this again. I thought when he was locked up I would get my life back. But now I see, that won't ever happen. He didn't murder me, but he sure as hell took my life."

As if he heard me, Preston looked across the aisle between our tables and winked. The bailiff had moved away after Montoya returned. Now, my face burned with anger. No, not just anger, all I once I became consumed with fury, a bright red burning that coursed through my veins like fire.

24

AFTER

ADA Montoya gathered his things and placed them neatly in his briefcase. I tore my gaze away from Preston's smirking face and looked at Carrie instead. I remembered how she had instructed me to look at her from the witness stand and so I did that now. But I could feel his gaze on my skin. It felt like insects crawling all over me.

I shivered and the rage welled up again. Without thinking, I allowed my eyes to meet his. This time he didn't wink. This time he saw a different person than the one he had victimized in the woods. This time, he saw the real me. The me beneath the terror. The girl I had become after months of seclusion and therapy and self-defense classes.

Staring into his face I made that girl come out. I allowed my gaze to harden. I did not look away. Neither did I wink. This may be some sick game to you, I thought, but not to me. I'm done being scared. I straightened my spine, my eyes never leaving his.

Preston's gaze faltered.

Someone stepped in between us and the moment was broken. When next I saw them, his father had clasped his mother's upper arm and they were leading Preston out of the courtroom.

My attorney took his time, deliberately placing things in his briefcase as if in slow motion. Every now and then he would stop and glance at his phone. I finally realized he was stalling to let Preston's bunch clear the area.

It also occurred to me that I still had my phone turned off so while we were killing time, I pulled it out and turned it back on. A message alert popped up. Lana wanted me to call and let her know how it came out.

I didn't want to try and carry on a conversation while we were walking, so I decided to call her after we got back in the car.

After a few more minutes, we made our way outside. In the distance, I could see Preston getting into the back of a Mercedes. Several news crews were filming spot promos here and there in front of the courthouse. A couple of reporters broke away and headed toward us, but once again ADA Montoya held them at bay. "Call my office if you need a statement," he said. Then he hugged the three of us, said he would be in touch, and helped us into Carrie's vehicle again.

And then we were on our own.

"It's like a circus, isn't it?" Mom murmured, looking out at the people standing in knots.

"A dark carnival," I replied, quoting a Ray Bradbury book.

Carrie maneuvered us out of the parking space before she spoke. "Thank goodness you both live in Denver now. The look on that guy's face..."

"I know. I can't believe I thought he was so good looking when I first met him." My phone beeped in my hand, reminding me of my waiting message. "I need to call Lana." I pressed her name and sat back in my seat. She answered immediately.

"You're not going to believe this..." I told her about the hung jury and new trial.

"You're right," she said. "I don't believe it. How could they possibly—"

"Money," I interrupted. "They buy their way out of everything."

I heard Lana murmur something. Then I heard a voice in the background.

"Who's that? Is someone with you?"

"It's Jim Allan," she said. "I've got Jimmy here with me. I found him, Mar."

A million images rushed through my head. I didn't know which ones to focus on first. I chose the one most problematic. "Does he know?"

Lana remained silent long enough for me to guess the answer.

"Lan? What's going on?"

In answer I heard a familiar voice say, "She told me." Then the deep voice cracked. "Marlie, why? Why didn't you tell me?"

My mind flashed back to the memory of those awful days immediately after the hospital. "I was such a mess," I said. "I sent a message, but you didn't reply." I took a quick breath. "And when I called, it just cut off." Mom and Carrie were silent in the front seat, obviously listening.

JIM DIDN'T RESPOND at first. Then he said, "But why did you go with him, Mar? Why did you go out with him as soon as you got back to school? And why did you send me that awful text saying you loved him, and not me?" He cleared his throat. "Did you want to hurt me for some reason? I thought—I thought—that night—"

"What do you mean? The only message I sent you was the

one asking you to call me after I got out of the hospital. But you never responded."

"What?" He sounded incredulous. "I don't understand. I got a message from you the night you got back to school. It said you never wanted to see me again, that you loved someone else." He stopped talking and for a moment I wondered if we'd been disconnected.

"Jimmy?"

"Marlena. I don't know what happened. I tried to call and text you before I gave up and went up the backcountry for a few days. My phone died but I didn't care. When I never heard back from you, I just no longer cared."

His voice rushed into my ear and into my brain and into my heart. It had all been a mistake. Just a huge mistake. Someone had sent him a message from my phone.

Understanding dawned on me. "He did it," I said. "He must have taken my phone after he—when he left me for dead." I took a deep breath, relieved to know the truth. "He did it, Jim. He must have."

"Oh, Marlena. I'm so stupid. I believed the message. I didn't want to, but I just didn't kn—."

"It's okay," I mumbled. "You couldn't have known."

"We need to talk," he said. "In person, not on the phone. I need to see you, to hold you, to make sure—"

"Make sure I'm still the girl I was?"

"No. Not that. I know you aren't the girl you were before, who could be after what you've been through?" His voice cut off again, and then he whispered, "I need to know if you can forgive me for not being there. Lana told me how horrible it was, how you're lucky to be alive. I can't believe I didn't hear a thing—"

"Rape victims names are not released to the public unless given permission. And I didn't until the trial. Then I had no choice."

"I'll kill him," Jimmy said. "I heard you and Lana talking about a hung jury and how you have to go through everything again. "But that won't be necessary if I get to him first. He needs to pay for what he's done."

His words burned in my ears, the idea burned in my mind. "Jimmy, you can't say that."

He grew quiet, but he didn't take it back. Of all the things I thought he might say if I ever got to see him again that wasn't one of them. "Yeah," I said at last. "As tempting as it would be, we can't even entertain the thought."

"Where are you?" he asked. "Lana said you live in Denver now."

"We are still in Austin, where it happened, but the three of us will drive back to Denver tomorrow. I live with Carrie and Dix now. Mom and Dad live nearby."

"Everything changed so fast," Jimmy said. "I camped in the mountains. No phones, no amenities—"

"I know," I said. "You don't have to explain."

"Yes, I do. It's the least I can do." He hurried on. "I've been sort of living in the backcountry since all this happened. I go to my classes, and then I get on Big Red and take off. I've been on hold almost the entire year since it happened."

"You, too?" I couldn't believe he'd just said exactly what I'd been feeling.

"But then Lana and Dash got together and found me. They told me everything. That's when we came up with this plan to meet up with you and your mom and sister. Lana and Dash just picked me up at the airport. In Lubbock."

That got my attention. "Lubbock? Is that why she took off after her testimony? I thought she said it was because of school... but Lubbock? We have to go right through there on the way home."

"That's our plan," he said. "Lana's a great friend, Mar. If she and Dash hadn't contacted my roommate, I would be in the backcountry again, unaware of everything. Instead, Daniel caught me at the stables, gave me their message." He hesitated. "Will you meet me in Lubbock, if I wait?"

My heart soared. "Of course I will." The terrible events of the trial faded a bit, but were immediately replaced by the worry that things would be different with Jimmy. That he would look at me and see something ugly, as ugly as the things Preston put me through. I took a deep breath and told him where our favorite Cracker Barrel restaurant was located. "We'll meet you on the front porch tomorrow."

"We'll be there," he said.

Lana got back on the phone and I scolded her and thanked her all at the same time. "I thought you said you left Austin to go back to school—"

"I tried to get him there before the trial ended," she interrupted. "I think he could have helped, you know, as a character witness, but he was just too far away."

"I can't believe you did all that."

"That's what friends are for, besides, you and Jim both helped me after Dash scared me that night."

"You don't have to keep repaying—"

"Don't say it," she interrupted. "Just come on up here and start putting your life back together. Jim is the one, isn't he? That's what you told me before all this happened."

"Is he right there beside you?" I could only imagine what his expression might be, hearing all this.

Lana laughed. "No, he's not right beside me. But so what? It's the truth, isn't it?"

I closed my eyes and leaned my head back. "I don't know anymore, Lan. I'm not that same girl. Preston took more from me than just my dignity."

"You had to toughen up, that's all. That's what you're feeling.

You had to harden your heart a bit to survive. Anyone would have."

Yeah, I thought. I had to harden my heart. That's exactly right. So does that leave any place for Jimmy? Or anyone else? I wanted to ask Lana what she thought but she began to chatter again.

"You won't believe this, but Dash has been going to AA and he got to that step about making amends and he called me up. We went and had coffee—"

"Jimmy said y'all were in this together. Has he really changed?"

Lana continued in a somewhat dreamy voice, "Yes. He is so much better, Mar. Now I remember why I had a crush on him all of senior year."

"Wow. Just. Wow. That's something I never expected to hear."

Carrie glanced at me in the rearview so I told Lana I couldn't wait to hear more, later.

"Okay," she said. "I hope you don't mind that Dash came with us. He insisted. Said he owed it to Jimmy to help the two of you get back together." Her voice changed. "They're coming back now. I'm taking them to find a hotel room. We will meet you at Cracker Barrel. Drive safely!"

I relayed all the information to Mom and Carrie. "Well," Mom said, "that is amazing. Lana is such a good friend to go to those lengths. It also goes to show that Jimmy knew something about Dash, too. Knew there was something in there worth saving."

That's right, I thought. Even back at the street dance last year, I remembered wondering why Jim bothered with Dash when he caused so much trouble.

I closed my eyes. Jim Allan. All a misunderstanding. Why did Preston do that? *Did* Preston do that? It had to be him. He was the only one who could have.

My mind imagined the awful scenario of Preston texting Jimmy until I finally felt myself beginning to doze. I jerked awake. Thanks to Lana, we would get it straightened out. Shouldn't I be way more excited than this? Jimmy had my heart. I didn't doubt that. He was the only boy I'd ever felt such a connection with.

So why didn't I feel over the moon excited? Today's horrible courtroom drama had obviously dulled my senses. Or maybe that had happened during and after the attack itself. I wondered if it would last forever, this apathy, this unrelenting feeling of dismay? Maybe seeing Jim again would bring me back to my old self. Maybe then I wouldn't feel like damaged goods anymore.

Dozing off again, I recalled my therapist saying excessive sleeping could be a coping mechanism. But not necessarily a good one. Whatever, she had no idea what I'd been through the last couple of days.

I pulled my travel pillow into a U shape around my neck and let my mind drift down into slumber. Sometime later the sound of my phone chiming softly awakened me. I immediately thought of Jimmy. I pressed the talk icon and held it to my ear. I didn't put it on speaker. I wasn't ready to share him with Mom and Carrie.

"Hello?" I hated that my voice sounded so timid.

"You were supposed to die in the woods. I'm not finished with you."

My heart slammed into the back of my throat. I looked at the screen. UNKNOWN CALLER. Preston. Who else could it be?

What should I do?

I sat still for a second. Should I call the police?

"Marlie?" Carrie's eyes sought mine in the rearview mirror. "You okay?"

My hand shook as I held up my phone.

"I know," she said. "I heard it ring. Who called?"

I swallowed, but it didn't help. My mouth had gone dry.

Mom swiveled in her seat. "Honey? What is it? You're as pale as a ghost."

"Him," I croaked. "He said I should have died in the woods. Said he isn't finished with me."

Mom grabbed the phone from my hand. "Are you sure it was him?"

I nodded.

"He can't do that! He can't call you. Isn't there a restraining order?"

"Call Montoya," Carrie said. "He'll know what to do."

Mom scrolled through my contact list until she found ADA Montoya. She pressed the icon to call but he didn't answer. His voice mail came on instructing callers to leave a message. Mom told him who she was and what had just happened. Her voice didn't shake until the last few words.

"He can't do that to you," Mom murmured. I noticed she didn't hand me back my phone.

"He's a monster," I said. "He can do anything he wants." Tears filled my eyes. "He should be in jail. They should have put him in jail."

Mom twisted around and put her hand on my knee. "We'll get him," she said. "He can't do this. There must be repercussions for breaking the restraining order."

Carrie pulled the steering wheel to the right, swerving us back into our lane. She had allowed the car to drift as she listened to Mom leaving the message. "Does he know you live with us?"

I shrugged. "I don't know. I don't even know how he got my new phone number. He had to have gotten it somehow today. It's the first time since—"

My phone chimed in Mom's hand. "Hello," she said. "Yes, I'm the one who called. We couldn't believe it either. Yes, we're still

in the car. No. Of course we don't know how he got the number."
She listened for a moment then pushed the MUTE icon and
looked at me. He thinks the creep's attorney may have carelessly
allowed him to see your number on the court documents.

Shock squeezed my brain until I couldn't even think. But
inside my skull a neon sign flashed on and off, on and off.
ADDRESS the sign read. ADDRESS. If he saw my phone
number, he probably saw my new address, too.

I yanked the phone from Mom. "Did he get my address, too?
Did he?"

"I'm sorry," Montoya said. "There's no way to know. I'll call
the judge. This can't happen. We'll put a stop to it." He disconnected after assuring me he would call me back.

"I can't go to Denver," I said. "He probably has our address."

"You don't know for sure—" Mom said.

I grasped her fingers so she would have to look at me. "Mom.
He will come for me. He said he wasn't finished." I shook my
head. "I'll go somewhere else. I'll make sure he knows it. I know.
I'll tell ADA Montoya to tell his attorney I moved. He can't come
to Denver. He can't."

The next time my phone rang, more bad news. Montoya said
it couldn't have been Preston calling because he had no access to
my file. "The judge thinks it's some crazy person who has read
about the trial or something."

I closed my eyes. "That's impossible. How would some
random person get my phone number? That certainly wasn't
published in the paper or online. Besides, I recognized his voice.
I'll never forget it no matter how hard I try."

"Marlena, you know how it works with social media. It isn't
that difficult anymore."

"Maybe you're right, Mr. Montoya. I pray to God you are, but
you don't know how careful I've been since I got my new
number. After I lost my old phone, just knowing he might have

it made me extremely paranoid. I cancelled all my social media accounts." I inhaled and tried to keep my thumbnail from digging at the cuticles on my left hand. I'd just got that compulsion under control recently.

"You did?" he said. "All of them?"

"I did." I almost hated to admit it. "He destroyed the life I had. I've been living like a hermit hiding in a cave ever since he attacked me. You just don't know. I quit school, moved to another state, got a new phone number, and cancelled my online life. There's no way some random person found me. It's him. I know it." I felt a drop of moisture on my thumb. Blood had welled up where my nail had been digging. "I put everything on hold. I thought – I thought after the trial I could start all over." My voice gave out as I thought of all the ways I'd let Preston take over my life.

"I'm sorry," the prosecutor said again. "I'm waiting on the judge's office to call back and see if we can force him to let us look at his phone. See if it was him."

I could feel Mom and Carrie's anger mounting even though they didn't say anything from the front seat. All this had taken place in the fifteen-minute trip from the courthouse to our hotel where we had planned to spend the night before heading back to Denver the next day. "Even if you could search it, I'm sure he will just delete everything."

"If we can get a warrant, we can get his phone and his phone records."

A sigh escaped my lips. "Okay. I guess that's it then. It probably doesn't matter anyway. I'm sure it isn't his regular cell phone. Probably one of those TracFones like I bought when he stole mine." We pulled into the parking lot of the hotel and Carrie drove slowly looking for an empty slot. My eyes scanned the lot for his car. It had become a habit ever since that night.

"Stay with your family," the attorney said. "Don't do anything alone while you're still here in town."

I chuckled harshly. "Don't worry. I know the drill. I've been living it for almost a year."

"I'm sorry," he said again. "I wish I could do more, but trust me, I'm going to do everything I can to stop—"

"It's okay, Mr. Montoya, you don't have to say any more. I know you will do everything you can, but ultimately, this is my problem. It has been since I met that creep."

"Trust me. We *will* work this out. Don't give up on the system, and whatever you are thinking, promise me, you won't do anything rash—"

I laughed again. "Of course not, what could I do? I'm just a girl. What could I possibly do?"

The assistant district attorney told me to stay positive and let him know if anything else happened. I agreed that I would. He couldn't hang up fast enough.

We got out of the car, looking behind us the entire time, and made our way to the elevators. My phone buzzed in my palm. I looked down and there was a message. I touched the screen and a picture of a bloody knife appeared. I looked over my shoulder again, and then I closed the screen. I wanted to show Mom and Carrie. I wanted to forward it to ADA Montoya but something stopped me. Something Montoya had said.

"Don't do anything rash." What did that mean? What could I possibly do that would make a difference? Without thinking too much about it, I pulled out my phone and scrolled through my emojis. I found the raised middle finger, clicked on it, and wrote this message, "I'm not your victim anymore." Then I sent the middle finger along with it.

Before I'd even formulated my reply, his message had dissolved and disappeared. It looked like one of those cartoon special effects. First the image was there, and then it disintegrated right in front of my eyes. How could that happen? Must be some kind of app. Now I had nothing to show ADA Montoya except for a random call from an unknown number.

My heart began to race. What have I done? Was that smart, taunting a madman? I turned the volume down and left the ringer on vibrate. If another text came in, or a call from Montoya, I didn't want Mom or Carrie involved. I wanted to end this mess. One way or another.

The outline of a plan began to take shape in the back of my mind.

25

REUNION

We decided not to spend the night in Austin. The call had left us all feeling vulnerable. Carrie said, "If we drive on, at least we'll be doing something. And between the three of us there's no reason we can't take turns driving and napping."

I think she wanted to get back to Dix and her home. I didn't blame her. I was so worried now. If he hurt anyone in my family there would be no place for him to hide. My mind pictured the .38 revolver packed away in my suitcase. Of course I hadn't been able to take it to court with me, but other than that, I never went anywhere without it.

Dix and Carrie had gotten their Concealed Carry permits and I wanted to talk Mom into going with me to the range as well. It wasn't an option for me anymore. I'd been forced into making it more of a lifestyle.

I went into the bathroom to gather my things. My phone buzzed again. Another call came in from the UNKNOWN NUMBER, but I chose not to play that game. Let him text me or leave a message on my voicemail if he had something to say. I knew he wouldn't be ignored. For some strange reason, that idea alone gave me a modicum of control.

I clicked the IGNORE icon to send the call straight to voice mail. I would listen to it later—to see if he left a message—when I could plug in my ear buds and make certain no one else could hear.

I didn't have to wait long. When I didn't answer, another text came in.

"You're dead." Simple and direct.

I smiled. "Obviously, I'm not." I hit send and stuffed the phone down in my pocket. Maybe if I baited him, he would get angry enough to show himself. ADA Montoya had said we still had a restraining order in place, so if he showed up anywhere near me, I could have him arrested. If I could even prove he was the one calling, I could have him arrested, but so far, no word on that search warrant for his phone.

I knew it was a risky plan, trying to force him into the open, but better than no plan at all. Thinking about spending the next year of my life the same way I'd spent the last year of my life sounded torturous. I didn't think I would survive. And if he didn't show himself soon, then I would move on to plan B, move to a deserted island somewhere, change my name, subsist on coconuts and fish. Anything to protect my family.

Of course plan B was really no plan at all. These ideas were occurring to me as we packed, in direct response to his threats.

A sudden urgency took hold of me and I threw all my toiletries into my overnight bag and rushed into the room where Mom and Carrie were gathering their things. I grabbed my few articles of clothing and stuffed them into my wheeled suitcase. "Okay," I said. "We'd better go. The sooner we get out of Preston's town, the safer we will be."

They must have heard the near panic in my voice. Both of

them stopped folding and began to shove things into their bags. Within minutes we were back in the car and headed out.

Driving took my mind off everything. At least it did once we left the Austin city limits and I could stop looking over my shoulder.

On the highway, I felt my bones relax into their sockets. Just being in the same city as Preston made me imagine how it would feel at the bottom of the ocean without a submarine—all that pressure, crushing.

Feeling somewhat better, I rolled down my window, turned up the Sirius radio, and drove us all the way to Lubbock. We only made one pit stop on the way, at a truck stop the size of a small city. I felt safe there. Safer than pulling in to any of the roadside rest stops we passed.

We neared the outskirts of Lubbock quite late. I picked up my phone and touched Lana's name in favorites. Her voice sounded sleepy and indistinct when she answered. "So glad you came tonight," she said. "Do you want to call Jimmy's phone, or should I?"

"Where is he?" I asked. I pictured him across the hall in another room.

Lana laughed. "The last time I saw him he was pacing back and forth around the parking lot with Dash."

"Go ahead and call him, please. Tell him we will be there in about ten minutes. We're just coming into town and I have to concentrate on driving. I know the restaurant is on this side somewhere."

"See you soon," she said. "I think we can just make it before the restaurant closes. Our hotel is right next door."

I breathed a sigh of relief. Thank goodness Cracker Barrel stayed open until ten. From the back seat Mom raised her sleepy head from her own travel pillow. "Are we there yet?"

Carrie and I both burst out laughing. "We're here," I said as I spied the big oval restaurant sign.

"Oh, my," Mom said. "It got dark, didn't it? Look at my hair."

Carrie handed her a hairbrush from her purse and then pulled down the visor mirror to apply fresh lipstick in the lighted mirror. I hadn't even thought of my own appearance. If I had, I might have made Carrie drive when we left the truck stop, then I could have touched up my makeup, too.

But too late now. I could see Lana, Jimmy, and Dash on the front porch of the restaurant just like when I'd met Carrie and Dix there months earlier. This time Lana and Dash rocked in the rocking chairs and Jimmy paced back and forth like a caged animal.

At the sight of him, I grabbed the hairbrush and ran it through my hair in the dark. "Thanks." I gave her back the brush and my hand automatically went to the z-shaped scar on my neck. I should've tried to cover it with makeup, but I pulled my hair across it and hoped for the best.

My heart fluttered in my throat as I searched for a parking space. I could see Jimmy from the corner of my eye. He looked almost exactly the same. Tall and rangy, dressed in a western shirt and cowboy boots, he strode from one side of the wide porch to the other as I drove slowly down the row of cars.

Apparently he saw us first. Lana must have told him what we'd be driving. Before I even got the gearshift into park, he was there, opening my door, pulling me out, holding me to his chest, pressing his lips to my hair, my forehead, my cheek.

I turned my face into his chest and breathed in the crisp scent of hay and fresh air, just like I remembered. His pearl snap buttons were cool against my skin.

He tilted my chin up and I gazed into those storm cloud eyes and knew I was home. How could I have ever doubted what we'd shared? I felt something close up inside my chest, a wound

I hadn't known still gaped. For the first time in nearly a year, I felt as if I could breathe again.

When his lips found mine, the past fell away.

He held me to his chest. "I'm so sorry."

"There's nothing to be sorry for—" I saw Mom and Carrie crossing the parking lot to where Lana and Dash sat waiting. "I hope you understand when I tell you I felt almost relieved when you didn't answer my calls." I looked at the ground. "Oh, at first it hurt, thinking you'd got what you wanted and now you were giving me the brush off—"

"On top of everything else you went through—"

I clasped his hand. "Don't worry about that. When you didn't call, or answer my calls, I was sort of glad because I felt so horrible. So broken, that I didn't want you to see me that way. And I didn't want you to have to come to court."

A strangled sound escaped his throat.

When I glanced up, I saw moisture glistening in his eyes. He smashed it away by dipping his head sideways to his shoulder. "You shouldn't have gone through it alone." He touched his fingertip to the scar on my throat.

Shaking my head, I gestured at Mom and Carrie. "I wasn't alone, but oh how I missed you."

He pulled me to his chest again. "It wrecked me, Marlena. I thought I'd done something so wrong that you couldn't stand to see me, or even talk to me. I believed what that psycho said."

This time I pulled back to study his face. "I can't believe he tricked us so easily, but after it happened, I could barely function." I spoke into the narrow space between us. "I've had months and months of professional help to face the demons. It's made me a lot stronger but—it has also made me different."

Jim touched my hair. His usually kind expression hardened. A vertical line appeared between his eyebrows. "Lana said it was a hung jury. That he is free until the retrial. How is that even possible?" His lips touched my cheek just below my eye. "She showed me pictures. I can't believe everything you've been through."

"It's okay." I took his hand and pressed my lips to his fingers. "I'm okay now." I glanced over my shoulder again.

Jim followed my gaze, echoed the movement of my head as my eyes scanned back and forth across the parking lot, checking each car. "Except now you don't know exactly where he is and so you're back to looking for him everywhere you go." He checked the opposite side of the lot for me, although I hadn't told him what sort of vehicle to look for. "Lana said you moved to Denver because his rich parents bailed him out and put him right back out on the streets of Austin."

I shrugged. When he said it aloud, it made me feel like a wimp. Or a perpetual victim.

But Jim wasn't finished. I had to remember this was all new to him. I suppose he just needed to understand everything.

"I can't believe he completely derailed your college plans," he continued. "I wish I had known. Wish I had—"

My eyes closed involuntarily. "He made sure you didn't. That's the only reason I met him at the restaurant that night. To tell him about you. To tell him I could never go out with him again."

Jim nodded. "So that's why he sent me that message."

"Yes. Although I didn't know about that until you told me." I held his hand as we walked across the parking lot to where the rest of our little crew waited patiently.

Mom stood and took my other hand. She gave Jim a little hug and he hugged her, too. Then Dash grabbed me and smashed me to his chest in a bear hug that somehow felt like the most authentic thing that had happened between us. Carrie opened the restaurant door and Lana hugged me before ushering us all inside.

"Can't believe it's almost Thanksgiving again." My fingers lightly trailed the edge of a gorgeous platter depicting a regal turkey in all its glory. "Nearly an entire year." I glanced up at Jimmy. It almost felt like time travel.

After a quick but pleasant supper of comfort food, we were ready to drive back to the hotel where Jim, Dash, and Lana were staying. That's when Jimmy informed me that the three of them would be accompanying us to Denver the next morning. I had no idea they were going to do that, but Jim insisted. Lana grinned as if she'd known it all along.

When we walked out of the restaurant, Jimmy kept his arm firmly about my shoulders until we got back to the car. I saw him glance around the well-lit parking area a couple of times. "We'll meet you there," Carrie said as she and Mom walked on across the lot to her car.

Once we were installed in the backseat—Dash insisted on driving—Jim said, "I forgot something. Be right back." He patted my knee and then hopped out of the car and hurried back to the restaurant.

He came back carrying a large Cracker Barrel bag with a flat box peeking over the edge. "For you." He handed me the bag as soon as he sat down beside me.

"What did you do?" I took the brown paper bag by the handles and pulled out the flat box. It was heavy. "What is it?"

He took one end of the long box and held it while I opened the other end. "I bought something for us. For our first Thanksgiving after we're married."

I almost dropped the box. "Jim!"

He grinned like the Cheshire cat. "I'd get down on one knee but—" He looked at the small floorboard space.

My eyes cut down to the space as well.

Jimmy turned sideways on the seat so that one of his knees was in the floorboard. He held up his end of the box as an offering. "I didn't mean to blurt it out that way." His gaze travelled to Lana and Dash who were turned around looking at us with silly smiles on their faces. "But that is exactly what I had in mind when I bought it."

My hands scrabbled open the end of the box and my fingers found the edge of the turkey platter. It was cool and smooth, the heavy ceramic decorated with the colorful Thanksgiving scene. "Oh, Jim. I love it." I threw my arms around his neck almost dumping the platter in the process.

"Well?"

I could hear a smile in Lana's voice.

"Well what?" I released Jim, just a bit, to look at her.

"He's on one *knee*," she scolded.

Jim laughed and kissed me lightly. "Is it okay?"

Kissing him back, I whispered, "Better than okay."

He sat back on the seat beside me and kissed me again, lingering a bit this time. "We can talk about the rest of it later."

"Yes," I said. "We'll definitely talk later."

"Awww," Lana said.

Dash grinned and started the engine. For the first time in ages, I forgot to check the parking lot as we pulled away.

26

GOING HOME

C arrie booked the three of us a room at the same hotel where my friends were staying and she and Mom took our bags up. I accompanied Jimmy to his room and we walked out to the balcony and sat in patio chairs in the moonlight.

We sat side-by-side holding hands and feeling at peace even though it was full dark with stars blinking on like tiny night-lights. "I wish I could take you back to the ranch with me," he said. "Or stay in Denver with you."

I gripped his fingers and gazed at the twinkling sky. "I wish that, too. Don't worry, though. I'm not afraid anymore. The main thing left from that night is an awful feeling that it will never be over. But it isn't fear exactly. It's beginning to feel more like anger."

Jim looked at me as if he wanted to say something, but he didn't, and after a while his lips found mine and we rekindled exactly what we'd shared back at the ranch under the same stars on a different, much different, night.

When we broke apart I ducked my head shyly. "I thought

things might be strange. Ever since Lana said she'd told you what happened, I worried you wouldn't want—"

Jimmy put the broad pad of his thumb against my lips. "Never, ever worry about that. Everything is just the same on my part except—"

My heart froze. "Except?"

"Except I will never get over the guilt that I feel. I should have known something was wrong." His jaw clenched and he ground out the next words. "When I got that text, I should have listened to my heart and come to you on the run. I knew you weren't the type of person that would tear me apart that way. Not after what we'd shared." He pressed his lips to the back of my hand. "But I didn't listen to my intuition. I let my insecurities overwhelm me."

I grabbed his face and kissed him soundly. "It wouldn't have made a difference. By the time he sent you those messages I was creeping through the woods, trying to get back to my car, wondering if he had found me again—"

Jim squeezed my arm. I don't think he meant to. I don't think he knew how hard he held on.

The night air grew cooler and I tugged my sweater closer. It was the same maroon one I'd left in the front seat of my car that night. I'd worn it to court for good luck. Guess luck hadn't been in the cards this time. "I'm sorry," I murmured. "I didn't mean to go on like that."

I looked down at a babbling fountain in the hotel's courtyard. Frosted lights like small sunken moons lit the water from below. "My therapist calls it PTSD. Post-traumatic stress disorder. She says it may last a long, long time." I shrugged. "Maybe forever."

Jimmy stood and pulled me up with him. "That's why I should have been there." He pressed my head to his chest and wrapped me in his arms. "I'm here now. I'm not ever going to let you go again. Never." His breathing quickened. "I meant it when I said the turkey platter is for our first Thanksgiving together."

I clutched him like a lifeline. It felt so good to be in his arms again. So safe. "We have a lot to be thankful for, but you have to go back to school."

"You'll come with me. We can get married right away."

Tears I hadn't even known were falling dampened his shirt. "I want to marry you. But not this way, not out of worry about being alone." I took a deep breath. "I'm not going to let him control me anymore." Hugging Jim even tighter, I whispered, "I'm going to stay in Denver, get my real estate license, and start living. I'm done with him. Finished."

Jimmy sat back down in his chair, me on his lap. "I understand. But we can start making our plans, right?"

I nodded.

"We don't have to set anything in stone, not yet." He stroked my hair. "You don't want to live in Denver forever, do you?" His hand stopped stroking as he continued to speak. "When I finish school, I have a ranch to run. Dad says it's all mine as soon as I'm ready. I, um, I hope you like the idea of living on a ranch—"

"Yes, very much. That's the good thing about a real estate license. I can set up my office anywhere. But I've let a whole year slip away. It's time for me to get back to living. I want to accomplish something while you are finishing your degree."

Jimmy pressed a soft kiss against the scar on my neck. "That sounds like a great plan," he said. "And we'll be together every step of the way."

I caressed his face. "Okay."

He grinned. "Better than okay." Then he put his lips to my ear. "I need you, Marlena Matthews. Don't ever let me go."

"I won't," I breathed. "I won't."

27

DENVER AGAIN

The next morning we all shared a quick continental breakfast in the dining room. We were like an extended family at a small reunion. It felt both wonderful and strange. As if I were on the outside looking in. I was relieved when holding and kissing my Jimmy didn't trigger any flashbacks the way the counselor had said it might, but at the same time I couldn't fully let myself enjoy it the way I had before. I felt a layer of cellophane between us, keeping me safe, perhaps.

There'd been more ugly messages on my phone during the night, but Jimmy didn't know about those. They dissolved as soon as I read them so showing them to anyone wasn't an option anyway.

In the most recent texts, Preston had begun to threaten specific things involving weapons and pain. He didn't even worry about me showing the messages to the police. He apparently considered himself bullet-proof. And maybe he was. But I had my plan.

I touched reply on the last message. "You don't have the guts to finish me off," I typed. "I saw you in court with your family.

You're nothing but a mama's boy. Even your own sister looked like she despised you. What'd you do, practice on her before you attacked me?"

For a few minutes, no reply appeared.

But I could see the ellipses that meant he was typing. "You leave my sister out of this. Someday she will pay for those lies."

Wow. My instincts had been right.

And that was the scariest thing of all. That bothered me more than anything he could have said. I checked my phone incessantly as we loaded our luggage into the cars and prepared to make the final leg of our journey. I didn't respond to his texts anymore. I didn't want anyone to see them.

But I couldn't get them out of my head.

Jim wanted me to ride with him, Lana, and Dash, but I felt guilty leaving Mom and Carrie to drive without me.

"Don't worry about it," Mom said. "We'll have you to ourselves in Denver. You ride with your friends and get caught up on everything you've been missing."

I hugged her, hard, and got into the backseat of Lana's car. Once again, Dash drove and Lana sat beside him. Before I knew it, my head found Jimmy's shoulder and I slept more peacefully than I had in months. I didn't even jerk awake once.

When I finally did open my eyes, Jim smiled and stretched his arm, rubbing the feeling back into it. He kissed the top of my head and together we whispered about our future plans.

"I'll have to fly back home for my semester exams," he said. "Just like the first time we met."

"What a difference a year makes, right?" I leaned my head back and closed my eyes, no longer the happy-go-lucky college girl I'd been the night of the fall dance. In some ways, I felt stronger. In other ways, still broken, deep down inside, where no one could see.

I slept most of the way back to Denver, but I remember

Jimmy offering to drive so Dash could rest. Dash had just smiled in the rearview and shook his head. "Nah," he said. "I'm good. Now that I'm sober," he'd glanced over at Lana. "Driving makes me happy."

"They're really a couple, aren't they?" Jim whispered.

I nodded. "I guess so. It's kind of recent, though. I didn't even know about it until now." I studied the back of Dash's head. Could he be that changed? Had alcohol been the only thing that made him so scary and reckless before, or were some people just inherently evil? I dozed off thinking about bridges and forests and I came awake certain Preston's Mustang followed us.

Glancing out the window, I did see a Mustang. It would get up beside us, then drop back, then accelerate again. It wasn't the same car Preston used to drive, but it looked just like it, only newer.

"Look at this idiot," Dash said. "He must be texting and driving. I'd let him pass if he would, but he just keeps falling back and then speeding up again."

That must be what had awakened me. Dash must've said something.

Jim still dozed, but I watched that car for a long time. I even memorized the license plate number. I couldn't see the driver at all. The windows were tinted black.

Dash's comment about the driver texting and driving made me want to check my messages, but I didn't dare. Not with Jim at my side.

The car finally fell back and took an exit ramp a few miles before ours. The exit sign read Old Telephone Road. How could that be? Another Telephone Road? Did every city have one? We were awfully close to Denver, but it appeared to lead to a wilderness area. Paranoia gripped me. It looked very similar to the place near the hidden stream outside Austin. I felt as if we were entering an episode of the Twilight Zone.

I made myself face forward. It couldn't be Preston. It couldn't be. Just my paranoia, that's all. Who wouldn't be a little paranoid after the threats he'd made? Besides, isn't that what I wanted, to lure him out?

I glanced out the rear window. I could see Carrie a couple of car lengths back. Everything's okay, I told myself. Don't panic. Just breathe.

Within the hour we were pulling into the driveway of Carrie and Dix's Craftsman style cottage. Dix stood in the doorway, a big smile on his face. Carrie must have called and told him we were close. He had probably dropped everything and gone straight home to wait. That's what I want, I thought. I want Jim to watch for me to arrive safely home. I want to be the one calling him and telling him I'm on the way.

Dix drove Mom home so she could check on Dad, and we all agreed to have dinner together at their apartment the next day.

Carrie invited Jim to stay in their second guest room. She and Dix had bought a three bedroom so there would be room for the children they hoped to have someday.

After dropping us off, Lana and Dash went to a hotel. I sort of thought Jim and Dash might room together and let Lana stay in the room with me, but maybe Dash and Lana needed some alone time. I didn't press them.

ADA Montoya called a few minutes after we arrived and told me the judge denied the request for a search warrant to look at Preston's phone. "I'm sorry, Marlena. But you yourself said the messages disappeared as soon as you read them."

"They did," I said. "So, what can I do?" My anxiety boiled to the surface.

"If you really think it's him, then I would turn that phone off completely. If he is as tech savvy as you say, he could be tracking it. Especially if it is connected in any way to your old account. Get another phone. Stay with someone else for a while—"

"You're saying run again, aren't you?" I couldn't keep my voice from shaking. "You're telling me you believe it's him and you think I'm in danger."

"I can only tell you what I would tell my own daughter. Better to be safe than sorry. And off the record? I do believe it's him. I wish we had the manpower to follow him, stake out his house, something. But the law prevents that. We'd have a harassment suit on our hands." He sighed. "If only we could see some of the messages."

"They really do disappear as soon as I read them," I said.

"Perhaps you could take your phone to the Denver PD before you click on the message. Then they could take a picture and send it to us. That way the judge would have irrefutable proof—"

"I understand." I glanced down at my phone. "The thing is, I've discovered that even if I don't click on the message, it disappears within a minute or so. Who knows how many he's sent that I haven't even read." There was complete silence on his end. "Are you there?"

He cleared his throat. "I'm here. Just dumbfounded. I had no idea that technology even existed."

I had a feeling he didn't believe me. I felt my credibility taking a nosedive. "Think of Snapchat."

"Oh," he said. "I see what you mean."

But I wasn't certain that he did. "It's not the same, but similar. Just more immediate."

"Well," he said, "I suppose you could go to the Police Department and sit there until the next message comes in. Let them witness—"

"That's not a bad idea. Oh, I don't mean sit at the PD, but what if I had Lana or my mom snap a picture of it with their phone and send that to you?"

"Hmmmm," he thought about it for a minute. "It would be worth a try. Let's do it. Make sure they get you holding the phone. If it isn't enough to convince the judge to issue the search warrant so be it. But at least we will have tried."

I agreed. Doing anything was better than doing nothing.

As soon as we got everyone settled into their respective places, I ducked into my room and checked the messages on my phone. "I saw you."

I thought of asking Lana to photograph me holding it up for Montoya and the judge, but then I realized how silly that would be. This wasn't a threatening message. I would look like a fool. And they still came from UNKNOWN. I'd tried blocking but apparently he had more than one phone number to send from.

Even before I clicked on reply, the message dissolved. I typed, "You exited on Old Telephone Road." If he could be cryptic, so could I. "Maybe I'll drive out there, too."

I hit send. Immediately self-doubt gripped me. But it didn't matter. Once the message had been sent there was no going back. I refused to be the hunted anymore.

From now on, I intended to be the hunter.

It gave me a dark sense of satisfaction picturing him driving up and down Old Telephone Road, looking for me. Of course, I could also picture him watching the house. Waiting for me to be alone. Or Carrie. Or even Mom. That scared me, but I had to do something to lure him out into the open while all my friends were here, and then when I had pictures of his vehicle, or even of him, with my witnesses to back me up, I would call 911 and show the responding officers the restraining order. I had it right here on my phone. Montoya's secretary had sent it to my email just like she'd promised.

It might not be sophisticated, but at least it was a plan.

From now on, whatever comes next is on me.

I took my .38 out of my luggage, made sure I had it loaded, and placed it in the top drawer of my bureau alongside my stun gun flashlight.

No more victim.

Not anymore.

28

THREE DAYS

Jim, Lana, and Dash stayed for three days. It was so wonderful having them there, like a mini-vacation, or a return to near-normality. It also lifted my heart to find that Jimmy hadn't changed, and his feelings for me hadn't changed. Everything I'd experienced at the hands of that monster had changed me, but not Jim. I could live with that.

I was almost certain the cellophane would fall away one day and I'd be able to really feel things again. Like before.

The first morning after we got back, I walked down the hall toward the living room just after Dash and Lana arrived. As I approached the doorway, I overheard Carrie telling them about the parts of the trial that occurred after Lana left. I stood right outside the living room door when I heard Dash's expletive-filled response.

He finished up by saying, "If I hadn't been in rehab all those months, I would have found out what was happening a lot sooner."

I peered in just as he jumped up and strode about the room before plopping down beside Lana again. "I can't believe he can lie like that and get away with it. And then just walk out of court as free as a bird." His eyes flashed and he smashed one fist into his opposite palm. "If I'd got hold of that pretty boy there wouldn't have been anything left to drag into court—"

That's when I cleared my throat to let them know I was there.

Dash dropped his head as if embarrassed by his tirade. But I noticed his shoulders didn't go down, they were still hunched up around his ears like the hackles on a mad dog.

Lana patted the sofa on her opposite side. "Sit here," she said. "Carrie was just filling us in on everything you've been through. None of us can believe it." She cut her eyes toward Dash.

I reached across her and patted his forearm. "Thanks for saying all the things I've been thinking. It's like a nightmare that won't end." I didn't ask, but I wondered if Carrie had told them about the threatening phone call back in Austin. I hadn't even told Jimmy about that yet. "I'm sure everything will be all right now, though. Denver is a long way from Austin, thank God."

Carrie piped up, "And we're here. We'll keep her safe until the next trial when we will have a new jury and a new outcome." Her sunny tone soothed me, a little.

"Yeah, or maybe his sister will get a conscience and come forward to tell what a fiend he is."

"His sister?"

I shook my head, closed my eyes. I'd forgotten I was the only one privy to what he'd said about her. "I saw her at the trial and I'd swear she's a victim, too. I could almost feel her agony across the room. And then out on the sidewalk she couldn't take her eyes off me. It was weird. As if she were trying to send me ESP messages or something."

Carrie nodded. "I do remember that. Her eyes followed us all the way to the car."

I took a deep breath, uncertain if I should tell them about

the other victim, and then I plunged ahead. "I didn't mention this earlier because it wasn't allowed in court, but a girl named Mariah Leathers was supposed to be Joanna's roommate. From Chicago—"

"What do you mean was?" Lana interrupted.

"She never made it to school at all. An Austin PD Detective questioned us about her."

"What happened?" Carrie asked.

I looked at the door to make sure Jimmy wasn't coming from the shower yet. "They found her body in a park. In Preston's hometown near Chicago."

Dash said another curse word.

"She'd been raped and her throat was cut." I regretted telling them almost as soon as the words were out of my mouth. They would tell Jimmy and it would be even harder for him to leave.

"Oh my God," Lana whispered.

"Detectives are trying to connect him to it, but so far, no luck. At least none that I know of. They don't exactly keep me in the loop."

"This is bullshit," Dash said. "There's no justice—"

"Dash, I don't want Jimmy to know."

They all looked at me as if I'd lost my mind.

"I can't let Preston mess up all of Jim's college plans the way he did mine." I tried to make my voice stern. "Please don't tell him until I give the okay." I looked at each of them in return. "I'll contact Detective Lapuli and find out if they've learned any more. Then I'll tell Jim. Deal?"

They each gave grudging assent.

"Thank you," I said. "You know he wouldn't be able to concentrate if he thought Preston might actually be linked to a murder." Even though that's what he tried to do to me, I thought. But I didn't say that. I'd begun to take my plan a little more seriously. I decided to up the ante. Really do my best to lure him out before everyone left.

Just then, Jim walked in. Of course we all stopped talking.

"You guys are talking about me, aren't you?" He grinned.

"Always," I said. "Were your ears burning?"

He squished in beside me on the sofa. Dash excused himself to get a drink of water in the kitchen, and Lana scooted down into the spot he'd vacated.

"I know," I said. "Let's drive up the mountain today. I can't let y'all come all the way to Denver without taking you up to Rocky Mountain National Park." I patted Jim's knee and Lana's arm on the other side of me. "We'll have a picnic lunch at one of the overlooks. You won't believe the view. It's just so beautiful up there."

Everyone agreed it was a great idea.

Carrie helped us pack a lunch and even helped us map out a route on Jim's phone. "There," she said when we had the route locked in. "Dix and I hiked many a mile in the park when we first got married. Still do on weekends." She smiled and I knew she hadn't been doing half the stuff she really loved since I had moved in. I vowed to stop being such a hindrance. I know she felt she had to take me everywhere since I'd been so afraid of being alone at first. Then I think it became something of a habit.

In no time at all, we were ready to go. I called Mom and told her our plans in case she came by and found no one home, and then we were off.

We had the most amazing day hiking and then throwing our picnic blanket down in a perfect alpine meadow. There was even a waterfall nearby.

"I can see why you've fallen in love with this place," Jim said, voice raised to be heard over the sound of the falls. "I've only been here one day and already I don't want to leave." He touched my chin as he said that and we all laughed.

I smoothed the wrinkles from the blanket. "It's too bad Trail Ridge Road is already closed. In a few weeks, this whole area will be closed for the winter." I lay back and enjoyed the high mountain sun on my face. Most of the wildflowers were gone, but a few braved the cool temperatures. "It's wonderful, isn't it?"

Lana and Dash wandered around, exploring, and Jim lay down beside me. "I wish I had Big Red here. He would love these trails."

I giggled. "Spoken like a true cowboy, longing for his horse."

A flush of red crept out of Jimmy's collar and up his neck. "We'll get you a little mare after we're married. She'll be a two-year-old, and I'll help you gentle her and break her to saddle and bridle. You'll be her first rider. You'll see..."

I laid my head on his chest. "It sounds great, Jim."

"It'll be okay," he said.

"Better than okay," I murmured.

Lana and Dash returned. "Look at this." Lana held up a rock that may have been a piece of bone. "It feels petrified." She passed it over to me. "Think it's a dinosaur bone?"

I made a show of hefting its weight, feeling its density. "Could be," I said. "Dinosaur Ridge isn't too far away. We should go there tomorrow."

"Hey, we should also try to get tickets to Red Rocks Amphitheater while we're here," Dash said. "I've always heard about that place."

Lana pulled out her phone and laughed when she had no cell service. "I forgot where we were. We can look at the website when we get back to Carrie's house." She glanced shyly at Dash. "I think that would be an amazing way to spend our last night here."

We laid out our sandwiches and drinks and had a feast before hiking back to the parking area. We were all looking forward to cramming in as many experiences as we could before the three of them had to head back home.

That evening we played cards with Mom, Dix, and Carrie at Mom and Dad's apartment. Dad barely looked up from his movie the whole time we were there. He seemed to be somewhere else. Mom said he had days like that, but not to worry. She at least seemed to enjoy our company.

Back at Carrie's house, we put on a movie, but Carrie and Dix went on to bed and Lana and Dash went for a drive. That left Jim and me on the couch, alone. It was wonderful, peaceful, all-I've-ever-wanted heaven.

The next morning we slept in while Carrie and Dix headed to the office. After an unimaginative breakfast of cereal and juice, Dash arrived and we drove up to Dinosaur Ridge and took the tour to check out the footprints and fossils. No matter what we did together, we had fun. Whether snuggled up on the couch watching an old movie on TV or eating a bowl of cold cereal in the mid-morning light, I enjoyed every moment.

Jimmy in the morning, hair all scruffy and face unshaven, could have been a new synonym for sexy. Added to my memory of turquoise knit boxers in the moonlight and I felt I could have written a whole new dictionary entry for that particular word.

He never tried to move past kissing and cuddling, though. For that, I was glad. Glad and thankful. I knew I still loved him, but the physical aspect of our relationship would have to wait a while longer. It made me love and trust him even more to know he would never rush me.

We spent all day hiking and exploring the mountain trails after Dinosaur Ridge. We had dinner at the Ship Rock Restaurant with its stunning cliffside tables and endless views, and then it was time for the concert. Big Head Todd & the Monsters were set to take the Red Rocks stage around seven p.m. I hoped they would open with my favorite song, "Wipeout Turn." It's all about remembering your dreams.

We took our seats and waited. The evening air felt cool, sliding toward cold, and the atmosphere tasted like a sweet dream. The natural red stone stage and backdrop, sitting out in the open between Jimmy and Lana, with Dash on the outside near the aisle, was another chapter of a new life I hoped would never end. Even the cold couldn't dampen our spirits. We had layered on long johns and flannels beneath our down jackets.

At first sitting outside in the open proved difficult, even surrounded by my friends—especially since Preston had begun to taunt me, saying he was watching every move I made—but I got over it when I realized nothing could happen on a mountain surrounded by people. That's when I finally relaxed and let myself enjoy the music.

The band played all my favorites plus some new material that I knew I would soon be adding to their playlist on my phone.

When the concert ended, we all milled about, making our way slowly back toward the parking areas. I turned my cell phone back on and an all caps message came in immediately. YOU'RE MINE, it said. JUST LIKE MARIAH.

I gasped and looked for Lana to ask her to snap the picture for Detective Lapuli, but she had made a beeline for the restroom.

Even though I had vowed not to involve Jimmy, I knew this one had to be shown to the police. It was practically a murder confession. But always the gentleman, Jim had plucked Dash's keys from his hand and hurried ahead to warm up the car.

Only Dash stood beside me. Making a split-second decision I said, "May I borrow your phone?" I figured I could snap the pic myself, and then delete it from his phone as soon as I sent it to the detective's number.

But it didn't work out that way.

As soon as I opened the message again, Dash leaned over my shoulder. "What the hell?"

The message began to dissolve the way they always did. "Oh," I said, "it's—"

"Just like Mariah? Does this mean you're next?"

Dash took my phone from my hand. "And now it's self-destructing? Good God, Marlena—"

"Don't tell Jim," I begged, reaching for my phone. "He has to get back to school to take his finals. He can't flunk out. I can't have that on my conscience, too."

He surprised me by giving me back my phone and wrapping me in a hug. "Marlie, you can't ignore it. This guy is a murderer."

I gave up. I couldn't help it. Something about his sympathy did me in and I told him my whole sorry plan for luring Preston out into the open to get him arrested. "But now I'm not even sure he's around here." I shrugged. "He's probably just taunting me from his plush condo in Austin, keeping me tied up in knots when he's really hundreds of miles away."

Dash's face clouded up. "I have to think about this." We walked slowly, keeping an eye out for Lana's head in the crowd. "I owe Jim my life," he said. "Literally. If not for the way he picked me up and took me home so many nights, I would definitely be dead by now. And I sure wouldn't have got up the nerve to enter rehab." He smiled. "Of course a lot of that also had to do with Lana."

I squeezed his arm. "I am so glad. She is crazy about you." Did I want to deflect the topic onto something else? Maybe. But it didn't work. Just then, another message popped up. This one was from a number I didn't recognize. Yet, it wasn't a threatening text. Not at all. Just the opposite.

"You don't know me," it began, "but we need to talk. He has to be stopped."

Dash read over my shoulder. "Who's that?"

"I'm not sure," I said. "But I have an idea." So I typed, "Sister?"

The reply came immediately. "Yes. I knew we connected."

Before I could type anything else, another message came in.

"We're both in Colorado. I followed him but now I've lost him. You and I need to meet. I think we can help each other."

I showed the messages to Dash, and then I typed, "What's your name? Where can we meet?"

I saw some emotion flicker across Dash's face. "It could be a trick. Or a trap."

"I don't know," I muttered. "It feels real. She says her name is Destiny."

Dash shook his head. "I think we make our own destiny."

"Exactly," I agreed. Then I saw Jimmy coming and typed a quick message telling her I had to go but would talk to her soon.

"You are quick." I pulled my winter gloves over my cold fingers.

Jimmy acted hurt. "You didn't even miss me."

I laughed and tried to avoid looking at Dash. I could sense his gaze trained on me to see if I would tell Jimmy what happened.

Thankfully, Lana came back from the restroom and saved me from having to say anything.

We all made our way out to the parking area where most of the crowd still milled about. No one seemed in a hurry to leave even though it was growing colder by the minute.

Dash bumped my arm with his elbow. When I looked up, he whispered, "You have to tell him."

"Okay," I said. "I'll do it when we get home."

But of course I had no intention of following through on that promise. I couldn't let Jim get on the plane tomorrow thinking that he was leaving me in danger. In fact, if he knew what I had in mind, I didn't think he wouldn't get on the plane at all. And therein lay the crux of the matter.

At the car, Dash held the door open for me. "I'll check with you later, okay?"

I nodded. "I'll take care of it." I ducked my head and slid into the backseat beside Jim. The night was beautiful, soft and dark, and as long as I remained encased in the cave-like interior of the backseat with my Jimmy, nothing could go wrong.

Outside the window the black shapes of trees grew and diminished as we passed. Streams of concertgoers were leaving with us so all the cars created a long row of headlights going down the mountain. When I looked back, a bright chain snaked around the curve behind us.

It looked like a page out of a fantastically illustrated book, one that I never wanted to end. And yet I knew I had to get to the last page. If I ever wanted to have my life back, I would have to skip past all the illustrations and write my own ending, no matter how ugly, no matter how twisted.

29

THE QUESTION AND THE AIRPORT

We all went back to Carrie's house. Dash and Lana stayed a while and then returned to their hotel. After they left and everyone else went to sleep, I sent another message to Preston's sister, but she didn't respond. I wondered if it could be a trick like Dash said.

Oh well, I thought, it isn't as if I'd revealed anything. As a matter of fact, I hadn't told her anything at all, yet.

The next day the time came for Jim to leave. I didn't want him to go, and yet I couldn't wait for him to be gone. There were things I had to do.

Lana called and said she and Dash were loading their car to head back to Window. Jim had farther to go, so he planned to fly. Being Sunday, Carrie and Dix were getting ready for church. Then they planned to come home and snuggle up on the couch in front of Netflix. I think they'd had enough company for a while.

On the way to the airport, Jimmy made me promise to invite him back for Thanksgiving and Christmas. "Of course you're invited," I laughed. "But what about your folks? Won't they expect you at home? It's only a couple weeks away."

"Yeah," he admitted. "But since we're going to be married someday, we've got to figure out a schedule for holidays anyway. Especially after we have kids. Might as well start now, right?"

I rolled my eyes and slugged his shoulder. Secretly I was both thrilled and terrified. I loved the notion of marriage and a family, but not with this shadow following me around, hanging over me like Black Death.

"Have you named our first born yet?" I joked. "Or would you like to discuss it?"

He tilted his head to one side, a contemplative look on his face. "I've given it a lot of thought, actually. I think Sam is a good name for a son. Or maybe Lane. Good, solid, cowhand names, you know?" His expression grew serious. "I even like Lane for a girl. Male or female, doesn't matter. I'll have that baby on a horse before it can walk." He pressed his lips together to keep from laughing. "But seriously, I still haven't talked to your dad about us getting married." He picked up my left hand. "And I haven't even bought you an engagement ring."

I shook my head. "I have a turkey platter and that's even better. Besides, Christmas is coming. That would be a good time to go ring shopping wouldn't it?" I entwined my fingers with his. "I just hope you aren't getting your cart before your horse. I mean we just got back together. Are you sure—"

"Of course I'm sure. I've been thinking about it since the day we met. Even during the last few horrific months."

That surprised me. "You did? Even though—"

He nodded. "Even though." He kissed the back of my hand.

I felt tears sting my eyes. "I'm not that girl anymore," I said. "You just don't know. It feels like my insides are rotten, mushy." I felt stupid telling him my innermost feelings, but I couldn't let him leave thinking he had the same carefree girl he'd first met. No matter how I had seemed the last couple of days, it just wasn't true. Not by a long shot. I glanced out the window, embarrassed. "Do you think I'll ever be okay again?"

"Better than okay," he said. "I promise."

"But—"

"Nope." He squeezed my fingers. "No buts about it. You'll be much better than okay. I *promise*."

I leaned across the console and kissed the side of his face. "Have I told you I'm in love with you?" The words slipped off the end of my tongue like butter off a warm knife.

"What was that?" He smiled and tapped the side of his face where my lips had planted the kiss. "Go ahead," he said. "Tell me again."

I leaned across the console again and whispered in his ear. "I love you, Jimmy Allan. Thank you for coming to rescue me."

He turned his head and kissed me quickly. "I didn't come to rescue you." He glanced in his rearview mirror and my belly tensed.

"I didn't come to rescue you because you didn't need it. Lana told me how you rescued yourself. Smacked that bastard with a wine bottle, got yourself back to your car, then back to town." He looked over at me. "I'm in awe. Seriously."

I shook my head. "It was just luck." I closed my eyes, reliving the nightmare stumble through the dark woods. "What they put me through in the courtroom was almost as bad. And I had no defense against that. No wine bottle or anything." I laughed at my own morbid joke. "Thank God Lana found you."

He touched my chin with our folded fingers. "You're one of the strongest people I know." We passed a semi and got back in the right-hand lane. "We make a great team."

"Yes," I agreed. "We do make a great team." I thought about the night he helped with my dad, how gracious he'd been. But at the same time my eyes were tracking a Mustang in the side mirror. It passed the semi, too.

To my relief, it sped on by. It appeared to be a dark metallic green, not black like I'd first thought.

On our way to the airport we stopped by to visit Mom and Dad. Mom hugged Jim warmly, but Dad is the one who really surprised me. When I leaned down to hug him he looked over my shoulder and said, "There's the boy who picked me up."

Mom and I glanced at each other. It almost seemed as if the last year hadn't happened. As if he didn't even know we'd been there only a day or two earlier.

Jim held out his hand, going with the flow. "Good to see you again, Mr. Matthews." They shook like old friends.

"What brings you to our neck of the woods?" Dad asked.

Jim sat on the loveseat nearest Dad's chair. "Well," he said. "I came to Denver to visit Marlena. You see..." He licked his lips nervously. "I've fallen in love with your girl. I want to marry her someday. With your permission of course."

Mom and I had retreated to the kitchen. It was only a few steps away, on the other side of the large island. I almost giggled. Almost fainted, too.

Clearly surprised, Dad said, "Well, I think that'd be fine. Just fine." Then he leaned forward and looked at Jim again. "She wants to?"

Jim smiled. If he'd had his Stetson he would have been worrying the brim of it between his knees. "Yes sir, she does. We haven't talked about a date yet. I've got to finish my degree at Sul Ross before I take over the ranch."

"Then you have my blessing," Dad said. "Just always take care of her." He seemed to run out of steam then. His eyes shifted back to the western he'd been watching on TV.

Jim looked up. Our eyes met across the island.

He winked.

My heart did a funny little dance. I never dreamed there

would be someone as special as Jimmy Allan for me. It felt like the *Once upon a time* start to my very own fairytale.

Mom grabbed me and hugged me.

Jim excused himself from Dad's side and came into the kitchen area where we were still hugging. He leaned down and whispered to Mom, "I wanted to ask the two of you together, but when he recognized me right away like that, I decided I'd better strike while the iron was hot."

"You were right," Mom replied. "You did great."

Jim shook his head. "I want your blessing, too, Mrs. Matthews. I want everything to be perfect from here on out. Your daughter is very important to me." He looked down at the floor. "She's pretty much my whole world."

Mom pulled him down and hugged his neck again. When she released him she said, "I can't imagine a better son-in-law than you, Jim Allan. Of course you have my blessing."

Jimmy made an exaggerated gesture of wiping his brow. "Whew," he said. "I'm glad that's over. I don't know what I would have done if y'all had said no."

Mom laughed, Jimmy grinned, and my heart settled in to a new and happy rhythm. The only thing tempering my joy was the knowledge that Preston had followed me to Colorado. Dash might not think so, but I believed the person who texted me was Preston's sister, and I believed what she'd told me.

I'd heard of stalkers harassing their victims for years. I hoped I was doing the right thing, baiting him the way I'd been doing. I couldn't let it go on forever. Something had to change. If his sister would agree to meet me, perhaps I could get some information from her that I could pass along to Detective Lapuli.

But I didn't tell any of that to Jim. After having lunch with Mom and Dad we strolled through the carefully manicured gardens of the assisted living complex. "Your dad looks good," Jim said. "Really good. You and your family are tight. Taking care of each other this way. It's another thing I really love about you."

"Will I ever get to meet your folks?" I asked.

Jim pulled me to him. "I can't wait for you to meet them. And them to meet you." He laughed. "You haven't even met Big Red yet—"

I elbowed him in the ribs. "Is that what you call him? I thought we met that night out at the old ranch... don't know about the 'red' part though."

"Hey, now!" He blushed. "I'm talking about my old gelding."

"Gelding?" I giggled. "I don't think so."

His face turned an even darker shade of crimson and I finally took pity on him and stood on tiptoe to kiss the corner of his mouth.

It had been a great visit. Although he had to leave, it would soon be Thanksgiving and I'd be with him again. I hoped his folks understood about everything, because I expected this one to be the best holiday of my life.

By the time it got here, the problem of Preston would—hopefully—be behind me.

FROM MOM and Dad's place, we went straight to the airport, the traffic as congested as always. Once there, I wanted to park and go inside with Jimmy, but he said no, since I couldn't accompany him all the way to the gate, he'd rather I simply go on home so I didn't have to walk back across the huge parking lot alone.

We said our goodbyes at the curb until a taxi behind us beeped its horn for me to move my car. After another kiss or two, Jimmy laughed, climbed out, grabbed his duffle from the backseat, and waved at the driver before blowing me one more kiss.

As soon as he got out of the car I began to miss the feel of his smooth cotton shirt beneath my fingertips. Only then did I realize how I'd been holding on to him.

When he disappeared into the terminal, I felt a pressure settle onto my chest that seemed as if it had been there all along, simply waiting to return.

The taxi went around me with another beep of its horn. I didn't bother to look up; I was too busy digging my stun-gun flashlight out from under my seat. I'd carried it to the car while Jim said goodbye to Dix and Carrie this morning.

I pushed my old TracFone back into the bottom of my bag. I didn't know why I'd kept it even after getting a new smart phone all those months ago, but like the equalizer, I had it if I needed it again.

I didn't trust my flashlight as much as my .38, but I could leave the flashlight lying on the seat beside me and no one would give it a second glance.

Checking my rearview mirror, I put on my blinker and got in line behind a Dodge Ram waiting to exit the airport.

It had taken an Act of Congress to convince Mom to let me take Jimmy by myself. She'd wanted to call an Uber, but I wouldn't hear of it. I'd wanted a few more moments alone with him before he left. As well as some time alone to contact Preston's sister.

"Don't worry," I'd told Mom. "I'll be on the freeway. Nothing could happen there." Of course I hadn't told her about the most recent messages. In fact, I'd pretty much lied and told her there hadn't been any more messages. I was tired of living like a prisoner. He should be the one constantly looking over his shoulder, not me.

Waiting in line to exit, I turned on my phone. I'd kept it off around Jim, just in case. Now the time had come to start the dance.

Sure enough, as soon as I turned it back on, a new message from Preston popped up. It reiterated what all the others had said, that I would soon be dead. "I'm going to enjoy seeing your red blood speckle the thin white snow."

I clicked reply. "No matter how poetic you get, you don't scare me anymore. The cops are watching. It's only a matter of time before you're arrested again." I hit forward on his message, but it dissolved as always. That's what made me think it really had been his sister on the other thread. Her messages didn't disappear.

Tossing my phone into the cup holder, I placed my hand on the flashlight. I lied. He did scare me. But I'd never admit it. Jim's words kept echoing in my head, *I didn't come to rescue you. You saved yourself. You're the strongest person I know.* It felt like a mantra, a truth. Words to live by. *Or die by,* my subconscious murmured.

The Dodge Ram turned the corner onto the highway, and then came my turn. I checked the oncoming traffic and left the airport. I needed to get the next part of my plan behind me.

30

DESTINY

H alfway home, a new text popped up.

"I found your messages," it read. "Now you're both dead." The letters began to fade before I fully understood their meaning. It originated from a totally different number than any of the others.

When the words disappeared completely, I knew they'd been from him. It must be true, then. He must have multiple "burner" phones at his disposal.

My hands began to shake. Blood rushed to my face as my heart pounded it through my veins. My cheeks burned with heat. Terror blurred my vision.

I took the nearest exit and began to practice my deep breathing techniques. Jimmy should be boarding the plane by now. Carrie and Dix were probably snuggled up at home on the sofa. Mom and Dad might be enjoying an early dinner in their neat little kitchen and Dash and Lana were headed home to Texas. It's time. No more running.

I tamped down the fear surging through my gut and drove back toward the mountain, phone in my hand. "Come and get me," I typed. "I'll meet you wherever you want."

All night long I had lain awake, devising a way to lure him into the open. I planned to make him meet me in a public place and once I saw that he was there, I would press 911 and ask for a police officer to come and get him. Of course I had the restraining order on my phone. I also had my stun gun flashlight and my .38 in case things went south.

I never got a chance to put the plan into action.

Twenty minutes passed. I just kept driving, waiting on Preston to respond. Finally, another text came in.

I figured it would be him telling me where to meet. But this time the text didn't automatically disappear.

"Don't worry about that last message," it read. "I slipped some sleeping pills into his tea. I thought they would never kick in. But I have him now. He's in the back of the car with a tennis ball duct taped in his mouth. Meet me three miles up on Old Telephone Road near Intrepid Point. There's a sign that says closed—just drive around the barrier—it's the spot he had picked out for you."

Shock hit me so hard I nearly drove off the road. My plan must have worked even better than I'd hoped. He'd made himself visible, but it wasn't me or the authorities who had found him, it was Destiny. Drugging him hadn't been my intention, but when he came around I could hold him at gunpoint until the cops arrived. I thought he would have to be awake and alert for the restraining order to be valid.

Having Destiny as a helper might throw a kink in my plans but there was nothing I could do about it now.

I tapped my GPS and typed in Intrepid Point on Old Telephone Road. I had a vague idea where to go, but after all my driving, I wanted the quickest route.

A new text came in.

Dash's name popped up. "Where are you? Your sister is worried. She called Lana."

I hit reply and quickly told him what had transpired and where I was going. Maybe someone should know. In case I didn't come back.

Next, I sent Destiny another message telling her I would be there shortly.

"Hurry," she replied. "I knocked him out completely. He'll never bite anyone again. Now, he is going to feel what we felt. Afterward, you will put me on a plane. That's all I ask."

I hurried. One thought kept running through my head. It can't be a trap. Please, don't let it be a trap, and then my mind began to examine what she'd said. *He'll never bite anyone again. Afterward, you'll put me on a plane.* What did that mean? What did she have planned?

When I got there, Preston's new Mustang was parked on the other side of the Road Closed sign. Someone had used duct tape to attach a handwritten sign that read WELCOME BACK TO TELEPHONE ROAD across the barrier. A skull and crossbones had been drawn inside each of the Os. Bright red lips began and ended the message like real life emojis. The sign definitely had the look of Preston's artwork.

Destiny leaned against the fender of the car, smoking a cigarette. A thin covering of snow coated the earth. She'd left just enough room for me to maneuver my car past the barrier.

As soon as I came to a complete stop, she ground out her Marlboro on the hood of the car, broke off the filter, and stuck it down in her pocket. She strode over, opened my car door, and placed her suitcase in the back seat. I hadn't even noticed it sitting near her feet.

I got out carrying my special flashlight. Yanking the sign off the barricade, I folded the tape around the paper and stuffed the square into my pocket the way Destiny had done with her filter. I thought I would give it to the cops later.

Destiny grabbed me in a hug. "He did that," she said, indicating the square shape in my pocket. "He intended to bring you here." Her eyes were wild blue orbs. "We have to do this," she said. "We can't let him go on raping and killing."

My nerves thrummed beneath my skin. "We have to do what?"

She released me and hurried around to the back of his car.

I followed, my flashlight held at the ready. Instinct told me to keep my .38 out of sight for the moment. Destiny was way too agitated for a gun.

She pressed the button to open the hatch. He lay on his side, knees drawn up to his chest; drool leaking from beneath a wrinkle in the silver tape. She had shoved the tennis ball far enough back between his teeth that his face was distorted, his jaw stretched to the breaking point. The ball made only a slight bulge under the tape. His once perfect visage now wore the monstrous, elongated expression that should have been there all along. His mouth appeared to be opened wide to scream. Or to bite. It reminded me of all those strange lips he'd painted and sculpted.

"I can't believe you managed this," I said.

She glared down at him. "I've been on drugs for years. Sleeping pills. Anti-depressants, anti-anxiety, you name it. All because of him." Her gloved hands worked at the edges of her jacket. I could see she was on the verge of hysteria. "Trust me. I know exactly how much dope to give to get the results I want." She laughed and it sounded almost as frightening as his voice hissing at me in the woods that night.

"But you're so small. How did you get him in the car?"

"Just before he passed out, I convinced him he'd be more comfortable in here." She nodded toward the pillow she'd placed under his head. "He was so wasted, he just crawled in on his own."

Shaking my head, I tucked my flashlight under my arm and grabbed hold of his legs. "Help me get him out."

Together we tugged and pushed and pulled until we had his unconscious form poised on the lip of the opening. Then all at once inertia took over and he tumbled forward and hit the ground with a thud.

A moan escaped his throat and he began to cough and choke. Somewhere nearby, I could hear the gurgling sound of a stream. A hard sense of déjà vu threatened to overwhelm me but I fought it off.

One of us on either side, we got Preston to a sitting position and he stopped coughing and choking. "We have to turn him in," I said. "As soon as he comes around."

Destiny looked at me like I'd lost my mind. She opened her mouth to speak, but all at once Preston began to swing his head from side to side in an effort to dislodge the tennis ball. His arms suddenly gained strength and his fingers flew to his face and began to claw at the heavy silver tape. I didn't even notice she hadn't tied his hands.

Terror flooded my senses. I knew his strength, his depravity. My survival instincts took over. "We can't let him get loose!" I pressed my special flashlight against the side of his neck and pushed the switch backward the way I'd been taught. The crackling sound was accompanied by the smell of charring flesh.

Preston went limp and his bladder let go.

"I think you killed him," Destiny said.

I shook my head. "I don't think so, but I can't let him get up." I watched for a moment. Maybe I really had killed him.

Suddenly, he hitched in a breath and began to cough again. My legs trembled, wanting me to flee. "He's breathing. But we have to tie him up him if we're going to call the police."

"I wish you did kill him," Destiny said. Her voice was that of a little girl. "You don't know the things he's done to me. Strangled my only kitten when I was five. Said he'd kill me the same way if I ever told the things he did. Things he made me do."

Bile rose in my throat as I imagined the things he must've done to her as a child.

With supreme effort, we got him to the nearest pine and pushed him against it so he appeared to be hugging the trunk. She pulled a package of plastic zip ties from her coat pocket. "I should've done this earlier but I didn't think he'd come to so soon."

She fumbled several of the ties as she tried to fasten his hands together. "Damn gloves."

I pulled my own from my coat and slipped them on. At last we got his hands secured together behind the tree. We had to secure him that way to keep him from running off when he woke again. The ties were too short to go around both his ankles.

"He had these in his car." Destiny held up a zip tie. "Along with six cell phones." She pushed her blonde hair off her face. "He came right out and told me he would bury you where no one would ever find you. Said there was no way he would go through another trial."

Numbness crept over me. I'd known he wanted revenge, but hearing it spoken that way, from someone else, made it even more real. Even more real than the inert form we now had fastened to a tree.

By the time I'd finished picking up all the zip ties we'd dropped, Destiny had produced a large knife. "This was also in his car." She began sawing at his clothes. "I'll throw it in the lake on our way back to town, along with all those cell phones. I already took out the batteries."

Preston began to moan. "I'll kill you. I'll kill you both. Bury you alive—" Even lashed to the tree, he still thought he was in control.

I stuck my hand deep into my other pocket for the campfire lighter I'd brought from home. It was just like the ones Dix had bought at Cracker Barrel so long ago. Just like the one Preston had used to scare me, to spur me on as I ran.

Click, whoosh.

"Give me that," Destiny dropped the knife and held out her hand.

I gave her the fire starter. My flashlight lay near the tree. I grabbed it and stepped back as Destiny studied our victim.

I thought she meant to burn his clothes or singe his hair a little while we waited for the cops, show him how it felt to be terrified and helpless. That had been my half-baked idea, at least. I pulled out my phone to press 911, but Destiny had other plans.

She shoved the silver wand of the fire starter between the cheeks of his bare ass.

He cried out and began to thrash.

I stood there speechless, mortified, 911 forgotten. I needed to stop her before she killed him, but I was frozen.

A lifetime of pain and anger ran down her arms and into her fingers. All at once he let out a primal roar and I realized she had pulled the trigger on the fire starter.

Preston came fully awake, bouncing up and down against the trunk of the tree in a futile attempt to break free. I could see the flesh on his face being scraped away by the rough bark of the pine.

Destiny pulled the trigger again and even the tennis ball couldn't stifle his screams. His bowels let go and evacuated the mess all over the lighter and all over his sister's gloved hands.

She shrieked and began to kick at him.

Then I saw the knife gleaming from his pile of clothes. Destiny spied it at the same time. She grabbed it with her filthy hands, yanked his head back by the hair, and sliced open his throat. Blood splattered the tree and ran down his naked torso.

I thought she was finished, but rage had consumed her as surely as the fire starter had consumed her brother's insides. She kicked his body sideways, grabbed his penis, sawed it off, and shoved it down into the barely-pulsing wound in his throat.

His remains hung heavily from his still-fastened wrists.

Oh Dear God, what have we done? Even as the thought entered my head, I found myself kicking dirt and leaves over our footprints in the patchy snow.

Destiny looked at her bloody, shitty hands and burst into sobs. "Look what he made me do," she cried. "Look."

I wanted to comfort her, but at the moment I remember just being glad we'd both worn gloves. "Come on." I pointed to the north. "I hear a stream."

We scrambled up the slope and she fell down beside the water, plunging her hands into the icy flow of a small rocky waterfall. Somehow she managed to get both her hands and her gloves clean. The sound of the falls reminded me of the burble of the hidden stream. This one wound down the mountain a little way, heading for a steep ravine in the distance. Ice edged the stream with lace.

Destiny sobbed beside me. Using one of her gloves, she'd scrubbed her hands raw.

Panic shook my insides. "Where is your other glove?"

She looked downstream with a blank expression on her face. Did she even know what she'd done? I watched as her missing glove surfaced and bobbled along for a few seconds before being sucked into a small eddy beneath an outcropping of rock.

We watched for it to reappear, but when it didn't, we headed back to the scene.

Dash stood near the tree, staring at the mutilated body. The expression on his face was one of horror. It didn't change when he saw me. If anything, the expression deepened. I wished I had never replied to his last text. I should have kept my own secrets after all.

"You did this?" he asked.

Destiny had faded back into the trees. "It was self-defense."

And I really felt that much was true. He never would have left me alone. He wanted me dead. I didn't tell him about Destiny's part.

Dash remained silent.

"Thank you for coming to check on me," I said. "This is not the way I thought it would turn out."

He looked at me and shrugged. "I saw his threats, remember? I'm just glad it isn't you tied to that tree."

That's when the tears came, hot, heavy tears that momentarily blinded me. "There's a ravine," I sobbed. "For his car."

Dash understood immediately. I scrambled back up the slope and pointed to where he should position the Mustang. He pulled his jacket sleeves down over his hands, got behind the steering wheel, and drove the short distance to the ravine.

With adrenalin on our side, and the gearshift in neutral, we shoved the car over the edge. It crashed through the brush and came to a halt about halfway down. When the branches stopped shaking, the dark car was gone, covered by Mother Nature.

Dash told me to go home and let him finish cleaning up the tracks we'd made. "Did you use gloves?"

I held up my still-gloved hands. I also had the knife Destiny had used. She'd washed it clean at the falls.

Dash said, "Can you get rid of that?"

"Everything will go into the lake on the way home." I wiped at my eyes. "That's the best we can do."

When I got back to my car, Destiny was there, waiting.

We drove toward the Denver airport in silence. Along the way Destiny changed into the dry clothes from her suitcase. She stuffed her wet ones into the laundry bag already there. No one would think twice about it.

Several times we pulled over to the side of Old Telephone Road and got out to bury evidence. We had an unspoken agreement to distribute it in as many unlikely places as possible when no cars were around. Throwing it into the lake no longer seemed like the best idea. Especially not while it was still light outside.

At the airport, we said goodbye at the curbside drop off and she strolled in as if nothing had happened. I had seen her dry swallow some sort of pill when she thought I wasn't looking.

I drove away, still in shock, wondering what my new life would hold.

31

DASH

I didn't get home until almost dark.

"What took so long?" Carrie asked. "We were really getting worried."

I could hear the near panic in her voice. They truly had been worried. "I had to take some time to think," I said. "You know Jim hated to leave. He's worried about me being so far away."

She didn't even seem to hear me. "I'm glad you're back." Her expression told me something bad had happened.

My gut clenched into a wad of dismay. "What's wrong? Is it Dad?"

Carrie shook her head. "There's been an accident. Dash is in the hospital."

"What?"

She drew in a breath. "A car accident. Lana's okay, she wasn't even with him. But apparently Dash went through the windshield."

The room blurred. "I don't understand."

Carrie took my arm as Dix came in from the kitchen. "We just got the call. Here, sit down. You look pale."

"I'm—yeah." I put a hand on the arm of the couch to steady myself. "I do feel lightheaded. Where are they?"

Carrie went down the hall to the bathroom. I heard the linen closet door open and close, and then water running in the sink. Dix patted my back and turned off the TV.

In a few seconds my sister returned with a cold wet washcloth. I took it gratefully and pressed it to my face and eyes. I immediately felt better, less faint. "Thanks. Now tell me—"

"Dash was coming down the mountain, just outside Denver. He lost control on a curve, rolled the car. An ambulance took him to the ER. They admitted him directly into ICU. Lana is at the hospital now. She's the one who called me."

"I thought they were headed home by now—"

Carrie sat beside me. "We thought so, too. Lana said at the last second they'd decided to stay a little longer. She said they just fell in love with the place, didn't want to leave."

I nodded. "But what happened? A wreck?"

"No one knows for certain. Lana said Dash dropped her off at the hotel and told her he'd be back soon. She thought he went to buy her some sort of surprise. But he didn't come back and then she got the call from the police about the accident. Apparently he regained consciousness just long enough to give them the name of the hotel where Lana was waiting." She stood. "Let me get my purse."

Dix said, "I'll drive." He pulled out his keys and clicked the remote start.

I rose slowly. "I can't believe it." I'd just seen Dash an hour earlier, although my sister didn't know it. "I'm so confused. Will he be all right?"

Carrie shouldered her purse and guided me out the door and onto the porch. "You can call Lana on the way."

I nodded. What else could I do?

We climbed into Dix's car and drove toward the hospital. I

pressed Lana's name in my contact list and she burst into tears as soon as she heard my voice. "I called you and called you," she said. "You didn't answer. Oh, Marlie, it's horrible. Dash is on life support." Her voice tore apart into sobs and wails.

"Oh, my God, Lana. I'm so sorry. I dropped my phone in the car and it slid under the seat. I couldn't get it out until I got back home."

I could hear her struggle to get a grip on her emotions. "Oh, well," she said. "It doesn't matter now. You're on the way, right?"

"Yes. Carrie and Dix are bringing me." I felt awful for lying to her, but I couldn't tell her where I'd really been.

Dix made good time. We were there in a few minutes.

Lana met us inside the front door. When she saw me, she fell into my arms. "I can't lose him," she cried. "He just got his life together, Mar." She collapsed into a sobbing heap and I helped her to a bench inside the massive entryway.

I stroked her hair and patted her back and tried to think of something comforting to say. "Can we see him?"

She sat up and swiped at her eyes. "Yes, he can have visitors but only one at a time. There is so much equipment, so many tubes and machines."

"Does his mother know?" Carrie asked.

Lana nodded. "I called her." Her voice threatened to break again but she continued in a whisper, "She said I was the reason Dash turned his life around. Me." She accepted a tissue from Carrie. "She'll be here as soon as possible. The airline said they would get her on the first available flight."

I held her as her shoulders shook and she curled over into a semi-fetal position. After a moment, she regained some control and stood. "C'mon. ICU is this way." She led us to the elevators and pushed the button for the fourth floor.

When we stepped off, she directed us to his room, only a few steps from the waiting area. "I'm sorry," a different nurse said.

"The doctor is doing some tests, he will come out and speak with you soon." She said we should wait in the waiting area. We looked for unoccupied seats on colorful chairs and couches. A large screen TV showed the local news. The sound was low, but the closed captions appeared at the bottom of the screen for those who wanted to keep up.

I sat nearest the TV. Lana sat beside me and Carrie and Dix chose a small sofa near the coffee station.

"We just wanted a little getaway before we went back home," Lana said as if someone had questioned why they were still in Colorado. "The mountains are so beautiful." Her eyes filled with tears again. "He left me at the hotel and said he would bring me some sort of surprise. I—I thought maybe something really special, a ring, maybe." The tears spilled over. "He said I was the one. The only one. But then he didn't come back. I didn't know what to do—"

A BREAKING NEWS banner scrolled across the top of the TV screen.

A pretty brunette news anchor came into view holding what looked like an iPad. "This just in," she read. "A body has been found in the woods near Intrepid Point." She looked up at the camera.

There was a quick shot of yellow police tape near a wooded crime scene. A blurry shot of patchy snow and an overturned ROAD CLOSED barrier completed the view.

"Details are sketchy," the anchor said, "but a man's body has been found in these woods, obviously the result of homicide. His wrists appear to have been bound together with plastic zip ties." She stopped and caught her breath, apparently glancing at someone off camera.

On the TV, a shot of the Mobile Crime Unit van filled the screen. "We will keep you updated on this grisly story as more details become available." The woman shuddered and the camera cut to a dog food commercial.

"Oh, my God," Carrie said. "Another monster."

"What do you mean?" We always called Preston a monster, did she have some idea, or could that be my conscience talking?

Carrie looked at me, but she was saved from replying when the doctor, followed by a cadre of doctors-in-training, emerged from the ICU doors.

Lana stood. She'd been in the shelter of my arm as Carrie and I discussed the news report.

The doctor stopped in front of our little group. "I'm looking for the family of Dash—"

Lana interrupted, "I'm his fiancée. His mother is on her way from Texas."

The doctor nodded. "May I speak freely?" He glanced at Carrie and me.

Lana nodded.

"He's still on life support. The machine is breathing for him. The intracranial swelling is pressing on his brain stem. We're doing all we can to ease the pressure." He paused and checked his notes. "I will keep him on the ventilator until his mother arrives, then we will test again for brain activity."

Lana's face paled. "And if there is none?"

The doctor's demeanor softened. He stuck one hand in his coat pocket. "Then it will fall to his mother, and to you, to decide the best course of action."

Lana melted back down into my arms, laid her head on my shoulder, and sobbed quietly. The doctor gave me a sympathetic look. "You all may go in and spend time with him, as much as you'd like. Talking to him won't hurt. I don't know if he can hear you, but be positive. Upbeat. Miracles happen every day." He reached out and touched Lana on the shoulder. One of the young doctors looked away, eyes shimmering.

I nodded and helped my friend to her feet. "Thank you, doctor." Together Carrie and I led Lana through the big double doors to the unit. Dash's cubicle was the first one on the right.

"He said we could spend as much time as we wanted," I murmured.

Lana nodded and straightened her spine. "After this, you'd better call Jim. He doesn't know yet."

I looked at my phone. "His plane should be landing in Midland anytime now. Then he has a three-hour drive to Alpine. I'm sure he will call me as soon as he can."

She looked at me as if she had no idea what I was saying.

I gave her arm a little squeeze. "I'll make sure he knows."

Carrie pulled the orange plastic chair up to the bed so Lana could sit as close as possible. The ventilator whispered and fluid from an IV dripped from a bag into a tube that snaked into the crook of his elbow. Monitors with LED readouts tracked his heart rate, blood pressure, and oxygen level, and a catheter bag hung from the bottom of the bedrail slowly filling with red-tinged urine.

His head had been partially shaved and bandaged. A drainage tube peeked out from beneath the dressing. His eyes were swollen and black. "Is it him?" Lana asked. "Is it really?"

"It's him," I said. But I wondered. It could have been anyone under all that wrapping. I vowed to myself to have a look in his personal effects bag on the shelf beneath his bed. I knew from experience that it would hold whatever clothing they had cut off of him in the ER, and possibly even his wallet if it was in his pocket when they got him here. I didn't want to go through his things with Lana in the room. That might be too much for her to bear.

After a few minutes, Dix went back to the waiting room.

"You guys can go," Lana said. "You have work tomorrow. I'll be fine until his mom arrives." She gave us a tired smile.

I shook my head. "I want you to go down to the cafeteria with Carrie, get something to eat, and maybe a cup of coffee. I'll stay until you come back up. Take your time, okay? Then Carrie and Dix can go on home and I'll hang out here with you." I glanced at the still figure on the bed. "With you and Dash." I smiled, intent on being as positive as possible. "By the time you get back, Jim will have landed and I will call him."

"That's a great idea," Carrie said. "I could use a latte myself." She looped her arm around Lana and helped her stand.

"You'll let me know if he wakes?"

"Of course."

Lana bent down and kissed Dash gently on his face. "I'll be right back," she whispered. "And you will wake up and everything will be fine." She hiccupped as she finished speaking.

My heart broke for her.

Carrie led her gently toward the door.

As soon as they were gone, I tugged on a pair of purple nurse's gloves from the box on the wall, and then I leaned down and pulled the large plastic bag off the shelf on the bottom of the bed. The bag seemed heavy. I carefully opened the top and saw bloody jeans, a torn and bloody t-shirt, a single Adidas sneaker, and a fat leather wallet. I did not see his cell phone.

Panic squeezed my airway. For a moment, I could hardly breathe at all. I ran my hand down into my coat pocket and was surprised by what I found there. I fingered the single plastic zip tie with my gloved hand.

I closed the bag and put it back. It wouldn't do for anyone to think I'd been going through his things. But that phone. It had messages from me telling him what was going on. Where could it be?

Removing the purple gloves, I shoved them down in my purse, closed the clasp, and leaned over his still form. "I'm so sorry," I whispered. Then I sat down in Lana's chair, laid my forehead on the edge of his bed, and said a silent prayer.

After a moment, an idea bloomed in my brain and I grabbed the bag and opened it back up. Sure enough, his phone was in the single undamaged pocket of his jeans.

I breathed a sigh of relief and stuffed it down in my purse with the purple gloves.

A few minutes later Lana returned. "I ate," she said. "I promise, I did." She gave me that wan smile again. "Now, it's your turn. You go on down and get something for yourself. I sent Carrie and Dix home, but she said just to call and she would come back and pick you up at any time."

I nodded. "I'll get a coffee and look at the news, but then I'll be back to sit with you." I stood and gave her the chair. "And then we will try out that recliner in the corner. One of us can sleep there, and the other can go to the couch in the waiting room."

"I'll take the recliner," she said. "I don't want to leave him again."

I touched my lips to the top of her head. "I understand."

The hallway was too bright after the soft lighting of Dash's room. No one stopped me or questioned me. I went through the double doors, through the waiting area with its couches and tables, and turned the corner.

Standing near the elevator, I took out my phone and checked the time. Jim should be calling soon. If he didn't, I would send him a message to call me. I hated to be the one to break the news to him about his best friend, but there was no way around it.

In the cafeteria, I made myself a cappuccino from a machine in the corner. Then I ordered a club sandwich and sat down to watch the news. It played a different channel, but all the same scenes. They showed a quick glimpse of the crime scene barely visible through the trees.

Although the body wasn't visible on camera, the news anchor always made certain to let the viewers know how particularly gruesome it looked. "Be sure to tune in tomorrow for the latest—exclusive—updates on this horrendous crime."

The cafeteria lady slid my sandwich onto my table with one hand and clicked the OFF button on the TV with the other hand. "They'll put anything on the news these days." She frowned. "But they shouldn't. Bad enough the poor thing being murdered that way, but to have the whole world seeing where it happened—"

I stood so suddenly my red plastic sandwich basket hit the floor. I didn't bother to stop and pick it up. How dare she sympathize with "the poor thing." She had no idea what she was talking about. Behind me I heard her tell someone, "You see? Those reporters have no respect for the dead. Shouldn't be allowed to upset people that way."

In the elevator, I took a deep breath and tried to get myself under control. The lights flashed and the bell dinged and the door opened. I stepped out into the ICU waiting room where I knew the TV would be on the news with no one to change the channel. I had to know the latest updates.

This time, they were interviewing the detective in charge of the case. "We have a tentative identification but the name will not be released until the next of kin has been notified."

My phone rang. Jimmy's face appeared on the screen. Here we go, I thought. "Jimmy?"

"Marlena, I just landed at the airport—"

I couldn't contain myself. "Oh, Jim, the most horrible thing has happened." I sat further back in the waiting room couch and told him about Dash. "They don't expect him to make it, Jim."

I heard him inhale. "I'll catch the next plane back to Denver." His voice roughened. "Tell him to hang on. I'll be there as soon as I can."

"I will, but the doctor said it would be up to his mother and Lana—"

"Then tell them, too," he said. "Tell them I'll be there."

"Okay, just let me know when—"

"I will, Mar. I may have to get on standby."

I swallowed. "You've always been such a good friend to him, Jimmy. He told me more than once how much he appreciated your friendship. How he wanted to repay you for everything."

Jim cleared his throat. "I'll call as soon as I can."

We disconnected and I felt as if I'd lost something by being the one who had to tell him. I went back to Dash's room and told him to hang on for Jimmy. Lana smiled her sad little smile. But Dash couldn't hold on. As soon as his mom arrived and kissed him on the cheek, his eyelids fluttered and his mother gave the doctor permission to turn off the ventilator.

I think she had convinced herself he would start breathing on his own. But he didn't. He was gone within minutes. The brain injury proved too severe.

By the time Jim arrived, detectives had discovered tire tracks at the scene of the crime where the body was found. The tracks led from there to the scene of Dash's single car rollover right down the road.

The two scenes were so close together coincidence was impossible to imagine. I could imagine it, though. In my mind I could see Dash jumping into his car after one last look around the area. I could imagine him tromping the gas pedal in his haste, adrenalin pumping, hitting a single patch of black ice, sliding, rolling, going through the windshield . . .

Lana and I were in the room when a Detective Smith arrived and introduced himself and his partner, Detective Orinoco. We watched as they opened Dash's personal effects bag. A lone zip tie fell out. It appeared to have been right on top of the clothing.

The look on Smith's face was classic. He could have been an

actor the way he looked at his partner, one eyebrow raised questioningly. "Just like the ones used to fasten the victim's wrists
together on the backside of that tree." He pulled on a glove and
picked the slim length of plastic up off the floor. "And what's this
tiny spot on it, could it be blood?"

"We'll need to get that to the lab ASAP," Orinoco said.
"Wonder if it has anything to do with this photo Chicago PD
sent?" He held up his phone and showed the other detective a
picture of Preston. "Seems our vic is the number one suspect in
a murder near Chicago. Little town called Glencoe. That victim
was raped and bound with zip ties, too."

"Throat cut?"

"Yep."

"Well, isn't that curious?" Detective Smith leaned closer to
the phone pic. "And does that say his sister has gone missing as
well? Wonder if a fireplace lighter was used in Glencoe?"

His partner shrugged. "Guess we'll find out when I call
them."

Lana's eyes were huge. She leaned into me and whispered,
"What are they talking about, Mar?"

I didn't have time to answer. Jimmy rushed in at that
moment. I'd told him the bad news as soon as he landed and
called my phone, but before I could even give him a hug, the
taller detective stepped forward. "Friend of the deceased?"

Jim nodded, his eyes red with unshed tears.

"Sorry for the timing," Smith said. "But after you've said your
goodbyes, we'd appreciate it if you could answer a few questions." He handed Jim a business card with his name and phone
number on it. Det. Smith, DPD, Homicide. "We will give you a
few minutes." He glanced at Lana and said, "When you are able,
we'll need to visit with you as well."

Lana swallowed and nodded.

Jim, clearly confused, went straight to Dash's bedside. Mrs.

Scarborough embraced him. "I guess he had to go," she murmured.

They cried together, the two of them, holding onto Dash's hands, and then Lana moved into their midst and they created a triptych of grief beside his bed. I stepped up behind them and put my arms around Lana and Jimmy. It was all I could do.

Detective Orinoco—the one with the scar on his lip and the crooked part in his hair—cleared his throat and said he would wait for us in the hall.

Dash's mom turned loose first, but she wasn't ready to leave her son. Lana brought her a chair and they both sat back down as if they would never leave.

Jim and I walked out into the hall. The tile floor reflected the fluorescent lighting like a mirror. I squeezed Jimmy's hand.

"Sorry," Detective Smith said when he saw us emerge. "We just have a few questions. We want to interview the deceased's fiancée, but she is much too distraught."

"What sort of questions?" Jim still didn't know about Preston.

"We've discovered a body on the mountain not far from where your friend crashed his car." He let that information sink in.

"What?" Jimmy's voice was incredulous.

Both detectives nodded. "Gruesome murder. Sorry to say we think the deceased may have been involved." The older one slid a small notebook from his suit pocket. A pen magically appeared in his other hand. "What can you tell us about your friend?"

Jim blinked. "Detective," he looked at the card in his hand, "Smith? I have no idea what you are talking about. I just flew in from Midland, Texas, but I didn't get here fast enough. The deceased, as you call him, is Dash Scarborough, my best friend since grade school. He was a good guy, a track star at our high school. But—" His breath gave out and he clamped his hand across his eyes to hide the flow of tears he couldn't stop.

I gave the man what I hoped was a withering glance as Jimmy turned to stare through the door glass into the waiting area. "Can't you see he's in shock?"

"Our apologies," Orinoco replied. "We'll give him a few minutes." They turned and started down the stairs, then the one with the notebook looked up at me like a modern day Columbo. "Just one more thing." He tapped the pen against his lips and looked straight at me. "Did you also just arrive by plane, or were you already here?"

I went mute. Words jammed up in my throat, one on top of the other. I couldn't get them to line up so they could come out. My tongue lay useless in the bottom of my mouth.

"Ma'am?"

Jim looked at me. "Marlena? You okay?"

The air in the stairwell changed, grew thick with silent questions. Both detectives stiffened, their backs straight. The one nearest me transferred his little notebook to his other hand and reached inside his jacket in slow motion.

He's going for his gun, I thought. He's going for his gun.

"Marlena Matthews?" His voice was all business.

Still unable to speak, I simply nodded.

Jim must have sensed the change in the atmosphere as well. He moved half a step closer, shielding me with his body.

"We will need you to come with us," Orinoco said. He didn't pull his weapon but he did drape the edge of his jacket over the butt of it so we could see he meant business.

"What?" Jim looked from them to me to the gun and back again. "Why? What's going on?"

Smith glanced at Jim but directed his question at me. "Are you the same Marlena Matthews who accused Preston Stevensen of rape and attempted murder back in Austin?"

My knees began to tremble. "Yes." My voice came out a whisper.

I felt Jimmy's body tense. "What does that have to do with anything?" he asked.

"Preston Stevensen is the victim we found murdered in the same area where your friend wrecked his car. Stevensen's throat had been slashed." His eyes went to the scar still visible on my throat. "He'd also been sodomized with a campfire lighter. Raped, I suppose you could say." He hesitated. "His hands were fastened with the same kind of zip tie we just found in your friend Dash's personal effects bag."

His words were directed toward Jim, but his gaze never left me. "The victim's Mustang had been shoved over a cliff not too far away. When we ran the license plates we came up with Stevensen's name. That's when we learned about his recent court case. And how he got off."

Now his gaze went to my wrists. "Did he use zip ties on you, Ms. Matthews, that night in the forest. Was there a campfire then? I saw no mention of one in the trial info."

My heart hammered so hard it seemed to have no pause between beats. The world around me narrowed to a pinpoint of light. The light focused on the detective who still stared at my wrists. "No," I managed at last. "He did not use zip ties because I ran. I ran for my life." I didn't know what else to say.

"Good," the older detective said. "I hate coincidences." He cleared his throat and it sounded like an exclamation. "It's coincidence enough that you're both in Denver." He jerked his head toward the doorway, toward ICU. "Isn't that odd?" He grinned at his partner. "Especially since Ms. Marlena Matthews still has an active restraining order against our vic."

His grin faded and he gazed at me as if he wanted to put me in a jar to study later.

My hand went to my mouth. "Are you certain it was Preston?"

Neither detective made a sound.

"I hope it was," I said. "He was pure evil. He should've been in prison." I wrapped my fingers around Jimmy's bicep for strength. "Are you sure he's really gone?"

Orinoco pulled out his phone, touched the screen, then held it in front of me. "Is this him?"

It was a picture of Preston's face. His head hung backward, away from his body. Blood darkened the tree bark in front of him. The rest of the blood had flowed down his neck and drenched his torso.

Bitterness flooded the back of my throat. I covered my mouth with my hand. Squeezed my eyes shut. When I opened them again, Jim's jaw was clenched in anger.

"My God," he said. "Why are you showing us this?"

The detective put away his phone. "Surely you can understand our interest. Your girlfriend has a history with our victim. Your friend Dash wrecked his car near the place where Stevensen was murdered. It's like some unholy trinity. Some violent sort of triangle."

Jim looked at me and my heart sank. The detective seemed to be getting to him. Jimmy hadn't even processed Dash's death and now he had to listen to the insinuations that both Dash and I had something to do with it.

"No," he said. "No. There's nothing like that. It's just a fluke. A series of ridiculous coincidences—"

I put my hand on his arm. I couldn't stand to see him try to defend me without knowing the facts. "That's not exactly true," I said. I glanced up at Orinoco. "Preston had been sending me ugly messages. Threatening texts." I sighed. "You won't believe this, but the texts would disappear right after I read them. Some sort of app."

Jimmy looked astounded.

"Sorry," I said. "I told Mom and Carrie. And I told ADA Montoya. It happened right after the trial." I thought back to that awful day. "We were still in the car, on the way back to our hotel room." I recounted the entire conversation to the detective.

"Would you come down to the station and let us get an official statement? Maybe a DNA sample?"

I looked at Jim.

He shrugged.

"Okay, I guess it will be all right. There's just one thing."

Smith raised an eyebrow.

"I'd like to say goodbye to Dash's girlfriend and his mom. They'll be leaving soon, I guess."

The older detective gave a slight nod.

Orinoco said, "We will be in the waiting room."

I nodded but before walking away I said, "Detective Smith? Can you tell me something?"

He stopped, one hand on the push bar of the door.

"What did you mean about his sister being missing?"

He looked at his partner. "Chicago PD sent an officer to the Stevensen home in Illinois, to tell about their son. They told the officer they've been unable to contact their daughter since right after the trial."

The detective stepped aside as a nurse hurried through the door. "We'll talk more downtown."

I nodded and took Jim's hand. Together we walked back into Dash's room where his mom kept vigil with Lana. It was time to say goodbye.

32

THE RANCH

"We're going to bury him in Window's old cemetery beneath a giant live oak," Lana said.

The detectives had closed the case once I told them about the text messages and how upset Dash had been about them. The random zip tie that had fallen out of his personal effects bag had sealed that part of the investigation.

"I think it was his way of paying Jimmy back for saving his butt so often," I'd told the detectives during my interrogation. "He knew Preston was the reason Jim and I hadn't seen each other all year. And then when Lana told him about the hung jury, and he accidentally found out about the threatening texts I'd been getting—"

"I think that's a very astute observation." Detective Orinoco said. "Jimmy Allan told us pretty much the same thing when we questioned him." He leaned forward and literally closed the manila folder with Preston's name on it. "Your friend, Lana, confirmed it. She said he told her he had to do something to stop the guy."

He arranged the folder so that its edge lined up with the edge of the dull gray interrogation table.

"Yes," I said. "He told all of us the same thing."

I REMEMBER TELLING Lana how sorry I was. "I know he was the love of your life. I can't believe he did this for me. And for Jim. I'd give anything if he hadn't lost control coming down the mountain—"

Lana nodded. "But if he had survived, we'd have to go through another trial. For Dash this time."

I couldn't argue with her, although I tell myself I never would've let that happen. If he had lived, I'm pretty sure I would've had the guts to come clean.

We'd been in the parking lot of the airport once again. She was flying back with Dash's mother. He would be sent back by private ambulance after the autopsy was completed.

I hugged her and tried to soothe her, but I couldn't say or do anything to make it better. And as much as I loved Lana, Dash's mother really had my sympathy. Sitting all alone in the seats near the ticket counter, she seemed to have shrunk since she'd come to Denver. Thank God she had Lana to lean on—I think it was better for both of them.

Even Detective Smith seemed relieved to close such a sickening case. He said, more than once, how shocking it seemed that anyone would go to that length to pay back a friend. "Of course I'm not done with the Stevensen family yet," he'd said. "Now we have to concentrate on finding the sister." I remember how he'd tapped his pen against the table. "Do you think Dash could've been involved in her disappearance?"

In contrast to his conversational tone, his gaze had been sharp.

"Of course not. But I certainly wouldn't put it past her brother, would you?"

The detective had shrugged. "Just have to explore all possibilities." He'd tapped his pen on the metal table again, deep in thought. "Personally, I think her brother *did* do something to her. The parents were so evasive."

I'd felt the spring in my chest loosen its coil a bit, relieved that he'd seemed to believe me, to realize how truly horrific Preston had been.

THE NEXT FEW days were a blur. Jim and I planned to get a later flight to Window since the one Lana and Mrs. Scarborough caught was full.

Dix and Carrie told Jim he could stay in their home as long as he wanted. And I know he appreciated their offer. Still, he couldn't help feeling extremely sad, distraught, and angry.

I tried to comfort him, but I had my own guilt over Dash's death to deal with. If not for me, Preston wouldn't have been in our lives and none of this would have ever happened.

But Jim blamed himself. "If only I'd known about this from the beginning," he said. "Maybe I could have made Preston stay away. Maybe all of this would have been avoided. Maybe Dash would be alive."

I reassured him the only one to blame in any of this was Preston. He had hurt me, then followed us from Austin, determined to finish me off. And as I kept reiterating the facts, I soon realized one fact stood out from all the rest.

Even though everyone believed Dash had killed Preston, not one person blamed him. Not one. Not even the detectives. Detective Smith said once he'd read about my case he was convinced Preston had been in Denver solely to kill me and put a stop to a second trial. And the day we were set to fly back to

Window for the funeral, he'd called and told me Destiny had been located in Amsterdam.

Her parents called off the search as soon as she contacted them. They also said she would not be returning. And why should she? The case had been solved. Dash had killed her brother and then died trying to get away. There was no need for further investigation.

At Carrie's house we gritted our teeth and packed our bags one last time. Mom and Carrie wanted to fly back with us for the funeral, but instead they financed my round trip ticket. Bereavement fares only applied to immediate family members.

Both Jimmy and I slept on the plane. By the time his father picked us up at the Midland International airport to make the short drive on to Window, we'd each had a little more time to come to terms with what had happened.

It had also given Detective Smith time to wrap up the findings from the autopsy and release the details to the press.

That made it official. I had asked if he could keep my name out of it, and he said he would, but once the press back in Austin got hold of it, he couldn't make any guarantees.

I called Detective Lapuli to make sure he and ADA Montoya were aware of all the developments and he assured me they had been kept in the loop.

He also said Detective Andrews, from Chicago, had sent him the news that the DNA findings confirmed Preston as the one responsible for Mariah Leathers' rape and murder. It was Lapuli's opinion that Joanna would have been his next target, three girls linked by one apartment. "A sickening kind of symmetry," he'd said. "Something our killer would have sought, I think."

I had to agree with him on that, especially after remembering his artwork welcoming me back to Telephone Road that day.

When I told Lana about the DNA confirmation linking him to Mariah Leathers' murder, she whispered that Dash had died a true hero. She was still in a terrible state of shock and grief. After helping Dash's mom plan the funeral, there had been nothing left to do but fall apart.

When it came time for the viewing, Jim stood between them. He held Mrs. Scarborough up and I held up Lana. Later, she told me she'd developed a real connection with her would-have-been mother-in-law. It added another layer of poignancy to the whole sorry affair.

At least half the town attended the funeral. Most came to support Mrs. Scarborough, or to see their track star one last time. A few came because they'd heard he was a hero.

Sure enough, they laid him to rest beneath a large live oak. The crowd of people kept the service from being too maudlin. However, I don't know if it would have affected me any differently if it had only been the four of us. I'd gone numb. Completely, solidly numb through and through.

Jim seemed resigned. He and Mrs. Scarborough held onto each other and to Jim's dad. Lana had her folks there, and Jim's mom stood beside me and held my hand. She seemed to think I needed extra support since my own mom couldn't be there. I loved her for that.

A couple days after the funeral, Jim insisted on taking me back to the ranch. I had been staying with Lana and had also made my plans to fly back to Denver. Of course he needed to return to Sul Ross, too. Thanksgiving had crept up on us, but he thought he could go ahead and review some of the semester exam material he'd missed out on over the last few days. Then he planned to spend the holiday with us at Dix and Carrie's house. He would begin his final semester after Christmas. We talked about putting our turkey platter to use in our own home next year.

But that felt like a long way off. And I was glad. Because even though danger no longer lurked around every corner, I still couldn't start making plans. Everything felt different. Tainted. I worried that once Jimmy and I were apart, it would only get worse. Sometimes, in the deepest part of the night, I was terrified we might not have a future together after all. So much had happened.

Jimmy said we'd already weathered the storms, now we just had to wait for the rainbows to appear. I prayed he was right.

He took me for a drive the day before I had to go back to Denver. "I have something to show you." We drove past the old ranch road leading to the spot where we'd first made love. "I know Telephone Road is where he attacked you," he said.

I nodded. I didn't want to talk about that. He hadn't been dead long enough. And now, when I thought about Preston and how he'd died, that memory got all tangled up with Dash and how he'd died. It also made me think of how I'd let him take the blame because I knew he couldn't be prosecuted.

Did that make me a horrible person? Destiny is the one who should have been prosecuted, and yet, I protected her because I identified with her. Would she have been able to kill him if I hadn't been there to help tie him to the tree? I had a feeling those questions would haunt me forever. My very own *Tell-Tale Heart*.

Jimmy slowed the car and pointed to a green rural street sign partially hidden by live oak trees. It sat at the corner of a rutted, disused branch of the newer access road.

I read the sign out loud. "Telephone Road?" I couldn't keep the confusion from my voice. "I don't recall this being here. I thought I knew every road in and around Window."

"It's always been here," Jim said. "I think nearly every town or county has a Telephone Road, but this one is different."

I felt my scalp prickle. "How do you mean?" Panic nibbled at my nerves. The day turned brown. All the color faded away. Why would Jimmy show me this, what did he want to prove?

An odd expression crossed his face. "The difference is... I own this one."

"You what?"

He nodded. "I own this road. Well, my family, I mean. The county named it years ago, but it's actually on our private property. If we want, we can take that sign down right now. Give the road a new name. Anything you choose." A smile of hope played at the corners of his lips.

His words finally began to make sense. Color began to seep back in. "Are you serious?"

"Yep. Name it anything you want." He indicated the offending sign with a wave of his hand. "I'll pull it down right now if you say the word—"

I threw open the Camaro's door and ran to the silver pole. "Yes," I said. "Take it down. Take it down right now."

Jim backed the Camaro up to the sign. From the cargo area he pulled out a toolbox containing a giant bolt cutter and a heavy-duty wrench. "If one doesn't work, the other will."

He stood on the back of Betsy so he could reach the top of the sign. With great effort he removed the bolts fastening the green metal to the silver pole.

When he had it free he handed it down to me.

I threw it on the ground, grabbed the wrench, and hammered at the white-on-green words until my shoulders ached and most of the letter-paint had flaked away.

At last I stood, heaving, wrench dangling from my sore hands, strands of my hair plastered to my cheeks.

Jimmy waited. When he knew I'd finished, he pried the wrench from my fingers and dropped it on the ground. It hit the edge of the mangled sign with a hard clank.

Then he took me in his arms. "We'll petition the county to

rename the road." He brushed my sticky hair off my face. "We can name it anythi—"

"Dash," I murmured.

He pushed me back a bit to see my face. "What?"

"Name it Dash," I repeated. "Dash Road. In honor of my hero." In the back of my mind, I wondered if I should include Destiny on it somehow. If not for her, who knows what might have happened. Dash had taken the fall for both of us, but she'd been the one who ended the monster.

At the word hero, Jimmy crushed me to his chest. "I still can't believe what he did."

If you only knew, I thought. But I couldn't say it. Instead, I wriggled free, picked up the sign, and put it in the toolbox along with the wrench I'd used in my attempt to destroy it. "I'm going to keep it for awhile, if you don't mind." I glanced at his face. "I'm not sure why, but I think I want to hang on to it until I'm certain Telephone Road has no more hold over me."

Jimmy nodded. "I have something else to show you before we leave."

He put the bolt cutters in the toolbox and closed the hatch. Then he drove us to the ruins.

There, beside the foundation of the old ranch house, grew a pumpkin vine. One bright spot of orange peeked out from beneath broad, green, curlicue leaves. "It's from our dance pumpkin," he said. "I've been checking on it all year, every time I came home to visit."

"It's wonderful." I squeezed his hand. He'd been telling me the truth when he said he still thought of me with love, even after Preston sent him that horrid text.

I knew I should feel happy. I knew I loved him, too. But something still seemed to be missing. Or maybe something had been added. I told myself it should be okay now—better than okay—this future, this path. Going forward with Jimmy should be the best thing in the world. And yet, ever since the events of Old Telephone Road,

In the night...

Every night...

As soon as my breathing slows and my mind tells me all is well, that moment when I finally let sleep begin to take me down...

Rain.

Mist.

Towering trees.

Thick brush.

Cold.

Dark.

Someone screaming. Something burning.

Nightmare memories I can't erase, no matter what we do to a metal signpost out on Telephone Road.

Dear Readers,

If you need help call 911 or your emergency services number. If you need to talk to someone about past abuse, call RAINN, The Rape Abuse and Incest National Network 800-656-HOPE (4673). They will put you in touch with a sexual assault service provider in your area. You can also go to www.rainn.org to learn more or to engage in live chat. You are not alone. Young people age 12-24 are most likely to become victims of sexual violence or abuse. Call someone or tell someone. Don't suffer in silence. It isn't your fault.

Ann Swann

February 23, 2020

MEET THE AUTHOR

Ann writes about women mostly. Women who start out as uncertain victims and wind up as self-saving heroines. Along the way there are often Prince Charmings, sometimes they help the women, other times they simply have to step aside. Strong women aren't always born that way. Often, it's a learning curve. Sometimes they are forged in fire.